WORLD WAR II
FLYING STORIES

JACQUELINE PUCHTLER

CRANTHORPE
—MILLNER—

Copyright © Jacqueline Puchtler (2021)

The right of Jacqueline Puchtler to be identified as author of this work has been asserted by her in accordance with section 77 and 78 of the Copyright, Designs and Patents Act 1988.

All rights reserved. No part of this publication may be reproduced, stored in a retrieval system, or transmitted in any form or by any means, electronic, mechanical, photocopying, recording, or otherwise, without the prior permission of the publishers.

Any person who commits any unauthorized act in relation to this publication may be liable to criminal prosecution and civil claims for damages.

This book is a work of fiction. Names, characters, places and incidents are either products of the author's imagination or are used fictitiously. Any resemblance to actual events or locales or persons, living or dead, is entirely coincidental.

First published by Cranthorpe Millner Publishers (2021)

ISBN 978-1-912964-97-0 (Paperback)

www.cranthorpemillner.com

Cranthorpe Millner Publishers

Oh! I have slipped the surly bonds of Earth
And danced the skies on laughter-silvered wings;
Sunward I've climbed, and joined the tumbling mirth
Of sun-split clouds – and done a hundred things
You have not dreamed of – wheeled and soared and swung
High in the sunlit silence. Hov'ring there,
I've chased the shouting wind along, and flung
My eager craft through footless halls of air...

Up, up the long, delirious burning blue
I've topped the wind-swept heights with easy grace
Where never lark, or ever eagle flew –
And, while with silent, lifting mind I've trod
The high untrespassed sanctity of space,
Put out my hand, and touched the face of God

High Flight by
John Gillespie Magee Jr
No 12 Squadron RCAF
Killed 11 December 1941

To Mum, Dad, Hazel and the boys – Simon, Tim, little Beckett, Alan, the twinnies Carter Denny and Lawson Gray – and any future munchkins!

Acknowledgements

Heartfelt gratitude to the following:

Dr Jim Castner for finding time between explorations to proofread, what was for him, unchartered territory. My cousin, John Lewin, whose uncle flew in WWII, for his interest and attention to detail. Ian Wright, who worked for the RAF Veterans' Association. Former Luftwaffe Instructor pilot, Oberstleutnant Klaus Puchtler, for his technical expertise. My sons: Simon, for his faultless critical eye and Tim, who would rather be flying than reading about it. Alan Marchant, whose work at Bletchley Park proved invaluable. Rosa Fraterrigo and Jennie Woods for their encouragement. My publisher Kirsty and editor Lydia for their much valued support and belief in this project. Kettering RAF veteran and former Lancaster bomber wireless operator, Reg Payne and his son David for providing me with details of Reg's wartime career and for showing me Reg's aviation paintings, one of which I am using for the cover of this book. Special thanks to former RAF flight engineer Craig Moore, who, despite the frenetic pace of his life, has found the time and energy to read through my efforts and offer his expert and in-depth knowledge. Author Gill Cross (who I have the phenomenally good fortune to call Mum), for her unstinting support in all my endeavours. Appreciation also to members of all the sixth-form book clubs I've run over the last twenty years and whose lively and enquiring minds have fuelled much literary discourse. And manifestly, to all WWII airmen/women and ground crew irrespective of nationality, for their bravery and sacrifice.

Contents

Introduction 1

Anything to Anywhere 12

The German Pilot 85

The Pathfinder.. 105

One Too Many 175

Corkscrew Port Go 186

Lion Hearts 198

Into the Fray Goes Walter Pidgeon 257

Introduction

I

Although these stories are works of fiction, they were inspired predominantly by real people and events. Beatrice in *Anything to Anywhere* is a fusion of any number of the one hundred and sixty-six female Air Transport Auxiliary pilots, such as Diana Barnato Walker (1918–2008), who eventually became the first British woman to break the sound barrier, Jackie Moggridge (1922–2004), awarded the King's Commendation for Valuable Service in the Air, and Lettice Curtis (1916–2014), who flew ninety different aircraft and was one of the first female pilots certified to fly four-engined heavy bombers. Of course, it's impossible to forget the image of Mary Dunlop (1920–2012), who became a poster girl for the ATA after being photographed emerging from the cockpit of a Fairey Barracuda, and, perhaps the nation's favourite, the intrepid Mary Ellis (1917–2018), who flew over one thousand planes and died at the grand age of one hundred and one. These women, known as the 'Attagirls', contributed greatly to the war effort by transporting military aircraft from factories to maintenance units and air bases, freeing their male counterparts for battle. Many of these women felt that they too should be allowed to use their skills in combat. Although ATA pilots were only taught basic navigational skills, Diana Barnato Walker writes in her autobiography, *Spreading My Wings*, of being given advanced lessons from two fighter pilots who had flown in the Battle of Britain. Their instruction may have saved her life when she was suddenly caught in thick fog and forced to attempt a landing. She'd already decided that bailing wasn't an option due to modesty, as she was wearing a skirt! Haphazardly landing at the first opportunity, she, ironically, found herself at RAF Windrush, Navigation and Blind Flying Establishment. She and other female ATA pilots make no suggestion of having used advanced skills in any offensive, but there are many stories of thrill-seeking WAAFs smuggled into bomber aircraft to participate in night-time sorties.

I've remained faithful to the names of most of the crews in Operation Chastise (now commonly referred to as the Dam Busters or Dambusters raid), which are well documented, particularly in the iconic and titular blockbuster. But of course, the conversation between Air Commodore Ralph Cochrane (1895–1977), Wing

Commander Guy Gibson (1918–1944), inventor of Upkeep, Barnes Wallis (1887–1979), and Senior Commander of the ATA, Pauline Gower (1910–1947) is pure invention. It is true, however, that only nineteen of the original twenty-one crews took part in Operation Chastise in May 1943. The other two were listed as too sick to participate.

The honour amongst wartime pilots, irrespective of nationality, inspired the story *The German Pilot*. The book *A Higher Call* by Adam Makos tells the incredible true story of an American aircrew spared by the humanity of a German pilot, who risked being charged with treason to guide the bomber crew to safety. The ace pilot, Franz Stigler's justification for saving the B-17 bomber, was his recognition of the crew's helplessness, which he judged comparable to men escaping burning planes in parachutes. He spared them, despite being one kill away from receiving the coveted medal, the Knight's Cross. Whilst impossible to criticise his compassion, it is certainly a controversial moral judgement with consequences I wanted to explore.

The term 'flying ace' was initially a French construct to award military aviators accredited with at least five aerial victories. However, the significant divide between the number of German and Allied aces meant that five kills hardly registered in terms of aerial successes by Luftwaffe standards. The top two hundred and thirty aces of WWII were all German, with one hundred and seven of them having shot down over one hundred

Allied planes each. Germany's top ace was Erich Hartman, who scored three hundred and fifty-two aerial conquests. The highest scoring Allied ace was Major Richard Ira Bong (US Army Air Forces), who scored forty victories. This compelling statistic is perhaps not widely shared due to the fact that, as wartime Prime Minister Winston Churchill (1874–1965) was fond of saying, 'History is written by the victors.'

The reason why the German Luftwaffe produced so many high scoring aces is not easy to qualify. Being an excellent marksman and tactician, and possessing perfect eyesight, a superior aircraft and immense courage were all no doubt universal necessities for the successful fighter pilot. But unlike their American and British combatants, who could look forward to being 'rested' after a number of sorties, Luftwaffe pilots were unceasingly operational. More flying hours would have given greater opportunities to vanquish opposition and hone combat skills, but the additional pressure and chronic fatigue this must have inflicted is almost inconceivable and often resulted in *Kanalkrankheit* (Channel sickness), causing young Luftwaffe pilots to fabricate reasons for returning prematurely back across the English Channel to base. And who could blame them!

The Pathfinder is not only about a man in an elite Bomber Command squadron, but one who navigates his own personal trajectory. During WWII, six thousand African Caribbean men enlisted in the RAF. About four hundred and fifty of these volunteers were accepted as aircrew and a much smaller proportion as pilots. It is interesting that when the war began in September 1939, the colour bar – a social and legal system of segregation and racial discrimination – was lifted. It can be assumed that the primary driving force for its abolition was not a beneficent one, but one arising from necessity and self-interest. However, the RAF, unlike the US Armed Forces, were entirely intolerant to racism, as shown in this document written by the Air Ministry: 'All ranks should clearly understand that there is no colour bar in the Royal Air Force… any instant of discrimination on grounds of colour by White officers or airmen or any attitude of hostility towards personnel of non-European descent should be immediately and severely checked.'

Inspiration for the character of Jellicoe was easy to find in such characters as Wellington bomber pilot Billy Strachan (1921–1998), later a civil rights pioneer; navigator John 'Jellicoe' Blair (1859–1935), awarded the Distinguished Flying Cross; navigator Errol Walter Barrow (1920–1987), who later became the first Prime Minister of Barbados; and pilot ER Braithwaite (1912–2016), who, after the war, became an author and diplomat. In his semi-autobiographical novel, *To Sir, With Love,* Braithwaite writes about his post-war experiences and how, despite being highly qualified, with a doctorate in physics, he could not secure an engineering position and had to resort to teaching in the East End of London. However, he writes that he experienced no racial discrimination whilst in the RAF, where squadrons were integrated. In the United States Armed Forces, African American and Caribbean aircrew were forced to form an all-Black squadron, known as the Tuskegee Airmen, due to Jim Crow laws, which ended only in 1965 with the Civil Rights Act.

Jellicoe's love interest was also influenced by an article in the daily newspapers about a radio telephone operator called Maureen Stevens, whose soothing voice relayed instructions from a control tower, directing crews back to base. Maureen was also on duty during the night of Operation Chastise. Her husband Steve was one of the pilots who fell in love with her voice as she guided him back from a bombing mission. A recipient of the Distinguished Flying Cross, he described his wife as a happy and dignified person who 'remained beautiful to the last'.

One Too Many differs in style from the rest of the stories in that it is more ruminative and character-driven. Colonel Warwick suffers from a nostalgic malaise and the ever-increasing conviction that despite his distinguished career, his life has been squandered in a loveless union. Instead of seeking a new life with his *innamorata*, he remained both militarily and domestically institutionalised.

There are few pilots who flew in both the first and second world wars, but the Australian Sidney Cotton OBE (1894–1969) was one. He also invented the Sidcot suit, which enabled pilots to keep warm in the cockpit, and contributed greatly to photographic reconnaissance in WWII. Air Vice-Marshal Stanley Vincent (1897–1976) is the only recorded RFC/RAF pilot to claim victories in both wars, although German fighter pilot Theodor Osterkamp (1892–1975), Squadron Commander of Jagdgeschwader 51, also claimed aerial victories in both wars, for which he received the *Pour le Merite* (known informally as the Blue Max) and Knight's Cross of the Iron Cross. But it is perhaps the life of Wing Commander Louis Arbon Strange (1891–1966), who also invented a bomb chute and assisted in the planning of Operation Overlord – the code name for the Battle of Normandy – who most inspired the character of Colonel Warwick. Strange eventually separated from his wife Marjorie after she admitted him to a psychiatric hospital following increasing bouts of depression, in all probability caused by the war.

Corkscrew Port Go, named after an evasive manoeuvre used by RAF Bomber Command, is dedicated to local veteran Reg Payne, his deceased brother Art, his late wife Ena and their son David, and is based on Reg's wartime experiences. Reg, a wireless operator in Bomber Command and a talented aviation artist, survived a tour of duty, along with his brother Art, also a wireless operator. Reg later married his wartime sweetheart, Ena, whose contribution to his successful passage from the RAF to civvy street cannot be underestimated. Reg's frustration at the lack of support by those who governed the course of the war is apparent in his memoirs, so clearly and painstakingly recorded in pen and ink and crafted into Kenneth Ballantyne's excellent biography, *First Wave*. Here, Reg's opinion of later generations, scathing of Bomber Command operations, is equally glacial:

'The armchair moralists who blame the young men of Bomber Command for carrying out the decisions of our political masters, have no idea of the burden which we have carried down over the years to give them the freedom to blame us. Only those who have faced a violent death can understand.'

Mrs Muggeridge, from *Lion Hearts*, would have been one of nine hundred and fifty thousand women who worked in munitions factories during WWII, which involved the manufacture of a wide variety of armaments such as bullets, shells, landmines and torpedoes. Working with high explosives and toxic chemicals, often in poorly ventilated spaces, was highly dangerous and the cause of many fatalities. At the time, work shifts were unregulated, with some women working twelve-hour shifts, seven days per week. In *Lion Hearts*, I have concentrated on Mrs Muggeridge's domestic life, but her working life would have contributed greatly to her exhaustion and implied illness.

Gordon, her younger son, suffers from Down syndrome (previously known as Mongolism) and would have been almost certainly institutionalised at birth. The grim reality of such institutions has been widely recorded over the years with horror stories of beatings and neglect, and it wasn't until the 1980s that Down syndrome children were no longer consigned systematically into care. As this condition became better understood, the Education Act 1944, which had judged such children as 'uneducable', was replaced by the Education (Handicapped Children) Act 1970, which stated that every child in the UK warranted an education. Defying society to keep a Down syndrome child in the 1940s would have been an extremely courageous thing to do, particularly with a partner who rejected the child. American playwright Arthur Miller (1915–2005) abandoned Daniel, his Down syndrome son from his third marriage, not only having him institutionalised but also keeping him a secret. *Lion Hearts*, the story most indirectly related to flying, nevertheless identifies Mrs Muggeridge's courage as commensurate, not only to Gordon's act of valour, but also to that of her Spitfire pilot son Michael.

Into the Fray Goes Walter Pidgeon is a homage to the contribution of the unlikely hero – the common pigeon. About eighty thousand pigeons were used as messengers during WWII, and of the fifty-three Dickin Medals awarded to animals for their gallantry and devotion to duty, thirty-two of these were granted to pigeons. At Bletchley Park, the heritage site in Buckinghamshire, hailed as the principal code-breaking centre during WWII, an entire room is devoted to these implausible champions. The 2005 animated film *Valiant* also follows the humorous adventures of pigeons during wartime.

Though it may appear that the injuries Walter sustained on his return flight from Normandy would have made his safe return across the English Channel improbable, pigeons are in fact extremely hardy birds. The carrier pigeon Mary of Exeter survived four missions from France to England, during which time she was shot, hit by shrapnel and bombed in her own pigeon loft! She was also attacked by a German-trained hawk, after which she needed twenty-two stitches. She was made a special collar by her owner to support her damaged neck muscles and lived for a further ten years. WWI pigeon Cher Ami delivered a message that saved an entire American battalion. In the process, she was shot through the breast, lost an eye and returned with one leg dangling by a tendon. The medics who fought to save her carved her a new wooden leg and she became the heroine of the 77th Infantry Division, preserved by taxidermy and exhibited in the Smithsonian Institution.

During the Battle of Britain, RAF fighter pilots undoubtedly changed the direction of WWII by preventing invasion, a feat recognised by Churchill in his speech: 'Never in the field of human conflict has so much been owed by so many to so few.' These lone warriors were the inspiration for many feature films and documentaries, sanctioned as the real 'knights of the air'. However, as actor Brad Johnson – as Lt. Jake 'Cool Hand' Johnson – says in the film *Flight of the Intruder*,

'Fighter pilots make films, bomber pilots make history.' It's no doubt true that the strategic bombing of cities and industrial buildings devastates a nation's ability to wage war to a far greater degree than any number of fighter aircraft. But the image of the bomber pilot has always been ideologically troublesome, given the number of civilian deaths left in the wake of an attack. Yet the immense courage of the bomber crew, whose fatality rate has been estimated at times as high as sixty-five per cent, is undeniable. During Operation Chastise alone, fifty-three of the one hundred and thirty-three crew members were killed serving their country.

The quiet, understated heroism of the home front gained less formal recognition but, nevertheless, dealt with those struggling bravely with their own private battles, without the recompense of insignia or citation. Heroism is happily perennial, however epic or humble.

Like the injured pigeon homing, the mother negotiating her child's best interests or the crippled bomber crew navigating its return course, all seem to entail landing 'on a wing and a prayer' onto a flight strip already heavily scrambled by the valiant.

Anything to Anywhere

I

She tossed her blonde hair from the constraints of its tight knot in the same unbridled fashion that she hastened across the airfield, leaving the Tiger Moth behind her on the runway, spent of fuel, already forgotten. Those who passed her cast a sideward glance at the ethereal figure in the flight suit, striding blithely, a faint smile lighting her comely features as she made her way to the operations room. This was her third flight to Prestwick in two weeks – a long and tedious flight that had taken her two days in the tired, sluggish Moth. Although summer was on its way, the air was still chilled and the open cockpit afforded her no shield against the biting winds of the Galloway Hills, which permeated her pale skin to the very core. She knew the Scottish landscape well now, and flying over the Solway

Firth, the colours and curves of the lochs and forestry plantations now seemed almost as familiar as the meandering Solent nestled between islands, and the undulating Hampshire Downs. The Downs, peaked by the aptly named Pilot Hill, seemed to wink their salutations from their chalked ridge each time she departed and returned to Hamble Ferry Pool, where she was based.

As an Air Transport Auxiliary girl, First Officer Beatrice Barton had what she felt was the most enviable job of wartime. Along with her colleagues at the all-female ferry pool, she flew new and repaired military aircraft from factories to airfields, as well as returning the damaged ones to maintenance depots, which was a perilous task as they were sometimes barely flightworthy. Only six weeks ago she had been flying a defective Mosquito when both engines had cut out for no apparent reason. A double engine failure was rare and for a moment she had been stricken by panic before hastily trying to restart them. But the aircraft had responded with a short splutter, then deathly silence. As she'd surveyed the area below for a place to land, the plane had begun to lose altitude fast. Ahead had been an area of unpeopled, arable land, where she could attempt a forced landing and further still the Solent, a lick of aquamarine against the horizon. Upon approach of the stretch of farmland, she had discovered further complications – the landing gear was not releasing.

Beads of perspiration had collected on her brow but her instincts had kicked in. She would have no option but to land the plane on its belly. But the terrain, though unvarying and featureless, had presented another challenge. It was populated by cattle.

Instinctively she had lifted the nose of the Mosquito and headed toward the turquoise belt of water, willing the plane to remain airborne long enough to reach it. She would have to ditch. She braced herself as she cleared the last of terra firma, circled the dying Mosquito once more and landed in the tidal water, the wooden frame skimming the surface like a skipping stone, toward the bank of the mainland. After what had seemed like an eternity, it stopped, and before the twin-engined aircraft submerged, she'd alighted with only a few cuts and bruises to mark her damaged pride. She'd swum the few strokes to the shore, where she'd been pulled unceremoniously from the bracing waters by excited members of the public who couldn't believe the spectacle they had just witnessed.

'A girl,' one middle-aged woman had exclaimed, divesting herself of her trench coat and placing it around Beatrice's shoulders. 'Who would have thought that a little frail thing like you could fly a warplane! No wonder it crashed.' She had laughed riotously, though not unkindly.

'Yes, there are plenty of jobs in the Land Army if you're determined to be useful.' A man wearing a grey fedora had lit her a cigarette. 'But with your looks, you ought to be in the pictures. You could be the next Lana Turner.' He eyed her keenly. Even half-drowned and without lipstick she looked stunning.

'Hey,' the middle-aged woman remarked protectively, 'stop salivating. She's young enough to be your daughter.'

'A man can dream, can't he?'

The Mosquito had lain still, beached like a whale so that later, it had been recovered from the water by locals and repaired on-site enough for it to be returned to the skies once more by First Officer Barton, who this time succeeded in delivering it unscathed to Hatfield for a thorough inspection. The engineers had cited fuel contamination as the cause for engine failure and she had been exonerated of any flying error. In fact, she had been congratulated by her commanding officer for not only defying death, but for saving a precious Mosquito into the bargain.

'A textbook landing,' Commander Gower had said. 'I'd like to see any man handle that situation better. Well done, First Officer Barton.'

Her words had meant a lot to Beatrice, who was acutely aware, as were all the ATA girls, that they had to be better than men in order to be accepted. The idea of female pilots was not a popular one and there were many who felt that flying should remain the domain of men. This meant that a good track record was essential.

Reputations could be ruined by incompetence and, more significantly, reflect badly on the ATA.

Since the Mosquito incident, Beatrice had taken to wearing a lucky charm around her neck – a silver amulet of a bird in flight given to her by her mother. She never flew without it and it became as essential to her, in its way, as the *Ferry Pilots Notes* manual that allowed her to fly any number of planes, especially since her conversion to four-engined aircraft. In times of difficulty, her hand would automatically stray, in silent prayer, to her throat for the comforting sensation of chain and pendant. She touched it now as she signed a collection chitty for the Fairey Barracuda bomber, which she was due to fly to Lossiemouth. The dive bomber awaited her at dispersal. She threw her overnight bag over its high wings into the cockpit and checked the handbook. She had flown a Barracuda half a dozen times and knew it well, but she understood the importance of familiarising herself with these notes before the flight as it was easy to become confused when flying several different aircraft in the same day, and the Barracuda was known to be unpredictable.

The weather was due to change and the sky, which was presently clear, would soon fill with dense cloud. Without a radio and only a map and compass for navigational aids, she knew she had to make the most of the daylight. The topography of the flight was etched in her mind: the pine forests and the distinctive triangular inlet of the Moray Firth. She settled into the large cockpit and began the initial checks for take-off – trimming tabs, fuel, flaps, radiator shutters, direction indicator, engines. Satisfied, she began to open the engine to static boost when she noticed something by her feet. At first, she thought it was a glove but upon closer inspection, she could see that it was a small, knitted figure of a bulldog, the face puckered and the beady eyes endearing in the nuggety face. She smiled. It had undoubtedly been made as a mascot by a mother or a lover in the hope it would protect someone from harm. Either it had been forgotten or it had slipped from an overnight bag without detection. Knowing how important her own lucky charm had become, she could imagine how distressed the owner would be upon discovering its loss. She shouted to the mechanic below: 'Would you happen to know who this belongs to? Looks like a bulldog.'

'Ah that.' The mechanic looked up at her with a wide, toothy grin. 'Name's Churchill. The dog, that is, not me! Belongs to Squadron Leader Vere Knightly. Never flies without him apparently. He was here on some business a couple of days ago, but I guess he's back at Lossie by now. At least I think that's where he was posted.' He laughed. 'He won't like flying without Churchill, that's for sure.'

'I'll make sure he gets it. Squadron Leader Vere Knightly you said?'

'That's right, miss, but we can do that.'

'No, it's no trouble, really. I know how important these mascots are. I'm off to Lossie now.' She smiled down at him. 'It'll save the postage!' She placed the *Ferry Pilots Notes* ring-bound file next to her in the three-seater dive bomber. The long, continuous canopy gave it a greenhouse feel and she settled into its warmth. 'Chocks away!' she shouted, sliding the canopy closed so that the mechanic quickly withdrew the quivering wedge from beneath the wheel. He watched her guide the Barracuda around the perimeter track to the runway. After making the final checks for take-off, she released the brakes, opened the throttle and, easing the control column forward, then slowly back, roared into the distance toward the River Forth. The mechanic watched her until she became nothing more than a speck on the horizon. He had heard of her, her reputation having preceded her, but she had surpassed all expectations. He sighed and returned to the nearby hangar.

Beatrice flew the hefty aircraft beneath the grizzled clusters of gloomy clouds. She was used to low flying and had a sixth sense about the landscape. Her navigational skills were reputed to be second to none and had saved her on several occasions when flying through dense fog. As she flew through the dim, russet mist, which hung loosely beneath the umbrella of cloud, she grew curious and wondered what Squadron Leader Knightly looked like and whether he had realised yet that his mascot was lost. If he had, she wondered what impact it had had on his flying. The flight to Lossiemouth was uneventful but she would be relieved to land the Barracuda. It was a heavy and ambling plane known for developing leaks in the hydraulic system, which could easily render a pilot unconscious if they weren't equipped with an oxygen mask, which she wasn't. Some called it the Death Bird due to its number of fatalities, and several ATA pilots had refused to fly one, saying that its ugliness reflected its mechanics, believing it to be cursed. She remembered Millie, a friend at the ATA, who, despite being a natural pilot, had had the misfortune of being assigned one of these planes. It had been the last flight she had ever taken. An image of Millie dancing at London's 400 Club formed in her head. The club was a favourite haunt of many of the ATA girls, but despite its fabulous orchestra, Beatrice was now bored with it, filled as it was with well-connected but often supercilious types. Everyone was there for a good time and, just like Millie, to forget the war. For a while it had been what she'd needed too. Her parents had been lost in the blitz and her fiancé, a naval officer, had been killed at sea over a year ago. A couple of fleeting affairs had helped her deal with the lonely nights and her scuppered dreams, but she had decided that attachment was a game for fools, and the cost of loving, too great. Her own personal battle scars had refashioned her into a thrill-seeker. One of these kites would probably claim her too, at some point, but she wished it could be in the throes of battle rather than delivery. It seemed to her so unfair that the women pilots of the ATA, who were so often better and more experienced flyers than men, were deprived of combat. She felt she had nothing left to lose. Her greatest fear was not of death but of a life half-lived.

RAF Lossiemouth soon approached and she collected her thoughts for the landing, which, despite the weightiness of the plane, was surprisingly smooth. She was marshalled off the runway by a rigger who allotted her a space next to a Vickers Wellington and placed chocks under the wheels.

'Good flight, miss?' he asked, seemingly apprehensive about addressing a female pilot. 'We've been expecting you.'

She was used to the curiosity, especially when she emerged from the cockpit of a four-engined Lancaster bomber. She pulled the helmet from her head and her blonde hair fell loosely over her face so that for a moment, her green eyes were concealed. She swept it back so that he caught the full impact of them above the curve of her pale, smiling lips. 'Tickety-boo, thanks.' She looked around. 'I expect my Spit is in one of the hangars. I'll just deliver my chit and freshen up, then I'll be back to collect her. I'm flying to White Waltham.'

She was looking forward to flying the Spitfire. They flew like a dream and were every ATA pilot's favourite plane.

She looked down at the weight in her hand and suddenly remembered the mascot. 'I almost forgot.' She held up the woollen bulldog. 'I have this for Squadron Leader Knightly. Do you know where I can find him?'

'Squadron Leader Knightly? He hasn't been here for some time now.' The airman laughed at the sight of the bulldog. 'He was called to Scampton. Flew a Lancaster down there some time ago and I haven't seen him since. He'll be sorry to have left this fellow behind, though. Swore he brought him luck.'

'Oh I see. Well...' She looked down at the beady-eyed dog, disappointed. 'No matter, it will wait. It's just that people set great store by their mascots, don't they?'

'Don't worry, miss. We can post it from here if you like? Save you the bother when you get to White Waltham.'

'That's very accommodating, thank you.' She motioned to hand the bulldog over and then, as if moved by something in its expression, changed her mind. 'No, on second thoughts, don't worry. I'll keep him with me a bit longer. Who knows, a bit of luck might rub off on me.' She couldn't rid herself of her curiosity about Squadron Leader Knightly, and the fact that he had been transferred to another squadron only served to intrigue her more.

RAF Scampton was almost directly on her route home. Some of the ATA girls raffishly took an occasional diversion to see a friend, landing in a nearby field so they could luncheon together or share a secret tryst with a lover. If caught, they were grounded and risked losing their jobs. But ATA pilots also frequently landed when they lost their bearings as they had no instrument training. The weather was due to worsen in a couple of hours so it would be feasible to search for a place to land.

After a brief period of respite at the mess, she collected her Spitfire, eager to start the journey. It was cooler now and she tucked her hair into her flying helmet and put on her flying jacket. The cockpit felt small and compact after the Barracuda, and the Merlin engine so powerful that when she opened up the throttle, it almost felt as if the plane and she had conjoined, the roar of the piston engine an expression of her own eagerness, the elliptical wings an extension of her own limbs. This is what she'd been waiting for – soaring beneath the clouds, following the lines and curves of railway and river, as much a part of the landscape as the flow of the Witham or the beech trees of the Wolds. She was so exhilarated that she couldn't help but fly a victory roll. Any aerobatics were strictly forbidden, but the power and agility of the sleek aircraft she piloted demanded she challenge its capabilities. As she approached Scampton, the sky conveniently darkened and mild rainfall sprinkled the canopy. She knew exactly where she was without the aid of a map or compass, but she still meant to land. She approached the airfield and landed smoothly on the tarmac, where she was quickly met and ushered off the main runway by a mechanic who was obviously surprised by her sudden appearance. She too was surprised, as lined up by the perimeter track were more Lancaster bombers than she had ever seen. They looked, with their colossal stature, like magnificent warlords joined in council, growling occasional orders at each other as their minions, the ground staff, rallied around, checking engines and undercarriage, propellers and fuel, guarding their masters with deferential pride. Obviously, an operation of some sort was imminent. She wondered if Squadron Leader Knightly was involved in it. In the darkening light, dressed in her flying jacket and helmet, the engineer didn't at first realise that he was addressing a woman.

'Not expecting you, sir. Important to keep the runway free at the moment.'

'Why? What's going on with the Lancs?'

Upon hearing the softness of her voice he adjusted his gaze, somewhat taken aback. 'No idea, miss, and I wouldn't be able to say if I had. Hopefully it's something that will put Jerry out of action for a long time one way or another.' He eyed the Spitfire. 'Flown off course, have we?'

She could tell by his tone that he was one of those men who felt that women were better suited to a kitchen sink than a cockpit.

'There seems to be a fault with the oil pressure,' she said. 'I thought perhaps you could take a quick look for me?' Before he could answer she added, 'By the way, is Squadron Leader Knightly about? I have something belonging to him.'

At this, the engineer smiled. 'Oh, I see, miss. Well yes, he's here but you won't get to see him. He's probably in the briefing room as we speak, or the mess. You could try the mess, I suppose. But I imagine he's pretty occupied.'

'I'll try anyway. No chance of a lift I suppose?'

'Sorry, we're understaffed as it is and you can see how we're fixed.' He eyed the Spitfire. 'But I'll take a look at her as soon as I get a chance.'

'Don't worry, the walk will do me good.' She made her way to the mess. It was rather a grand building that seemed all the grander, juxtaposed as it was, by corrugated iron Nissen huts and the flat-roofed operations block. She had put the mascot in her overnight bag, intending to freshen up and sate her appetite first, but the sight of so many crews staved her hunger, replacing it instead with a gnawing curiosity. She kept her flight jacket and brown leather helmet on, the flaps covering the feminine line of her jaw and her high, prominent cheekbones. Knowing that her presence would have been prohibited, she kept her head low but no one gave her so much as a cursory glance, immersed as they were in conversation.

'It must be the Tirpitz. What else?'

'Could be any number of targets – viaducts, bridges, ships. Who knows?'

One of the members of a nearby crew was in visible distress, his face contorted with a fear he made no effort to disguise.

'I have a bad feeling about this op. I'm telling you it doesn't feel right. I just know we're not coming back from it.' The others tried to calm him, but hysteria had seeped into his bones and he couldn't be silenced. 'All this low flying, it just won't work. It's impossible to sustain that kind of level above the sea in pitch darkness, even with the lamps attached. A momentary lack of concentration and we're done for. And even if we do get there in one piece, we'll be like sitting ducks, all lit up like beacons. Talk about announcing your arrival.'

A striking, dark-haired man chipped in. 'Come on now, old chap! That type of talk doesn't help anyone.'

'That's right. Come on, Spike, you'll turn the milk sour. It's not like you.'

Beatrice beckoned to the girl at the bar. 'Do you know if Squadron Leader Knightly is here? If so, can you point him out to me, discreetly?'

'Oh yes.' Her face lit up at his mention. 'It's the dark-haired one over there.' She gestured with her eyes. 'The one who's trying to calm ole Spike. Very good-looking, isn't he? We've all got a crush.'

At that point, an NCO arrived and called everyone to the briefing room. Squadron Leader Knightly walked past Beatrice, brushing her arm as he passed, and she knew that she should have said something then, returned the mascot and left, but the conversations she had overheard had intrigued her and instead, she followed him with her head bowed to the upper floor of the art deco building, into the main briefing room. The room was darkly lit, filled with airmen who only seemed aware of their own crews, so she settled at the back of the room until every seat was taken. Two RAF police officers now guarded the door, which they closed behind them and locked. Then Wing Commander Guy Gibson addressed the men. Though not tall, he was an imposing figure. No one could deny his charisma. As soon as he stood, the room fell silent and the air was alive with an intense and palpable energy. Beatrice listened in amazement as he spoke with authority and candour of the task that awaited them. He could now reveal, Gibson said, why this special squadron had been formed and what its mission entailed. It became clear to Beatrice that these bomber crews had been training for weeks, flying at night at low level, to enable them to release a bomb that would skim the surface of the water before hitting its target. No stranger to low flying herself, Beatrice understood how difficult it was to discern exactly how close you were to the ocean at night. Any lack of concentration could mean that you were suddenly in the drink, as Spike had noted. But to combat this problem and help maintain altitude, two spotlights had been fitted to the nose and fuselage of each aircraft, so that the shafts of light would merge on the water's surface when the plane was flying at the correct height. It was a simple but effective solution. But that wasn't the only modification. Amongst other things, the mid-upper turrets of the Lancasters had been removed to make the plane lighter, and a nose blister had been added to improve visibility for the bomb aimer. Beatrice marvelled at the ingenuity of the bouncing bomb and the dexterity of the pilots and their crews. She longed to be a part of this band of brothers but realised it was nothing short of a miracle that she had managed to remain undetected in the briefing room, let alone accompany them on their mission. If they knew she was an ATA pilot, and worse still, a woman, she would be removed immediately and, probably, severely disciplined. She looked over at Squadron Leader Knightly, listening intently to instructions from Gibson while nearby one of his team shook visibly with fear. She sensed that this man was at breaking point. If he was like this on their mission, he would spook the entire crew and undoubtedly thwart the entire operation.

The targets of the bouncing bomb were three of Germany's major dams – the Möhne, the Sorpe and the Eder – with the objective to create as much devastation to the Ruhr valley infrastructure as possible. If successful, the flooding would annihilate power stations, transportation systems and factories, and cause immeasurable disruption, as well as lowering enemy morale. Knightly and his crew were to fly in the first formation, which comprised of ten aircraft flying in groups of three, four and three. Knightly was to fly in the second group, which would take off ten minutes after the first. Their intent was to breach the Möhne dam as quickly as possible and, after that, any aircrew that hadn't used their bombs were to proceed to the Eder dam. She looked at the large flight map in the briefing room. The route led them over the North Sea to the Netherlands then into North Rhine-Westphalia and the Ruhr district, where they would make a detour to avoid German defences before turning south and following the Möhne river to its great dam.

The idea that a dam could be destroyed by a bouncing bomb was hard for her to conceive, so freshly placed in her psyche, but this squadron had obviously been practising for this operation by flying low over a number of reservoirs around the country for some time. The inventor of the bomb, Barnes Wallis, seemed convinced that if it ricocheted and hit the dam directly, it would sink against the wall, its explosions causing massive shock waves. When the briefing was over, crews studied models of the dams and excitedly discussed the logistics of the operation, before making their way to the transport trucks that delivered them to their aircraft. The aerodrome was a hive of activity now, with ground crew battling against time to correct any errors and ensure the safety of the aircrew. Armourers fitted the great mines winched from tractors, and instrument fitters, riggers and mechanics worked tirelessly, checking instruments and making repairs on the modified aircraft now draped with scaffolding and mounted by devoted technicians. Relatively inconspicuous amidst such enterprise, Beatrice followed Knightly and his crew at some distance, electricians and mechanics crossing her path in hurried concentration. Near dispersal, they stopped and one of the men lit a cigarette.

'Aye, it's mad,' she heard him say, in a broad Scottish accent. 'Ye had better settle yer affairs. We may nae be a comin' back.'

Knightly seemed dismissive. 'Nonsense, don't listen to McDuff here, the merchant of doom and gloom. This time tomorrow I'll be standing you all a drink at the mess and we'll be high from the thrill of it all.'

'Aye mibbie, but ye'v got tae admit it sounds nigh impossible, breaching a dam that size wi' all the flak 'n' spotlights 'n' whatnot. Ah cannae quite get mah head around it.'

Spike was beginning to crack. 'It's a crazy idea, crazy!' His voice grew louder and quivered with torment as he spoke. 'We're all going to die; I know we are.'

Beatrice had witnessed before the decline of men pushed beyond the threshold of reason. She could only imagine what he had experienced in the theatre of war. Anyone could see he was a sick man.

Knightly grabbed him by the shoulders. 'Now look here, Spike. You've got to pull yourself together. We'll all be fine. We've got a top crew and that's why we've all been chosen. It's a great adventure we're all going on and a great privilege, and we're all going to come back, do you hear?'

'Yeah, Spike, you're gonna spook us all if you carry on like that. We'll be fine. We always are.' A short man with a shock of ginger hair patted him on the back. 'And anyway, I don't know what you lot are worried about. I'm the rear gunner so if anyone's likely to cop it, it's probably gonna be me.'

'Dinna worry, Ginny. Ye'r so wee no one will see ye.'

'Better short than ugly.'

Knightly persisted. 'It's just the waiting around that's got to you Spike, that's all. It's no disgrace to get scared. God knows you'd be a fool not to be, but it's just how you deal with it. Now take ten minutes to get yourself together and join us at Her Ladyship. We can't fly without a navigator and it's a bit late to find a substitute now. They're already one Lancaster down due to sickness.'

Spike turned and walked away; his shame evidenced in his faltering gait.

'Shall I go after him, Skipper?' a burly looking man with thinning hair cut in.

'No, Crouch. I'll give him ten minutes to calm himself. He's no good to us as he is. If he isn't back by then, well, we may have to abandon the mission. Hopefully it won't come to that.'

Crouch raised his hands in despair. 'We've been training for this for nearly two months and as crazy as the mission seems, I want to be a part of it, even if McDuff here doesn't. We've shown more accuracy at Eyebrook than any other crew. We've had enough to put up with from the other squadrons thinking we're having an easy time of it with no operations, and I'm not missing out on something we've put our heart and soul into these last weeks, just because someone's gone yellow-bellied all of a sudden.'

'Ah didnae say ah wanted tae call it off. Just that we've got a nigh impossible job on oor hands.'

Knightly raised a hand to silence them. 'That's enough, Crouch, McDuff. What you said about Spike wasn't fair. You know as well as I do that he's already flown over fifty operations with no problems. He deserves a damn medal, not your condemnation. He's just overtired that's all.'

'We're all tired and scared,' Ginny scratched his red locks. 'Jesus, I've got a wife and two kids waiting for me at home. But I'm here, aren't I? Just like the rest of this crew and the nineteen other crews. We know what the chances of returning in one piece are, but we're here.'

A tall, fair-haired man addressed Crouch. 'Skipper's right. Spike's been a hero. You know that. He's on his second tour and has flown more sorties than all of us, except the skipper. In his last couple of sorties, he saw the rear gunner get shot up and the wireless operator burn to death. Everyone's got their breaking point. Now, I'm going to go and check out the hydraulics. Come on Shortwave, you'd better inspect your wireless. Make sure it's up to all that Morse code nonsense you do. Anyone else coming?'

Knightly checked his watch and beckoned toward the peri-track. 'Okay, chaps, Dobby's right. Enough idle chit-chat. Go and sort yourselves out and I'll catch up with Spike.' He sighed. 'I'm only glad I picked you all for your skills and not your optimism. We're leaving in half an hour and we'll need to have our wits about us. I'll be back shortly and you'd better just hope that I've got a navigator with me.'

He strode off in the direction that Spike had headed, and Beatrice followed. The ground crews were thinning out now and most of the aircrews had dispersed, heading to their aircraft.

She knew that Spike was presently unfit for purpose and that any attempt to skewer him into submission would prove futile. She quickened her pace, eager now to desist with any duplicity. 'He went this way.' She nodded toward the barracks. 'I watched him go.'

'A girl!' Knightly looked astounded. 'I saw you out

of the corner of my eye at the mess and wondered who you were but it didn't register. Too damn busy with Spike, I suppose. Who are you? And what are you doing here? You know of course that you shouldn't be here?'

Beatrice pulled off her flight helmet, as if her gender were still in doubt. 'I'm an ATA pilot. I came here to give you this.' She pulled out the bulldog mascot from her overnight bag. 'I thought he might be important to you. I had no idea that I'd be arriving in the middle of such an important operation.'

'Good God, it's Churchill. Where did you find him? I never thought I'd see him again. What a great omen, and just when we need a spot of luck.'

'He was in the cockpit of a Barracuda that I flew to Lossie. I know how important these mascots are so thought I'd stop by in the Spit on my way home.'

He laughed loudly now as he took in her small frame. 'You flew a Barracuda to Lossie and survived to tell the tale? Well, I never! I knew you ATA girls were something else but I never thought… Anyway…' He was drawn back to reality. 'I'm eternally grateful to you for bringing me Churchill. It means more than I can say.' He put the bulldog under his arm and smiled at her and she noticed, even in the darkness, that the worry lines on his forehead temporarily dissipated. 'Maybe we can catch up sometime when I get back. We can swap stories. You can tell me about the different aircraft you fly and I'll tell you…'

'About the dam raid? That doesn't really seem a very fair exchange, does it?'

'You know about that?'

'I was at the briefing. I heard it all.'

'Good God, talk about a security breach. Still, I suppose you realise the importance of keeping silent. Unless of course you're a German spy. I guess I really ought to have you arrested or at least interned until the mission's over.'

'There is one way you could stop me from talking.'

'Oh? What's that?'

'You could take me with you.'

Knightly laughed. 'Really, in what capacity may I ask?'

'Navigator.'

'We already have one. I'm just about to fetch him now.'

'I saw him. He's a wreck. There's no way that he's capable of even boarding a plane, let alone navigating one, and I think you know that.' She gestured to the operations block in the distance. 'He needs to be in the sick quarters.'

Knightly strained his eyes. There was certainly nothing wrong with her vision. Spike was sitting on damp grass, rocking from side to side, and as they approached, his choking lament punctured the still air.

'Jesus, we can't leave him here wailing like a banshee.' Out of his depth, Knightly resorted to the language of understatement customary of his class and status. 'I can see you're a bit under the weather, old chap. Let's get you to your room, shall we.'

Slowly cajoled into submission, Spike was led to his room, almost monastic in its lack of adornment, where, like a weary pilgrim, he collapsed onto the linen blanketed bed.

'Well, I suppose that's it. I'd better go and tell the boys that ops are off.'

'You don't need to do that. I can take his place.'

'You *are* joking? I mean, I don't doubt that you're good at what you do but we're talking about flying in combat. And you may well be acquainted with British terrain but, in case you've forgotten, it's Germany we're flying to, and not for a vacation.'

'I've studied the routes many times. My father was a cartographer for heaven's sake. He read me maps for bedtime stories! I know the Ruhr valley well and I'm used to low flying. We're told never to go above the clouds so most of our flying is low level anyway. And I've flown over seventy different planes should you need a break.'

'That's impressive! But you're not a trained navigator.'

'A friend of mine gave me some advanced instrument training at White Waltham. Spike has no doubt already plotted the course. I'm a natural navigator. Always top of the class at geometry and calculus. Took to it like a duck to water. Look,' she sighed, 'I fly alone. I'm used to depending on my instincts. Let me try. It's either that or you're all grounded.'

'This is different. The noise of the plane and the vibrations alone at that level can make you sick. But that's the least of your worries. It's the flak and the fighter planes…'

'I've delivered several Lancasters so I'm already conversant with their rhythm. As for the flak, I'll take my chances.'

'And what do you think the chaps would say if I brought a female ATA pilot on board? Do you really think they'd be happy about that?'

'I think at this moment in time they'd fly without a navigator at all rather than not go and you've got to admit, even the most cynical man would think my navigation better than no navigation at all. You don't need to tell them about me until we're on the way if you don't want to, and then it'll be too late for them to complain.'

'You're crazy! Have you any idea how dangerous this mission is going to be?'

'Yes, I do. And if you're putting your life on the line for it then why shouldn't I have the right to make that choice. I'm not afraid of dying. But I want to make each moment count.'

'Well,' Knightly shrugged, 'I don't think I've ever met a woman who thinks like you before. You really are certifiable.'

'Apparently so.'

'I don't even know your name?'

'Beatrice. Bea to my friends.' She noted the time on the wall clock. 'So, what do you say?'

Knightly looked at Spike, destabilised and broken by his experiences, then at Beatrice, eager to encounter the thrill of danger, at any cost. He had neither the time nor inclination to disabuse her of her somewhat callow notions, and he was willing to admit to some self-interest. He and his crew had been training for this mission for months, with conversion flights to cope with as well as low flying and the trials of Upkeep, the bouncing bomb. The men were fatigued already with only a few hours' sleep each night and weighted by the expectation of success. Yet, if they couldn't now go, all this would have been for nothing – the intensive training, the isolation, the indignation of other crews and the constant fear in the pit of one's stomach. He nodded at her. 'Check his kit.'

'There's everything I need – maps, navigation log, sextant, compass. Here's the course to the Ruhr, all plotted. Weather check complete and destination. I'll give you latitude and longitudinal readings on point of departure. Give me five minutes when we're in the Lanc to get prepared and complete the pre-flight data. It's child's play.'

By the time Knightly and Beatrice arrived at the

Lancaster, the crew were looking dejected.

'Only three minutes to go, Skipper. We thought you weren't going to make it. Where's Spike? Who's this?'

Beatrice already had her helmet on and the oxygen mask hung, covering half her face. Her flight jacket rendered her shapeless and in the dusky evening she was unrecognisable.

'This,' Knightly said, 'is our last hope. So if you really want to go on this crazy mission, don't ask any more damned questions. Introductions later.'

'Let's get on with it, Skipper.' Crouch eyed her suspiciously. 'The rest of your crew sick, I suppose?'

Beatrice nodded. She was unused to sitting behind the pilot and engineer, a curtain drawn between them so she could check her maps with a light, but she quickly arranged her instrument kit on the navigator's table, maps for easy access, dividers and compass, drift meter, air position indicator and dead reckoning computer. Within minutes they were taxiing along the perimeter track to the runway. She secured her oxygen mask for the sake of concealment, though she knew at some point she would have to communicate over the intercom. The wireless operator seated nearby smiled at her and she nodded.

'Good to have you with us. I'll stand you a drink when we get home.'

She smiled; her head lowered. He must think her a mute.

The engines thundered their readiness, on full power now, as they cruised to the take-off point, and Beatrice could not rid herself of the sensation that she was involved in something monumental, something much bigger than all of them. The pitch of the Merlin engines now changed to shrillness.

'Let's have a crew check, shall we? Make sure we haven't left anybody behind.' Knightly smiled to himself. 'Bomb aimer?'

'Bomb Aimer Crouch present, Skipper.'

'Flight engineer?'

'Flight Engineer Dobbie here, Skip.'

'Wireless operator?'

'Present and correct, Skip.'

'Tail gunner?'

'Here, Skipper.'

'Front gunner?'

'Aye, Skipper.'

The Merlin engine droned happily as they sped along the runway.

'Navigator?'

'Navigator Beatrice Barton present, Skipper.'

'What the…' Just then the plane's massive bulk turned weightless and lifted off the runway. It never ceased to amaze Beatrice how such a heavy plane could seemingly defy the laws of gravity to fly.

'Mah God!' McDuff spluttered. 'Yer wee navigator sounds like a lassie.'

'Steady, North Sea ahead. Approach in five minutes. Air speed 160. Drifting to port. Adjust heading, Skipper.'

'Thank you, Navigator.'

'Jesus, ah cannae believe it. We need tae land the plane. We cannae hae a lassie on board.'

'Too late I'm afraid! We already have. Her Ladyship will just have to put up with it.'

'We've really got a girl on board?' Crouch, Ginny and McDuff already secured in their turrets could do nothing but exclaim, while Dobbie looked over at Knightly with a quizzical expression, and then over his shoulder to the curtain, which he hesitantly pulled back to see Beatrice studying her maps, tendrils of her long hair now escaping from her flying helmet. Next to her, Shortwave's mouth was agape.

'She found Churchill. Brought him over from Lossie in a Spit. Thought we could do with the luck. Nice, eh?'

'An ATA girl?' Shortwave took in the escaped blonde hair and curving lips.

'You've got it, Shortwave. She's flown more types of aircraft than you or I could name so she must've picked something up.'

'Yeah, but navigation?' Ginny interjected. 'They only give the female ATA pilots the most basic instrument training. And women just aren't good with maps. No offence meant, I'm sure,' he added with a belated sense of courtesy.

'What about if you let me do my job and you concentrate on yours?' This was just the kind of attitude Beatrice had fought against ever since she'd begun flying. 'Calibrated airspeed two-forty. Stay on heading, Skipper.'

'Thank you, Navigator.'

'Her Ladyship wilnae like it,' McDuff persisted. 'Another lassie.' He sighed loudly.

Beatrice continued studying the maps. 'For your information, McGruff, I've flown at least a dozen Lancs in the last two years and we've always got along famously.'

'McGruff! She's got your number.' There was some laughter.

'Aye, well! Ah will be the first tae eat ma words if the lassie manages tae navigate Her Ladyship back in one piece.'

Beatrice could hear McDuff mumbling his disapproval. 'Sounds like you're overheating in that altitude suit, McGruff. I'd be careful not to get too worked up or you might just short circuit.' There was more laughter from the crew.

'Ach!' McDuff adjusted his oxygen mask irritably. 'By th' way, ye are aware that our destination is Germany, nae France or Poland?'

Beatrice laughed good-naturedly. 'I'd just concentrate on rotating that turret if I were you, McGruff, before some Junkers blows you out of it.'

The mood of the crew was positive now as confidence in Beatrice grew. Nervous energy translated to high spirits but as they grew closer to the Dutch coast, the mood grew more sombre and silence pervaded. Beatrice, behind her curtain, wondered how Knightly was coping. She realised the concentration he needed to fly so low over such a long stretch of water was enormous. One momentary lapse and the North Sea would claim them.

'Crossing enemy coast in five minutes. Standby gunners for possible defences around point of entry.'

'Thank you, Navigator.'

They flew over the Dutch coast without incident. Beatrice wondered how long it would be before they were intercepted by fighter planes. They should have been picked up by enemy radar by now. She hoped that Ginny and McDuff were as good at aiming as they were complaining.

'Should be a railway intersection coming up starboard, Skipper. New course due east.'

'Okay, Navigator.'

'There it is.' Dobby pointed it out to Knightly.

'Information a little thin here. Watch out for pylons and kites just in case.'

'Will do.'

'Pylon coming up now,' Dobby said, and Beatrice felt the aircraft lift as they flew over it.

She switched out her light and drew back the

blackout curtain that separated her from Knightly and Dobby. She was tired of the darkness and it was reassuring to see outside again. Vision was good and the moon lit the canopy so that the faces of the two men were illuminated as they might have been if they'd been sitting around a candlelit table.

'Feeling claustrophobic?' Dobby smiled at her. 'You're doing a great job, so don't give up on us now.'

'Not a chance. But I've memorised the rest. That body of water you're approaching is the Wilhelmina canal.' She observed the new landscape, eager to commit it to memory. The terrain raced past at speed. It was difficult to navigate from sight this low but not impossible. 'Change course, Skipper. North-east avoiding Dortmund.'

'Thanks, Navigator. Everyone okay? McDuff, you're unusually quiet.'

'He hasn't got over the shock of having a woman on board yet. Hey, McDuff, I wonder if there are any female front gunners that we could replace you with!'

'Shortwave, have ye nae heard th' Scots' phrase, "noo yer bum's really oot the windae"?'

Beatrice was enjoying being part of the crew. It was a different experience altogether to flying alone with only your thoughts for company, but there was little time to relax. 'Okay, change course south. Prepare for heavy defences around target area. We should approach the Möhne river in five minutes.'

'Thanks, Nav.'

Suddenly, Beatrice heard bursts of anti-aircraft weapons and the sky lit up with colours. Charged with adrenalin, her heart racing, she was adamant no expression of fear would set her apart.

'Try to think of it as a firework display navigator,' Dobby said kindly. 'I find it helps.'

'Yes, in our honour,' laughed Shortwave. He felt surprisingly at ease in Beatrice's presence. She obviously had guts and that was half of it.

'The good news is that flying on the deck, the heavy guns can't reach us,' Knightly added.

She realised that they were trying to reassure her. Having a female on board had altered the dynamics of the crew and brought out their protective instincts, despite her best efforts at stoicism.

'Don't worry, I'm enjoying the show,' she joked, watching the colourful bursts turn into smoky, impotent puffs that dispersed into a foggy trail high above the canal.

'Aye, but we cannae take evasive action so near tae th' groond,' added McDuff with his usual cynicism. 'Sideslipping and skid turning are oot at this height 'n' in formation. Ye could say we're sittin' ducks.'

'That'll be all thank you, McDuff.'

Beatrice saw they were now flanked by other Lancasters and that they had caught up the first three planes from the first wave. Some distance behind them, she caught sight of the final group. They followed the line of the canal closely, so low that had she been in her Moth with its open cockpit, she felt she could have reached out and touched the water. She realised that the area was more heavily defended than they had anticipated and the mood was one of controlled unease. The noise of flak was endless now, accompanied by violent eruptions of colour all about them. Just then, one of the Lancasters ahead of them was hit.

The aircraft plummeted. There was an almighty explosion as it hit the ground. Evacuation had been impossible and Beatrice and the rest of the crew could do nothing but watch in horror, the thought of their burning comrades quickly dismissed as they fixated on the mission ahead.

'Searchlights ahead.'

The searchlights were blinding and disorientated Knightly and Dobby. The plane wavered as it struggled to maintain height. Knightly, aware that he had little margin to play with, shielded his eyes against the dazzling rays as best he could, the bright orange and red of the flak exacerbating his already blighted vision. Beatrice returned to her maps.

'Hold course. Target should be sighted in two minutes.'

'Can't see it.' Dobby searched the horizon. Beatrice pulled back the curtain again. She recognised the shape of the canal from her brief glance at the model in the briefing room.

'Over there!'

'Yes,' Dobby shouted in excitement. 'There's the dam. My God, look at the size of it.'

'We'll ne'er destroy that monster.'

Crouch, in his bomb aimer's blister, sounded incredulous. 'You really think we'll be able to breach that, Skipper?'

'No problem. Like blowing over a deck of cards with these beauties.'

'Hope you're right, Skip.'

'Well, we'll soon find out. Leader's about to go in. Intercom to radio switch, Shortwave.'

'Done.'

Knightly orbited with the other planes as Wing Commander Guy Gibson went in for the first offensive under heavy counterfire. 'Going in to attack. Stand by to follow in order at my command.'

'Good luck, Leader.'

They circled in observation as his bomb released and bounced across the stretch of ebony, forbidding water toward its gargantuan target, willing it to hit the front of the dam, but it bounced too high and detonated over the top, causing a tsunami that almost caught the tail of his aircraft. The next assault was made by Flight Lieutenant 'Hoppy' Hopgood, but the heavy defences from the towers of the dam and other anti-aircraft guns overpowered him and just as the bomb was dropped, he was hit. Heroically, Hopgood managed to climb to an altitude that enabled some of his crew to evacuate the plane, but it then exploded, falling on the power station below, leaving the dam firmly intact. The crew fell silent, knowing this could be their fate next. Wing Commander Gibson bravely declared that he would fly beside the next plane to help draw off some flak but despite this, Flight Lieutenant Micky Martin's plane veered to the left to avoid burning shells just as the bomb was released and it failed to reach its target.

'Okay, F for Foxtrot,' Gibson called. 'Your turn. We'll fly with you and take some of the punishment. Good luck.'

'Okay, Leader.'

This was the moment they'd been waiting for. It seemed to Beatrice, in that instant, that life and death stood shoulder to shoulder. Who knew which would prevail. As they circled and dived down toward the uninviting mass of water, she could see the towers looming ahead and the sinister eyes of the sluices beneath. This crew had replaced the family she had lost and the camaraderie she craved. She heard the flak gunners as they approached beginning their chorus and McDuff's answering call. She caught sight of Churchill the mascot, who had brought her to such adventure, and watched Knightly pat his head, turn to acknowledge her and wink.

'Tail-End Charlie?'

'Ready, Skip.'
'Front gunner?'
'Aye, Skip.'
'Bomb aimer?'
'Ready.'
'Navigator, keep me posted on the height and speed please.'
'Skipper.'
'Okay, in we go,' Knightly said. 'Bomb doors open. This one's for our lady.' Beatrice instinctively knew that he didn't mean the plane.

Knightly flew the aircraft so low Beatrice thought they would hit the water but at the last moment the spotlights were switched on and he levelled. At this point, the Lancaster could be clearly seen by the artillery gunners and they were at their most vulnerable, but two other bombers were flying with them at a higher altitude and some of the flak was diverted. Beatrice was too engrossed to feel fear. The correct height and speed were imperative to a successful hit.

'Seventy, sixty-five, sixty. Hold her there. Keep her steady, two-ten, two-twenty, two-thirty. Right on course, Skipper. Perfect speed. Hold her steady.'

The flak lit up the canal and flew past the cockpit at an alarming rate, the colours changing in brightness as the shells burnt themselves out. Amidst the constant eruptions of shells were the blasts from the cannons below and their own guns drumming their angry response into the nebulous realm of sky. Crouch, in his horizontal position in the blister, now assisted with the navigation. 'Port a fraction. Now starboard a little more. Straighten. Okay level. Steady. Perfect.'

At precisely one thousand two hundred and eighty feet from their target, Crouch, the towers in his sights, released the bomb. 'Bomb gone.'

'There goes the cookie, don't want it back, duckie!'

They felt the plane rise as the weight of the bomb was released. Knightly wasted no time in retreating. He turned to examine the target. Direct hit. A massive wave rose up in furious response and then settled. They could see a distinct crack in the dam wall but it miraculously held steady.

'Perfect. We've cracked her. You could knock her over with one finger now. One more should do it.'

'Well done F for Foxtrot.' Gibson's praise was emphatic. 'Terrific, chaps.'

'Thank you, Leader.'

'Perfectly executed. Hope you got a good photograph.'

Beatrice felt elation as she observed the crack in the giant wall. Thanks to Knightly's unwavering nerves and Crouch's skilful aim, they had been the first to directly hit their target as their gunners had fought valiantly to protect their aircraft.

Next in was Squadron Leader 'Dinghy' Young.

Knightly knew him well. He was a great pilot. 'We'll fly alongside and take some of the flak.'

'Good,' Gibson said. 'You too, Martin. Let's give Young a chance to finish off this Godforsaken dam. She's holding on by a thread thanks to Knightly and his crew.'

Young, with three other aircraft diverting the flak, released his bomb on target. The dam wall shook but appeared to stabilise. 'She's a stubborn one.'

Gibson then sent in Squadron Leader David Maltby, but just as he was releasing his bomb, the wall of the great dam broke.

'It's gone. The wall's collapsed!' shouted Dobby. 'We've done it.'

There was jubilation from the crew. 'I've got to admit,' Crouch said, 'I didn't think she was ever going to move. Look at that surge of water. Jesus, I've never seen anything like it.'

'Okay, boys, you've done well, all of you.' Gibson congratulated them. 'Now, those of you who've dropped your bombs, head home, and those remaining, follow me to the Eder.'

Knightly turned and Beatrice set their course back to Scampton. For a while, the crew was silent other than when instructions were imperative. Beatrice realised that they were all trying to take in the enormity of what had just happened – the breaching of a seemingly impossible target. They were not yet safely home but for a few moments they could reflect on the success of the mission and how it would affect the Ruhr district's vital water supplies.

Factories, power stations and fuel plants would be demolished and to reconstruct the dams would mean diverting armies of manpower from other crucial areas that the enemy would no longer be able to protect with efficacy. But it was the thought of the impact on their fellow countrymen that gave them the greatest sense of achievement, and whether they now returned safely to base or not, they had at least accomplished that and would take it to their graves.

Part of their silence too was reserved for those comrades who had not been so fortunate and for the families who would grieve for them. It was now that the images of their burning planes became real.

'Do you think anyone got out of Hopgood's plane?' Ginny finally asked.

'Yes,' Beatrice said. 'I saw three parachutes.'

'Hopgood's a hero.'

'Aye, that he is.'

'I was only having a drink with him yesterday,' Dobby said. 'He was looking forward to visiting his parents. He was going to take his mother a few eggs from the poultry farm that he'd started. It's down to him that we got double eggs and bacon to set us up for the flight.'

'Not all of us,' Shortwave said, smiling at Beatrice. She suddenly realised how hungry she was.

'Aye well, if ye will jump onto planes uninvited what can ye expect.'

'Thank God she did,' Knightly said, 'or ops would have been off for us.' He thought about Spike and wondered if he was still cocooned in bed, oblivious to their departure. 'You're right, though,' he continued. 'Hoppy was one of the best. Fearless and a true friend to all.'

'We'll raise a glass to him when we get back to base. Poor sod.'

'Yes,' Dobby said, 'and to our new navigator who's proven to all you sceptics that women *can* navigate.'

'You're right,' Ginny said. 'I never would have believed that of a girl. I'll have to eat my words.'

'Aye, but the lassie's still got tae get us back.'

The crew groaned in unison. They were happy and Beatrice felt privileged to be with them.

'You're right, McGruff,' she added. 'But if I steer you safely home, you owe me a couple of eggs for breakfast, even if I have to take them off your plate. Deal?'

'Och, okay, ah suppose that's fair,' McDuff said reluctantly.

Beatrice settled into the role of navigator. She felt more relaxed now that their mission was complete and she had the confidence of the crew, but it instilled in her an even greater responsibility to guide them home. She directed the Lancaster with ease, avoiding paths that were known to be heavily defended. She and Shortwave worked well together. He was a likeable man, quiet and industrious. She observed him as he sent and received coded transmissions from time to time and was impressed by how deftly he managed the Morse code. Every so often he would forward her fixes to help confirm their position. She thought how much easier life would be for her ATA colleagues if they had access to full navigational aids and how some of their lives, including Amy Johnson's, might have been saved when flying into dense cloud.

Knightly had now changed tactics and was flying the Lancaster above twelve thousand feet and climbing. Beatrice guessed that he was preparing for the inevitable onslaught as they approached the coastline. No doubt the enemy were aware of the damage they had wrought and would be keen for vengeance. At intervals, he would check on the crew. She knew that he needed them awake and alert. Out of formation and unescorted, she knew they were highly vulnerable. Unfortunately, the mid-upper turret had been taken out due to modifications, but McDuff had adapted well as a front gunner and Crouch, when in his blister, had a better view below than in the unmodified version.

'You okay, rear gunner?'

'Okay, Skip,' Ginny replied, 'but freezing.'

'Afraid it's only going to get worse for a while. Reaching fifteen thousand feet. Keep an eye open for the Hun. We don't want any nasty surprises!'

'Will do, Skip.'

'Approaching North Sea in two minutes, Skipper.'

'Thank you, Navigator. Here it comes everyone.'

Sure enough, the sky lit up with high explosive compound, so close that their plane shuddered fearfully, before the aggressive red flashes burnt themselves out. Beatrice knew that on the ground below, their position was being traced and that Knightly was now weaving in an effort to outsmart the trackers. In addition, the gunners would be firing ammunition randomly in the hope of getting lucky. It was an unhealthy lottery that these men faced most days of their lives. She thought of Spike and what he must have endured before his mind unravelled with the violent and continuous yaw of their absconding aircraft. The flak clouds were dense now, new flashes of explosion snapping angrily amidst them like rabid dogs, any one of which could have claimed them. So, this was the adventure that she had sought. She was here of her own volition when she could have been safely in her rented room fast asleep in ignorance of the entire operation. Perhaps it was her own sanity, she thought, not Spike's that needed consideration.

'This flak's the worst I've seen. Hold tight everyone.' As Knightly spoke, the deafening sound of exploding shell resounded beneath them.

'What the hell was that?' Crouch asked.

'Looks lik' a wee piece o' flaks hit th' starboard wing.'

'Any serious damage?'

'Well, th' wing's still there so it cannae be so bad.'

'Thanks, McDuff, that much I could ascertain. At least it's obviously missed the fuel tanks or we'd know about it.'

There was another explosion and the bomber shook forcefully from side to side before stabilising.

'Port wing this time,' Dobby said. 'Hole shot right through it.'

Beatrice felt sick with anxiety.

'We'll be out of the storm in a minute,' Knightly said, 'then we can properly assess any damage. But don't worry, I've had bigger dents to my ego.'

Beatrice knew that the reassurance was meant for her and felt an overarching sense of shame. Knightly had enough to do without carrying anyone emotionally.

The sky darkened as they retreated from the dying embers of ack-ack, the sounds of battle now muffled, like the distant rumble of thunder. The damage to the Lancaster was evaluated and deemed minor, though Beatrice marvelled at how a hole in the wing could be viewed so casually. With the Dutch coast now markedly behind them, she felt the tension slowly drain from her taut and anguished frame. But her relief was short-lived.

'Snappers!' Ginny shouted. 'Astern attack. Three of them. Out of your sights I'm afraid, Duffy.'

'Dinnae fret yourself. A'm ready when th' are.' McDuff inwardly cursed the fact he was no longer in his mid-upper turret.

'109s, Skipper. Prepare to corkscrew starboard.'

Knightly began jinking the plane violently and Beatrice felt nausea rising up in her throat. They had no escorts and several enemy fighters giving chase. The odds were against them. She heard Ginny fire and then a massive explosion as one of the fighters blew up.

'Corkscrew starboard. Go!'

Knightly used the ailerons to bank steeply, slicing through cloud, noctilucent in appearance, so that he feared their concealment would be reliant upon speed and agility, rather than camouflage. Heaving the aileron controls to port, he ascended into a left turn, manipulated the other aileron and dived again. He repeated this process several times, shouting out each manoeuvre he took to alert the gunners. Beatrice had flown Lancasters on many occasions but had never tested their capabilities in combat. She couldn't help but be in awe of the deftness of its movements, despite the fact that the spins and jolts made her wretch and addled her mind.

'One down, two to go,' Ginny shouted. 'Hopefully we've lost them.'

Just then, there was a deafening burst to the left of the Lancaster. 'Quarter attack port!' Knightly shouted. He threw the plane into a vertical bank so its descent, fast and furious, cut through the air like a knife. It seemed an age until it levelled, just behind the 109 that had followed them down and overshot. Short blasts from McDuff and the sky ahead turned red, orange and purple, the flames dancing ahead of them in a billowing, blazing rage as the fighter burned.

This is what death looks like, she thought.

'Bottom strafe,' Knightly said, and he pulled back on the throttle as the third fighter flew beneath the Lancaster. 'Those 109s are like leeches – you just can't shrug them off.'

Beatrice heard the battle commencing but felt her eyes closing. Blood trickled from her sleeve and she realised with horror that she had been hit. The blood seeped through her flying jacket. She quietly acknowledged the small circle of red growing in orbit, but felt no pain, just a frightful cold. Voices over the intercom echoed inside her head. The plane continued its frenetic, evasive tactics. A spot of blood fell onto the map she was reading and she wiped it furtively with the back of her hand. Shortwave, witnessing the gesture, realised suddenly what had happened and reached for the first aid kit. He pulled the sleeve of her jacket off as they lurched and twisted through the darkness, and she flinched as he examined her arm. 'Thank God, it's a flesh wound. Hold still.'

Shell from the port attack had penetrated the fuselage and fragments had ricocheted into her seat. Shortwave stemmed the bleeding as best he could and bound her arm tightly. With her jacket partially removed, she was bitten by the cold, and, with difficulty, as the plane weaved and dived, he helped her slip her arm back into the jacket. Sadly, she had no flak vest to protect her and provide additional warmth. Giddy with nausea, she nodded her thanks.

'All okay back there?'

'Okay, Skip. Navigator's sustained a flesh wound is all.'

'You okay, Navigator?'

'Never felt better.'

'That's the spirit. Don't worry, we'll soon be home.' She could sense a veiled anxiety in his voice. The plane seemed to be on a never-ending rollercoaster ride and there was nothing she could do but put her faith in the crew. She understood now how important the relationships between them were. As hallowed as any marriage, their complete trust in each other was apparent in both silent and verbal communications. This kind of rapport was not accidental, she knew, but had been fostered through long periods of interdependency. Hers was now a passive role and she happily submitted. If they made it through this onslaught, she would soon be needed. Her Ladyship was getting a battering and the fuselage was peppered with holes. The enemy slugs pounded again and again as the Lancaster dived, levelled and throttled back, banked and dropped again, desperate to flee or annihilate its enemy. The hole in the left wing played on her mind, as so much was being demanded of the bomber.

Knightly was flying it like a fighter plane, using every trick he'd ever learned. If they were to be shot down, it would not be for lack of enterprise. Blinding curves of tracer now spewed their way and suddenly, Beatrice heard an almighty blast of fire ahead and McDuff's instant echoing response. New tactics, she thought – they're going for the pilot. Sure enough, the 109 flew toward them head on, guns blazing. It flew so close that she expected a collision and her body convulsed in terror. But despite the deadly sound of bullets spraying the nose of the plane, and the shattering of Perspex windscreen and canopy, the plane remained in one piece but swerved instead into free flight and then began a death dive toward the North Sea.

'Jesus,' Crouch shrieked, as his head was slammed against the top of the bomb aimer's blister. 'What's going on?'

'Skipper hit,' moaned Dobby in obvious pain. 'One engine on fire.'

Beatrice felt the plane beneath her hurtling downward. Knightly lay back in his seat, motionless, and Dobby next to him, now appeared to have passed out. She fought her way against gravity into the icy cockpit as the plane continued to plunge to ever greater depths.

Knightly was still breathing but had deep wounds to his chest from shell fragments.

'Quick, help me get him out of his seat.'

Shortwave, struggling to the front, cut his hands on the jagged Perspex fragments embedded in the backrest of Knightly's seat. Ignoring the painful gashes, he pulled Knightly awkwardly out of the pilot's seat as he quietly groaned. There was so much blood he wondered how he could still be breathing. Dobby too was covered in blood from broken shards, which had lacerated his face and shoulder, the blood flow impeded only by the below zero temperatures. But time was running out and there wasn't a moment to tend to either man. Beatrice took the controls and immediately her responses became intuitive. She heaved at the yoke with a wilful resolve, determined to level the burning plane as it spun toward the awaiting depths of ocean below. There was no response and she heard McDuff and Ginny cry out in panic at the thought of their plane being unpiloted.

'Do we bail?' Crouch clambered into the cockpit. 'Christ, what's happened to the skip?'

'Crouch, I need your help.'

Beatrice wrenched harder despite the debilitating pain in her arm, and she and Crouch, head bloodied from being smashed against the Perspex nose cupola, joined forces, the last reserves of their strength united in a desperate fight for survival. Despite the freezing cockpit, perspiration formed on her brow and her hands, clammy, shook from the exertion. Slowly, very slowly, the nose of the plane began to lift. Beatrice breathed a sigh of relief. 'Into level flight now,' she said. 'Recovering. No need to bail yet. Going to stopcock engine.' She shut down the fuel valve. Now that they were running on three engines, there would be an increased burden to keep the plane on a controlled flight path. She could feel the plane drifting.

'Any sightings of that fighter, Ginny? McDuff?'

Unbeknown to the rest of the crew, Ginny had been using a fire extinguisher to douse a fire that had started at the rear of the plane. He had succeeded in containing it but in the process had burned his hands and was in severe pain. But he was unwilling to demoralise the rest of the crew with news of his limited ability to turn the gun turret and fire the Brownings.

'No further sightings. We appear to have shaken him.'

'Aye, for now.'

Beatrice breathed a sigh of relief. Flying the plane was one thing, but she'd never been taught any evasive manoeuvres. Any attacks now would be fatal.

Crouch remained outside his blister and tended to Dobby, who was losing blood fast.

'McDuff, keep your position and report any

sightings.'

'Aye, Nav. But can ye actually fly this wee plane? Ah mean tae say…'

'How do you think we've just got out of that dive?' Shortwave quipped. 'By witchcraft?'

'Shortwave, can you get me a QDM to home field?'

'I'll do my best, Nav.' Amazingly, the radio still functioned. 'Heading two-eighty.'

'Good, then we're homeward bound. Let's just pray we don't meet any more bandits. How's the skipper, Crouch?'

'Stable I'd say, but he's lost a lot of blood. I've just given him a morphine shot.'

'Keep him awake if you can.' She willed the plane to fly faster. She needed Knightly to survive. She'd only known him for a few hours, but it now seemed like a lifetime. Knightly had believed in her, had given her a chance, out of expediency perhaps, but it had made her realise that this was no longer an escapade for her amusement but a fight for the lives of an entire crew. Little did these men know that they were the closest she had to a family. Her sole purpose now was to get them safely home with the help of Her Ladyship, who was staggering with her battle wounds marvellously, if inelegantly, back across the unwelcoming arm of the North Sea. The two functioning starboard engines were forcing an unwanted turn and she adjusted trim and reduced power on one side. She suddenly noticed the bulldog mascot beneath her controls, hooked partially on the undercarriage lever. She reached for it and threw it toward Crouch. 'Here, give Knightly this will you.'

Knightly lay still. Crouch was talking to him cheerfully as though they were returning from a joyride rather than the flight from hell. He put the bulldog in Knightly's hands and Knightly seemed to clutch it as a child might a treasured and comforting toy. The aircraft was freezing and broken, the holes in its shell along with the shot-out engine and shattered windscreen creating drag. The gusts of wind from the broken canopy hit her like a slap in the face. She was already exhausted. The plane was losing altitude and she was concerned that one of the fuel tanks had been punctured. She had no way of knowing how much fuel they had. Shells had ripped through the instrument panel and the excessive damage meant there would be a new stalling speed, which she could only guess at. It crossed her mind that, at some point, bailing out might be best for the rest of the crew, but she knew that Knightly wouldn't make it and Dobby seemed worse than she had first suspected. She had no option but to stay with the plane and hope things worked out in their favour.

She glanced back at Knightly holding the bulldog. If he was conscious, she knew he would be worrying about the same things that passed through her mind. They were now sitting ducks for any attack and he knew that her flying skills had limitations in terms of evasive tactics. The plane was limping badly. They were in serious trouble and he didn't need to be at the controls to recognise that. He would be able to tell from the motion of the plane, the sound of the engines, the tense voices and alternate silences of the crew. She needed to give him some hope. She began to sing.

'Pack up your troubles in your old kit-bag and smile, smile, smile. While you've got Lucifer to light your fag, smile, boys, that's the style...'

One by one the crew joined in.

'What's the use of worrying, it never is worthwhile, so, pack up your troubles in your old kit-bag and smile, smile, smile.'

McDuff was singing in a surprisingly rich baritone that temporarily drowned out the faulty engines, though the dying instrument needles disclosed the reality. The old girl was doing her best for them. If only she could stay airborne for a little while longer, then the riggers, fitters and mechanics would give her a pampering when they returned. She struggled to keep her on course and they had already descended about two thousand feet when Ginny shrieked.

'Bandits at eight o'clock. Two of them heading this way.'

Beatrice's heart sank but she tried in desperation to weave the damaged plane. She knew that they would not survive another beating and she guessed that they were virtually spent of ammunition and fuel. They were not far from the English coast now. The moon lit a dark shape on the horizon that she recognised as home. She glanced back at Knightly and knew that whatever happened, she would stay with the plane until the end, but the others must have the choice. 'Those of you that can, prepare to bail.'

The sea below looked a bleak alternative, but it was better than being blown to smithereens. She braced herself for what was to come but heard Ginny call out excitedly, 'Spitfires intercepting. Three of the beauties. Just look at that!'

Beatrice could have cried with happiness. Sure enough, before the two Me-109s were within firing range, the Spitfires swooped down like beautiful birds of prey. Even in the darkness, Beatrice could recognise their elliptical wings, the slender grace of them, and imagine the determined purr of their engines. She heard the dogfight commence and then the sounds grew more distant as they flew further from the action and closer to the dark strip of land ahead. Her arms were numb now from the effort of keeping the plane on course.

Already crossing her mind was the landing. She had no idea if the hydraulic system had been damaged during their beating and if the landing gear would release. 'I may need someone to crank the landing gear when the time comes,' she said, thinking out loud. 'I doubt it'll be a pretty landing.'

'They know we're coming,' Shortwave said. 'I managed to get a message through. And thank God for IFF. At least we won't get shot down by friendly fire. But the radio's stopped working now. I'm afraid I can't get another bearing.'

'How are Dobby and Knightly?'

'Dobby's asleep. Full of morphine. I can't remove the glass. I might not be able to stop the bleeding. Knightly's still with us, but he needs urgent attention.'

'Keep talking to him, Shortwave. McDuff! Ginny! Abandon your stations. We have to prepare for an emergency landing. Knightly and Dobby need to be kept as still as possible.'

'I'll be glad to get out of this damn turret. If you're sure, Nav?'

'Positive, Ginny. Enemy aircraft are not our priority now. You both need to get into a secure position.'

'What aboot th' snappers?'

'Forget them, McDuff. We need you here.' She scanned the horizon. 'We're coming in further north over the wash. And I'm going to try to make it to Scampton. They'll be ready for us there and have immediate help for our wounded.' She omitted to say that they would also be ready if their plane crashed, or worse still, exploded upon landing. 'And no doubt your ground crew have been waiting up for you all night.'

Looking down, she saw the breakers of the Lincolnshire coast meet the sands and peter into stillness. Beyond, the low-lying Fenlands, with their quirky patchwork shapes, greeted her like the best kind of friend, silently, without declaration.

The crew cheered. 'Well done, Nav!'

Beatrice smiled. 'I'd save your gratitude until we've landed if I were you!'

The final part of the journey seemed interminably long. The Lancaster was losing altitude so fast that the trees below seemed to greet them suddenly, as if the drag of the plane was a consequence of the dense copse as they brushed against their wings. Behind Beatrice, Knightly lay still, covered in blood. Shortwave cradled his head and spoke to him in a low voice, drowned out by the droning of the engine. Beatrice remembered his smile when they had first met, his gentleness with Spike, his disbelief that she wanted to trade places on a mission that seemed doomed for failure and which had been almost certain to incur crippling losses. He had believed in her and now she had to show him that his belief was justified.

Beside him, Crouch supported Dobby, holding his head in a vice-like grip that prevented the protruding shards of glass from moving too violently. Both men would need to be kept as still as possible when she attempted a landing. McDuff had now reluctantly withdrawn from his turret and was assessing the internal damage to the plane. Ginny too slowly extracted himself from the rear turret, his hands blistered and throbbing from quelling the fire, his limbs numb from the effort of lying for hours in the small, confined space. He was shocked by the sight of Knightly and Dobby so badly injured, prostrate and bloodied, so obviously near death.

Beatrice surveyed the moonlit landscape. She knew exactly where she was, the shape of each meadow and stream etched deeply in her memory. She was grateful for the Fenlands and their lack of undulation. The Lancaster would not have coped with a more elevated landscape in its ravaged state. She welcomed the sight of each hedgerow and river, each railway line and spinney as it carried them closer to home. Finally, the meadows formed the shapes she was awaiting – the darker pentagonal field juxtaposed by the smaller rectangular one and beyond that the lines of the flare path at Scampton, lit in greeting.

She needed to get the approach right as there would be no second chances. She reduced the thrust and the nose of the plane turned toward the landing strip. Ginny fired the flares with difficulty but without being prompted. Beatrice needed every ounce of concentration to land the lumbering plane.

'On descent path. Take up secure positions.'

McDuff helped the others with the injured, holding them as securely as possible, though Ginny, his hands in terrible pain, could do nothing but sit nearby and crook his legs around Dobby's prostrate figure.

'Lowering undercarriage.'

Beatrice waited and for a moment, her heart sank, then suddenly the three green lights appeared and the landing gear descended. Below, she saw the ambulances and fire trucks racing to greet them. She glanced back at Knightly. She was unsure whether he was still alive but Crouch was still talking to him. Hold on, she thought, just hold on, we're nearly home. The plane was degenerating and she knew it. The dead engine port side still attempted to throw the plane off course but Beatrice was used to it by now and adjusted the rudder and yoke accordingly. She could only hope and pray that the runway was long enough as there would be no chance to overshoot the crippled bomber and try again.

'Hold tight, everyone. Touch down imminent.'

The wheels hit the runway exactly on target and tore down the strip as if in formation with the pursuing fire and crash crews. For a moment, Beatrice thought the brakes were dead. Her hand hurt from the effort of jamming the lever. But despite its slow response, the bomber gradually began to decelerate and with the help of the wing flaps and the prevailing headwind, screeched to a halt inches from the end of the landing strip. There was applause from the crew and cries of relief. Beatrice switched off the engines.

For a moment, she tried to raise herself but realised that she couldn't move. Her hands now appeared glued to the yoke. She could hear voices around her, fire crews spraying the plane with foam and medics entering the hatch to tend to the wounded. With difficulty, Knightly was removed from the battered fuselage into an awaiting ambulance. Dobby was next, shards of glass still jutting from his wounds. McDuff and Crouch exited after them, then Ginny, who dropped to the ground and kissed it, his wounded hands held up as if in surrender. Beatrice, still gripping the control wheel, felt a hand on her shoulder and turned to see Shortwave, his face full of gratitude, smiling down at her.

'You did it! I reckon McDuff owes you a breakfast, don't you? We all do!'

'Knightly and Dobby?'

'They're being cared for. There's nothing more any of us can do but hope.'

'We need you to evacuate the plane now,' one of the medics shouted through the hatch.

'They want us out of here. Come on.'

Beatrice tried again to raise herself out of her seat, but she felt a searing pain down her back and thigh.

'I don't think I can move.'

It was then that Shortwave saw the blood on her seat and realised it wasn't from her wounded arm.

'Quick.' She could hear the anxiety in his voice. 'We need some help here!'

Within seconds, she was surrounded by medics who lifted her from her bloodied seat and away from the damaged plane. She had lost a lot of blood from an undetected shrapnel wound to her lower back, which adrenalin and necessity must have concealed. The wound now gaped and a nurse attempted to control the haemorrhaging. The pain wracked her entire body and she felt her eyes closing as she was put on a stretcher and rushed off for emergency treatment. She could hear the voices of the crew, words of gratitude and encouragement, promises of eggs and wine and celebrations and other words of exclamation. How had she managed to land the plane with those injuries? Where had she found the strength? Would she live? She fought to open her eyes but exhaustion overwhelmed her. She couldn't feel her legs and the voices around her became muted and then inaudible. Was this what death felt like? Her last conscious thought was of Knightly's smiling face as she returned his lucky mascot and the sensation of his hand as it brushed hers in the exchange.

II

Air Commodore Ralph Cochrane entered Wing Commander Guy Gibson's office and shook him by the hand.

'Good show, Gibson. Tremendous effort. This has been exactly the kind of morale boost that the country needs right now.'

'Thank you, sir.' Gibson, small and affable with a

handsome face, gestured to the tall man beside him, who moved his hands anxiously by his sides. 'Of course, without Barnes' ingenuity none of this would have been possible.'

'Nonsense, Gibby.' Barnes Wallis smiled kindly. 'I had the easy part. The credit must go to you and the men. Well, um…' He stuttered uncomfortably. 'When I say men…'

Cochrane extended his hand and Barnes Wallis, the inventor of Upkeep, the revolutionary bouncing bomb, shook it somewhat hesitantly.

There was a knock at the door and Gibson opened it and beckoned a small, resolute-looking woman inside. 'Senior Commander Gower, please come in.' He turned to the others. 'This is Commander of 5 Group in Bomber Command, Air Commodore Cochrane, and this is the inventor of Upkeep, Barnes Wallis. Please take a seat. I believe tea is on its way.'

Wallis held out a seat for Pauline Gower, Senior Commander of the ATA, who nodded her thanks and sat, her keen eyes taking in the three men. She took an immediate liking to Wallis, whose face emanated kindness and intelligence. Gibson seemed as amiable as he was dashing. His reputation as a fearless and loyal leader preceded him. She watched him light his pipe and the aroma of the tobacco relaxed her. Cochrane, as she had suspected, seemed somewhat hostile, but she was used to such men. He had a reputation for impatience and arrogance, characteristics that were seldom, in her experience, associated with a desire to please or an interest in making friends. However, his efficiency and commitment to duty were qualities so easily recognised in a like-minded soul and she was intimidated by no man.

As a woman who had single-handedly established a women's section in the civilian organisation the Air Transport Auxiliary, she made a gentle yet formidable opponent. She noticed the flight maps on the wall, no doubt relating to Operation Chastise, the attack on three German dams in the industrial heartland of Germany, which one of her girls had, incredibly, been a part of. She would have liked to have known how this had come about when First Officer Barton was supposed to have been delivering a Spitfire to White Waltham.

Beatrice, she knew, had a taste for adventure, but to fly in combat was foolhardy in the extreme. Not that she wasn't proud of her achievements. Beatrice had always been a hard worker and an exceptional pilot, but after she'd lost her parents, she had cut a lonely figure and when her fiancé had been killed, she had become more and more distant from her colleagues, pushing herself even harder at work, delivering record numbers of aircraft just to keep busy. She sighed. The problem was, there were so many fatalities in war that one almost became desensitised to the pain of others. Names were wiped from boards every day and those who knew them were expected to keep a stiff upper lip and get on with it.

Cochrane smoothed his hair, grey at the sides and darker on the crown, and cleared his throat. 'Well, what I propose is that the events of yesterday, regarding Knightly's crew, are eradicated. As far as I'm concerned, their bomber did not leave Scampton and only nineteen planes were operational. No one must ever hear about this.'

'Just one moment.' Commander Gower straightened her shoulders and faced him determinedly. 'One of my girls saved the life of an entire crew in that operation.'

'That's not proven.'

'The pilot and flight engineer had been shot. Who else but First Officer Barton could have landed that plane?'

'I'm sure Crouch would have had a damn good try. And they could have bailed.'

'Two members of the crew were too badly injured to bail and the rest would have most likely perished in freezing water.'

'She sounds like quite a girl,' Gibson said good-naturedly. 'A real looker too by all accounts.'

'I don't really think her looks are relevant, Gibson,' Cochrane said impatiently. 'The fact is she shouldn't have been there.'

'Lucky for some that she was.'

'If you'd been able to keep your girls in line, we wouldn't have this dilemma.'

'Please,' interjected Wallis. 'The point of this discussion is not to apportion blame but to consider what to do for the best... for everyone.'

'Hear, hear!'

'Look, it simply cannot come to light that a mere slip of a girl played a part in Chastise,' Cochrane continued. '617 Squadron has been training for this mission for months. To suggest that a girl, an ATA pilot for heaven's sake, had the ability to navigate a bomber over Germany and then recover a burning plane from a dive to land it successfully on British soil would undermine the very fabric of the operation.'

'It sounds,' Gower said indignantly, 'like you feel threatened by the abilities of women challenging the conventional stereotypes. The female ATA pilots are used to that. I can assure you that First Officer Barton is not a mere "slip of a girl", but a highly trained and superior pilot who converted to four-engined bombers some time ago. That means, sir, that she flew Lancaster bombers without a crew of six to support her.'

'My crews, Commander Gower, fly sorties most days of their lives. You can hardly compare that to your ATA pilots taking a jolly to Scotland. Take Gibson here...'

'Oh no, please don't, sir.'

'He's flown dozens and dozens of sorties over enemy territory. Can you imagine the courage that takes? And you want his reputation compromised by one over-privileged ATA girl who fancies herself as Biggles for the day?'

'Oh dear.' Wallis shuffled uncomfortably. 'That sounds a little unfair. She sounds like a pretty remarkable girl to me.'

'Yes,' Gower said, whose anger was visible. 'Not privileged at all as it happens, but an exceptional girl who saved a crew and a valuable aircraft. I believe fifty-three aircrew lost their lives on this mission. It could so easily have been sixty.'

'Oh dear, yes…' Wallis took out his handkerchief and dabbed his eyes. 'Such a large number of casualties. If only I'd known in advance, I'd have aborted the idea. Those poor young men.'

'Now don't fret, Barnes,' Gibson said kindly. 'We all knew the risks and most of those losses were not through bombing the dams, just awfully bad luck. There's not a man in the squadron who would put the blame your way.'

'No, I didn't mean to imply…' Gower softened her tone. 'All I really wanted to say is that First Officer Barton saved precious lives when dreadfully wounded herself. Something to be celebrated not denigrated, I would have thought.'

'She showed enormous courage,' Gibson said, smiling at Gower. 'I'd be proud to have her in my squadron any day I must say.' He turned to Cochrane.

'The men have nothing but praise for her, sir. Even McDuff, as it happens, and he never has anything nice to say about anyone. They're entirely beholden to her. And they're pretty cut up that she's taken a hit.'

'Look here.' Cochrane could sense that he was outnumbered. 'Of course, what she achieved was unprecedented for a woman but let us not forget that women are forbidden to fly in combat. What she did was unlawful.'

'There are many female ATA pilots who believe they should be able to fly in combat,' Gower proclaimed. 'They fly in extreme weather, generally to places where men don't want to fly because the journey is too long and too inclement. Anything to Anywhere is how I believe we are also known. Several of my pilots have suffered from hypothermia due to those "jollies to Scotland" you mentioned, and several have lost their lives because officials did not deem them worthy of investing money to train them on instruments. Amy Johnson who flew solo to Australia would be alive now if she had been taught to blind fly.

'Without the women's core of the ATA your damaged planes would not get delivered to maintenance units for repair so you wouldn't have any to fly in combat. Yet still, women pilots are derided, their heroism belittled. Many of my girls are flying half a dozen planes in a fourteen-hour day, with only half an hour to read the *Ferry Pilots Notes* manual and acclimatise themselves to different control configurations. They are confronted with prejudice every day from men who think they should be confined to factory work. Yet, my girls have far more experience and more flying hours than many of your male pilots, more adaptability and just as much courage.'

'They sound an extraordinary group of women,' Wallis said. 'And very undervalued. I must say I think…'

'I'm not denying,' Cochrane interrupted, 'that your women do a splendid job, as do their male counterparts, the Ancient and Tattered Airmen as I believe they're known. And perhaps your girls haven't received the credit that they deserve but there are more pivotal reasons why this incident must not come to light. First Officer Barton may well be an exceptional girl, but she is also a maverick, and whereas we may privately celebrate the achievements of non-conformists, there is no room for them in the warfare services or civilian organisations that are fighting for the common cause. Our very fabric is built upon following orders, orders that are sometimes controversial, orders that we may disagree with deeply on a personal level, but nonetheless that we must follow. We cannot be seen to be endorsing wilful disobedience, however much we may admire the end result. Otherwise we are left with anarchy and anarchy will not win us the war.'

Despite her reservations about Cochrane,

Commander Gower recognised that his argument was a cogent one and nodded her acquiescence.

'I do believe that her story will resurface,' Cochrane continued. 'Despite being sworn to secrecy, there are always indiscretions, in a public house or…' He hesitated. 'During moments of tenderness. But for now, publicly, we should celebrate Gibson's achievements and those of his squadron.'

'Really, sir, I'm not remotely concerned about any personal glory. But every crew that flew last night gave it their all and many paid the ultimate sacrifice.' Gibson turned to Commander Gower. 'I lost a good friend last night – Flight Lieutenant John Hopgood. Despite everything, he managed to reach a height whereby two of his crew could bail. Just before the mission, my dog was killed, run over by a car. He was our mascot you see so I didn't tell my chaps. To be honest, I thought it was a bad omen and that we'd had it, but instead it was poor Hoppy. He was probably the best pilot of all of us, but it didn't help him. So, you become quite fatalistic about things, I suppose. And war is rotten at times. I think what a grand group of boys I started out with and now I'm the only one left. It's so damned unfair. And here I am being decorated.' He glanced at the picture of King George VI on the wall. 'There will be lunch in the officers' mess with the king and queen attending, lots of photographs taken for posterity… and yet there are chaps far more deserving than me who didn't make it or who won't get the publicity, just like Knightly, who I know is a fine pilot and a great man, and your girl Beatrice, who, because of the sensibilities of the establishment, won't be publicly recognised for this mission. But it's alright you see because we know what she did, and it was a tremendous thing. That's why the crew love her and why her bravery wasn't in vain, because she touched the lives of others in a way that's far more important than receiving any acknowledgement or award.'

'Well, Gibby.' Wallis dabbed his eyes again. 'For someone who had already flown so many sorties over enemy territory before this operation, you are the most self-effacing man I know, I must say.'

'Are we agreed then?' Cochrane said restlessly. 'Gibson should be enjoying the party and I'm sure Commander Gower, you will be keen to find out if there's any news about First Officer Barton?'

'Agreed,' Gower said quietly. 'I think on reflection it's in the best interest of everyone involved to keep this matter amongst ourselves.' She stood. 'Now, if you will forgive me, gentlemen, I must visit the hospital. Beatrice has no living family and there may be arrangements to be made.'

III

Several weeks had passed since the raid but the nation

was still elated by the news. The small, woollen bulldog, which had played its part, sat in the winged chair in the spacious dining room, its puckered face and beady eyes seemingly staring at the table, which was covered with a white lace cloth. Mrs Knightly, an attractive, middle-aged woman, set about dressing it. She placed a large pot of tea in a cosy in the centre and pretty, floral crockery around it, then left the room briefly to fetch a newly baked walnut cake and plate of sandwiches, which she had cut into small triangles.

She stood back, briefly admiring her handiwork, then moved over to the window. A girl was moving slowly toward her front door on crutches, the pain of movement evident in each step. Her first instinct was to rush outside to help her, but she knew that this would be the wrong thing to do. Beatrice was very proud and one shouldn't underestimate the importance of pride. She turned from the window not wishing to be seen and busied herself by lifting a photo frame on the sideboard, dusting it with her handkerchief and returning it carefully to its place. The handsome young man within the frame smiled at her, almost as if he were reading her thoughts and approving of them. She could contain herself no longer and hurried to the front door.

'Come in, Beatrice. I've set afternoon tea in the dining room. I thought you might be hungry.'

'Well, I must admit, my appetite is returning. I didn't feel much like eating for a while but I'm much better now.'

'Well, you're still rather thin,' Mrs Knightly replied. 'Of course, I realise it's quite fashionable but you must try to keep up your strength or you may relapse.'

'Oh, don't worry,' Beatrice replied, eyeing the cake, 'there's no fear of that. I can assure you, I'm quite strong and getting more mobile every day. The boys keep visiting me, you know, and bringing me biscuits. I'd be quite enormous if it were down to them. Especially McDuff. You'd never think there was still rationing going on the amount of chocolate and biscuits he brings. I have no idea where he gets them all from.' She noticed the bulldog mascot in the chair.

'Churchill looks very solemn, doesn't he?' Mrs Knightly said. 'I find him a great comfort. Those little beady eyes seem most penetrating at times. He seems to have developed a life of his own since I knitted him. He has, after all, witnessed a great deal. If only he could talk, goodness only knows what he would say!'

Beatrice deepened her voice. 'Never in the field of human conflict has so much been owed by so many to so few.' She laughed and Mrs Knightly laughed with her.

'Oh, Beatrice, I couldn't be fonder of you if you were my own daughter.' She gestured to the table. 'Please do start. The tea will get cold.'

Beatrice sat down. 'Walnut cake, my favourite.'

'I made it specially.'

'You really are too kind to me.'

'Nonsense. You know when I first got the call about Vere I was quite inconsolable. You know, I lost his father last year. Of course, everyone has lost someone in this damned war, and I know we just have to get on and make the best of things, but it's hard. You know that more than anyone. But to lose one's husband, however dreadful, seems somehow more bearable than losing a child. It just doesn't seem right to survive one's children.'

'I'll probably never know.' Beatrice helped herself to a slice of walnut cake. 'The doctors say I may struggle to have children.' She paused. 'But then again, they said I would never walk again and look at me now.'

Mrs Knightly noted the fleeting look of sadness in her eyes. 'One thing at a time, dear,' she said. 'Let's just concentrate on getting you fully well.' She poured Beatrice some tea. 'Only a few weeks ago I thought my whole world was about to end, and now…'

Just then, Beatrice heard footsteps in the hallway. It was strange how familiar those footsteps had become in such a short time and how eager she was to hear them.

'Vere, is that you?' Mrs Knightly called fondly. 'Late as usual!' She frowned in mock reproof.

'Sorry, I blame administration!' Vere greeted the women warmly, his cheerful disposition apparent in his gait and broad smile. He gave his mother some flowers and planted a kiss on Beatrice's forehead. 'So good to see you, darling.' He reached for her hand and Mrs Knightly noted the gentleness in her son's eyes as he caught Beatrice's gaze. She had never witnessed before this demonstration of devotion in him, and it melted her heart.

'I'm afraid they've taken me off operations for the time being. They said I'd done my fill of tours. They've given me some dreadfully boring desk job.'

'Poor you!' Beatrice finished eating her last mouthful of cake. 'I hope to be flying again soon. Commander Gower is keen for things to get back to some semblance of normality.'

'Is that wise, dear?' Mrs Knightly said anxiously.

'You really needn't worry.'

'No, Beatrice is an excellent pilot and I don't think she'll be making any more pleasure trips to the Ruhr district in the near future!'

'Who knows,' Beatrice laughed, and the happiness that had once seemed so remote from her grasp was captured momentarily in the glint of her green eyes. 'You know what they call us ATA girls – Anything to Anywhere!'

The German Pilot

I

His eyes had that quality of absorption that denied access to the rest of his face for the first moments of introduction. Blue as flax, intense as lightning, they filtered through any competing features like sun through gauze. Rudi Schnell was unaware of the impact of them, devoid of that kind of vanity, competitive only in the sphere of aeronautics. He wanted to be the best pilot he could be, claim as many enemy aircraft as possible and his eyes, like those of a hawk, missed nothing. Not for him, the defensive role of escort to bomber planes. He actively sought out his prey, exploiting fearfulness, inexperience and weakness. He was thrilled when he found a challenge, a pilot as adept as he, whose nerves made the combat a game worth playing. It was just that, he thought – a game to be played until your luck ran out,

The German Pilot

which he knew was an inevitability. Even the most skilful and accomplished pilots had bad days, or were faced with overwhelming odds or the maelstrom of confusion that resulted in friendly fire. His days were as numbered as a clock face and time was running out. But not quite yet. Yesterday he had shot down three Hurricanes and he was hungry to claim the next, when his number of kills would establish him as the greatest ace in Jagdgeschwader 52, one of the most prominent fighter wings in the Luftwaffe.

At present, he was escorting a Heinkel bomber and he hated the tedium of it. It was rather like taking your grandmother to a party, holding her arm and leading her sedately to a chair, when all you wanted was the action on the floor. He was a hunter by nature, restless for combat and his eyes searched the skies avidly for some sign of action. He didn't have to wait long. A lone Spitfire, perhaps thrown off course by the heavy winds, lumbered through a distant cloud, spotted the Messerschmitt, dived steeply, fired a short burst into nowhere and turned tail. In an instant, Rudi's steely blue eyes noted the weakness of his enemy. The Spitfire had already been hit, which probably explained why the pilot hadn't made any serious attempt at combat.

Rudi observed the holes in his right wing, noted the random, ineffectual burst and recognised a pilot in distress, exhausted perhaps, inexperienced, hungry for home and the safety of a landing strip. He changed his

The German Pilot

course in pursuit of the travailing Spitfire and adjusted trim. His enemy was outclassed both by aircraft and pilot and he knew it. This wouldn't take long. He made a sharp wingover to the right, placing himself in the perfect position astern. For a moment, he was disappointed that the pilot didn't put up more of a fight. His aircraft didn't have the rate of climb of the Messerschmitt but his responses were sluggish at best. He gently turned the dial of his reflector sight to accommodate the wingspan of the Spitfire and noted the elongated, ovate wings and the distinctive roundels, now perfectly placed within range. His thumb slipped casually over the gun button. He waited until he was within four hundred yards, the perfect range, tension building in the pit of his stomach. With the hazy refuge of clouds only moments away, he fired. The cannon, expelled through the propeller shaft, together with the two machine guns, made a deadly symphony that resounded in Rudi's cockpit. A thick glycol trail momentarily obscured Rudi's view. He ruddered sharply to the right and, just before the Spitfire exploded, happened to glimpse its pilot, the sheer terror in his young face, white, then bloodied, then lost in cremation. He turned and rejoined the Heinkel. Back with grandma. A clear kill. He was now officially the highest scoring ace in his squadron. Cause for celebration.

That night he had his first nightmare. He had felt a sense of unease all evening but had been unable to identify a cause. Satisfaction at his top gun status had been surprisingly ephemeral. It was as if the realisation of a deeply coveted goal had rendered it suddenly inconsequential. It wasn't as if there was any reward apart from self-aggrandisement and a comforting legacy, perhaps the Knight's Cross with Oak Leaves and Swords, to the family he would leave behind. He was a credit to the Fatherland, they would say. He had served his country well, with honour, courage and distinction. Exhaustion was making him morose. His squadron had scrambled throughout the previous day and combat missions had been unremitting.

The camaraderie in the squadron was tarnished at times by a competitive element or else from fear of attachments and their possible repercussions. At dispersal, awaiting orders to scramble, tensions were usually high. Sometimes the wait seemed endless, allowing too much time for reflection. Cigarette stubs littered the grass by the chairs outside the dispersal huts, along with a sporadic spattering of vomit. Ball games offered a diversion but mostly less energetic pursuits, such as card games or chess, were preferred. Rudi drank coffee and skimmed the newspapers, avoiding discourse when possible. In his head, he was always somewhere up in the vast arena of fleecy sky, chasing the veiled contrails of a distant foe.

There was a begrudging respect for him in the squadron. He was without doubt an excellent pilot, instinctive, committed and detached in his attitude toward killing – a formidable assassin. But he was also self-contained and considered arrogant. He had flirted with death on many occasions, most recently when bullets had ripped into the fuselage and ricocheted, denting the armoured plating that had undoubtedly saved his life. On another occasion, his aircraft had caught fire, the mangled, heavily strutted canopy preventing his escape. While the plane buckled and spiralled, he axed his way to freedom, parachuting into the lugubrious depths of freezing ocean, to be rescued by the *Seenotdienst*. He returned to flying after only one day's rest, without swagger or complaint. For these reasons he was much admired, but the entire corpus of attributes that constituted popularity were sorely lacking. Those who sought fellowship and gaiety looked elsewhere.

The bright, innocent faces of young airmen in the early years of war were soon lost, some having died the fate of a spinster, never to be kissed, while others, deluged by romantic liaisons, lived each day as their last. Many coped with the help of alcohol, propping the bar whenever possible, loudly espousing their politics. But Rudi didn't drink and he had no girl. Flying demanded a clear head and he wanted no part of any tender trappings. He had nothing left to give. His aircraft was his mistress. His days and nights were spent with her – intimate, terrifying moments that bound them together in consummate trust. To inflict their burden, that terrible uncertainty, on another would, he felt, have been unconscionable. So he went to his bed alone, awoken from his nightmare in sheets unrumpled by night-time congress, dank only from the exertions of fear.

And that night it was the blanched, petrified face of the young English pilot he saw, who had looked, in the cursory glance that he had been granted, exactly like his younger brother, Hans. He had heard that everyone had a doppelgänger, but he couldn't quite escape the idea that he had just shot down his own blood. Hans was the one person who met his silences with ease, embracing his sombre moods and monosyllabic responses as though they were eager felicitations. He was in flight training now, despite Rudi's efforts to dissuade him, and would shortly be operational. Rudi knew better than anyone that his brother had no vocation for flying. He was doing this out of some misguided sense of hero worship and brotherly love. Of the two of them, Rudi recognised his brother as the better man – kinder, more patient, with the tenderest of hearts. A heart would weigh you down in this business like a millstone about your neck.

The German Pilot

He thought back to when they were very young on their parents' farm. It had been a childhood of happy toil, of threshing and harvesting, of sheering the thick fleeces of bleating sheep and wringing the gorged udders of unwieldy cows. He remembered how Hans had fought back tears as the realisation that these animals were sent for slaughter had registered.

He, Rudi, had teased him mercilessly for every kindness bestowed on those big, lumbering beasts, for every time he had released a trapped animal and tended its wounds. And later his open heart had been so easily cracked and broken by the giddy vagaries of love. How could he possibly face the enemy with the necessary detachment? In this war, you needed to be savage. One moment of compassion could prove your last.

Tormented by these thoughts, he drifted into a restless sleep, awoken time and time again by thoughts of the young pilot with Hans's face, the face he had so easily obliterated and been happy to do so. He was not a religious man, but he found himself praying silently for the safety of Hans. He would gladly sacrifice himself for his brother, who, in any case, gained so much more from life than he did. Hans would be inordinately grateful for the smallest favour, would help others selflessly without begrudging his time or expertise. He was an excellent carpenter, had a special way with children and the elderly alike, and would labour on the farm until his hands blistered from the exertion. He could cook better than their mother and would smile through the worst adversity. He was the most admirable man Rudi knew. Yet for some unfathomable reason, Hans revered his older brother, saw in him something he could not find in himself.

Rudi dreaded the day his brother would fly in combat. He knew the plight of the rookie pilot. He had to learn on the job and learn fast. The first half a dozen flights were crucial. If you survived them, you had learned something. It was one thing having someone explain the techniques of combat to you on a sunny training flight, but quite another to be out there alone, in an endless, livid firmament, buffeted by banks of sable cloud, with neither instruction nor vision. The unpredictable weather was as great an enemy as the Spitfire and the Hurricane.

And there were enemy flyers who could recognise a rookie immediately, as he did. The image of the English pilot, so young and vulnerable, played again on his mind. If only he hadn't seen his face. If only he hadn't been so keen to claim his next victory. It had seemed desperately important but suddenly it meant nothing except torment, his brother's life as retribution for all those young Englishmen he had shot down. Surely it was fair. He had deprived so many mothers of their sons, wives of their husbands and children of their fathers. They too would have the impossible burden of grief thrust upon them, a grief that he had caused and for which he should now pay penance.

He could visualise his mother's face as she was told of Hans's death, weeping inconsolably for her younger son. She relied heavily on Hans, who could sweep away her depression like dust from the mantel shelf and make her smile again with an impromptu remark or expression. Hans never forgot her birthday as he, Rudi, was inclined, and would feed her love of trivia by updating her on the most paltry topics. This wretched war couldn't last much longer and until it ended, he must find a way to protect him.

It was the following day that it came to him, this latent idea, incubated during his troubled sleep. As mad as it appeared to his fatigue-addled mind, he couldn't shrug it off. And despite the absurdity of it, he found consolation in its reasoning. The face of the young pilot, identical, in his perception, to his younger brother, haunted him and he felt the need to make some reparation. War was a barbarous thing. Every day men killed other men that in times of peace they would have befriended. He made a pledge, to whom he was not quite sure – some unknown deity or the memory of that lost, English pilot perhaps. The next young, rookie pilot he came into contact with, he would spare. Then perhaps, if there was a God out there, he would spare Hans. It was odd that he, who looked to science rather than theology for answers, and who had never suffered from superstition, should think like this. But his mind was made up. He felt a sense of calm at last.

He soon found that his resolution was more difficult to execute than he had imagined. His skills as a fighter pilot were finely honed and instinctive, and trying to suppress them was rather like asking a concert pianist to perform a musical composition in the wrong notes. It was contrary to every natural response. Later that afternoon, he was sent on an escort mission with his squadron. They had been flying uneventfully for a couple of hours when the skies had darkened quickly into a thick, hoary grey. Suddenly, half a dozen Spitfires had appeared out of the gloom. Barely visible, they came at all angles, their obvious intention to destroy the bombers. Several of the escorting Messerschmitts, along with Rudi, dispersed to engage with the fighters, leaving only a couple flanking the Heinkels. Should the Spitfires muscle their way through, they would be their last vestige of defence. Their adversaries were accomplished and the battle frenetic, resulting in aircraft from both sides rolling and diving in an effort to outmanoeuvre the other.

It was a struggle in the gloomy lighting, even with Rudi's superior vision, to determine which were the enemy aircraft. One Spitfire pilot, in a desperate attempt to escape a pursuing Messerschmitt, flew directly into the path of a bomber and collided. Rudi pulled back sharply on his control stick, ascending into cloud cover just as one and a half tonnes of vertically stored explosives, along with eight hundred and fifty gallons of fuel, detonated beneath him, incinerating pilots and crew and causing great chunks of molten metal to diffuse, annihilating a passing aircraft. Another pilot opened his canopy and deserted his burning plane, but his parachute, either faulty or mishandled, failed to open, so that he dropped like a stone to inevitable death. Bursts of ammunition broke out like a deathly symphony as an enemy fighter broke through the confusion of battle and headed for the Heinkels, firing wildly, forcing them out of formation and into vulnerable isolation. Rudi turned the yellow nose of his plane toward it, his Daimler-Benz engine growling furiously at full throttle as he closed in and blasted cannon fire. The shells cut through the Spitfire's propeller boss, tearing off its propellers and bursting the oil tank. He watched the Spitfire plummet backward, followed by a column of black smoke, into the spume of fermenting waves below. This was not the time for redemption.

Rudy checked his fuel tank. His opponents were playing a great tactical game, forcing him to consume his fuel in aerial combat. He would have barely enough left to complete their sortie. He heard a sudden burst of ammunition and caught sight of another Spitfire on his tail. Yanking up the nose of his plane, he arched over the top of it, settled in astern, the red dot of his gunsight aiming for the petrol tanks tucked discreetly behind the engine, and fired. The Spitfire burst into flames so close that Rudi was forced to sideslip violently to change his flight path and avoid becoming a victim of his own assault. Debris from the destroyed plane followed him as he dived out of the arena. An arm sailed past his canopy. Then, it was over as quickly as it had begun. The sky so suddenly abundant with aircraft was now empty and he retreated, back to the Heinkels, staying close, guarding their every sway until they returned to base.

Over subsequent weeks Rudi had many such incidents. He flew each day, sometimes several times, disabled from tiredness. He was still haunted each sleeping and waking moment by the face of the young English pilot so like his brother's. The occasion for atonement had still not arisen and the pact he had made himself remained unrealised. He grew more edgy the closer Hans came to graduating. He had already passed his navigation and aerodynamics exams with distinction and received his pilot wings. Now, he was at operational training and any time now, he would be in combat. Rudi grew more and more remote from his comrades, more isolated and reticent in his daily life. The only person he met with any regularity was Hans, and the more he heard him relaying the news of his forthcoming graduation, the more depressed he became. 'Perhaps we will fly together,' Hans would joke. 'Two aces from the same family, the fastest pilots in the West. And with a name like ours, yes... Schnell. Ha! It will be like old times, working together, like on the farm.' No, nothing like the farm, Rudi wanted to say, but said nothing.

Hans seemed happy and eager to get started. He got on well with his comrades, liked everyone and by all accounts, was liked by all. 'You should get home more,' he would say. 'They worry about you, you know.' With that he would slap Rudi on the back as if to signify an end to the solemnity. 'Let's go and talk to those girls over there. They're both so pretty and the one on the left has been making eyes at me all evening. Didn't you notice?' At this point, Rudi would make an excuse about an early start and leave, satisfied that his brother was well.

He tried each time to impart some advice about flying, various manoeuvres he had found useful, such as how to recover from a spin, the art of deflection shooting and ways to make your fuel last. He reminded him of the importance of having the radio transmitter on receive mode, to check his turn and slip indicator before firing and to keep his guns activated.

He mentioned anything that he felt might help to keep Hans alive. Whenever he did this, Hans would listen with intent, respectful of his more experienced brother, keen to learn. Occasionally, Hans would bring along a friend, introducing him to Rudi as if his brother were royalty. Privately, they had already heard of his reputation. *Hervorragende* pilot was the general consensus. An outstanding pilot but a bit of a *scheisskerl*, so arrogant and unsociable.

How could he be the brother of Hans, who was the nicest and most approachable of people. Even in looks they were different, both blond and good-looking but one with a stare of glacial blue, brimming with condemnation, the other holding a gaze of gentle brown that seemed capable of seeing only goodness in the world and everyone in it.

Two weeks passed and Hans began to fly in combat. His meetings with Rudi showed little outward change in him. The conversation was still cheerful and he would talk of his flying antics with an air of understatement. 'Yes,' he would say, 'had a little skirmish with a Spit yesterday, but nothing to write home about. I expect you've had much worse.' But Rudi, who knew his brother well, detected behind the warm, hazel eyes a barely concealed emptiness and a tremor in his handshake that was unfamiliar. The officers' mess was awash with talk of the rookies and he had heard several comments from those who didn't know their connection.

'Did you hear about young Schnell? He almost took out his wingman?'

The German Pilot

'All round good chap, wouldn't let you down. Dare say his responses will quicken.'

'A bit slow to scramble. Thought he was waiting for an invitation. Pity he doesn't live up to his name.'

Each time he flew, Rudi sought out the opportunity for restitution, but things were getting harder. Staying alive was harder. The enemy were a brave and steadfast people and defence was easier than attack. Radar defeated the element of surprise and sometimes, particularly during night flying when visibility was poor, the climate proved the victor. But then things changed.

Three weeks after Hans had graduated, Rudi was heading home across the North Sea when he spotted the faint gash of a condensation trail in the distance. The aircraft was moving rapidly toward him. His eyes narrowed in an effort to identify it between puffs of cumulus clouds. It looked like a Spitfire, though there was something different about it. He could usually discern the roundels at a great distance and occasionally the undercarriage had been painted a different shade to camouflage specific locations, but this wasn't the case. Then he spotted the girl on the side of the nose, blonde and scantily clad. This was unusual for Spitfires and the rarity of it distracted him momentarily, but the tell-tale vapour trail had prepared him for combat.

In contrast, the Spitfire pilot was surprised by the

sudden confrontation. He turned sharply at some speed and for a moment his engine stalled so that he spiralled briefly before gaining control and diving into the clouds. Rudi tore after him, his steely, watchful eyes never losing sight. He came out of the cloud above the Spitfire and saw the pilot cast a look over his shoulder into the blinding sun. He must have frozen with terror as he stayed flying in a straight line until Rudi was within perfect range. Until that point, Rudi had been carried along by adrenalin and the will to survive, but suddenly, he remembered his pact and the young pilot, so like Hans, who he had so easily shot down. This pilot was obviously equally inexperienced and out of his depth. Had he not heard of the Hun in the sun? It was the oldest trick in the book. And now he was purblind. In the seconds it would take him to retrieve his vision, his life would be lost. What a lame victory it would be. He glanced about him to check that there were no witnesses, then turned swiftly for home, firing an empty burst into the opaque clouds. A lesson learned. The Spitfire pilot, sight restored, saw his chance, opened the throttle and with a smile and a wave from Lady Luck, disappeared into the distance.

Flying back to base, Rudi realised he felt something that he hadn't felt in a long time, something verging on pure happiness. It was as if the demons that for the last few weeks had plagued his every waking moment had been exorcised. That night he slept soundly and awoke with renewed vigour. He drew curtains to a bleak mist. The landing strip was barely visible, yet it seemed to him a fine day. He enjoyed some light-hearted exchange with his comrades over breakfast. If they wondered what had brought about his transformation, they asked no questions, for which he was grateful.

His next flight was planned for noon. The fog had cleared by then and he greeted his plane with a sense of joyful reunion, as if the reason for his flight was recreational rather than combative. They flew together like a dream and no amount of flak could reach their elevation; no explosions blight their trail. The clouds cloaked them, the sun was their accomplice and the vault of heaven their playground. He felt untouchable. It struck him then that fearlessness demanded neither great courage nor great stupidity, just a perfect collaboration between man and machine. He engaged against the odds, intrepid and tireless, breaking formations, chasing stragglers, defending the bomber crews, returning to base only when the clatter and hiss of empty guns dictated. His keen vision judged the slow descent to the landing strip with the last drop of fuel. He pulled open the side-hinged canopy and climbed wearily, yet happily, out of the cockpit.

He was met by the unexpected sight of his wing commander, Oberstleutnant Schneider, a tall, slender man with heavy jowls that made him look older than his years. The skin on his face looked unusually ashen and when he spoke, his voice was softer than usual as if to compensate for the severity of his words.

'Hauptman Schnell,' he said quietly, 'Rudi, I need to speak with you.'

Rudi stopped in his tracks. He looked directly at Oberstleutnant Schneider, who held his gaze but with such obvious reluctance that Rudi knew in his heart that something was terribly wrong.

'Yes?' he said, his blue eyes intense and quizzical. 'What is it?'

'I really think that we should speak more privately.' The wing commander glanced at the passing ground crew. 'You're exhausted. You need to sit down, take some refreshment. I would have sent for you but...'

'*Bitte*, please, I need to know.'

'Very well.' Oberstleutnant Schneider sighed and raised a hand to his forehead to brush away the small beads of perspiration forming there. 'It's bad news, I'm afraid, very bad news, so you must brace yourself. It's your brother, Hans. I'm afraid he didn't make it back.'

'But that can't be. There must be a mistake.' Rudi wavered slightly, so that Oberstleutnant Schneider moved forward to steady him.

'I'm so sorry. He was...' he searched helplessly for the right words. 'He was so well liked, by everyone.'

Rudi moved aside and vomited on the tarmac. Oberstleutnant Schneider stood helplessly by, his head

The German Pilot

bowed, waiting. After a few moments, Rudi composed himself sufficiently to speak.

'How? Tell me. I need to know what happened.'

'It was after he scrambled this afternoon. He was keen you see… to prove himself. He went after a fighter. It was very courageous. He wanted to be like you… an ace, to make you proud. He said it all the time to his comrades. But it was just a case that this time he met a better pilot, or a luckier one. I'm so sorry.'

'I need to know the details.' Rudi's cool blue eyes demanded answers. 'I need to know everything.'

Oberstleutnant Schneider nodded. 'Of course. It was a Spitfire. That much I can tell you. It was all witnessed by Hauptman Klein. He said it was an act of great bravery. He could have let him go but he went after him, you see. He was keen to make his mark, to serve his country well. Klein saw it all. But it was the old trick, the sun… he was tricked into it.' He paused. He was not a man at ease with emotion. Words were always inadequate in these circumstances, but he was desperate to say something consolatory. 'Don't worry. He was so well liked, you see. There won't be a pilot around that won't put himself out to shoot down that Spitfire now. And it won't be difficult to spot. Had a blonde on the nose apparently. Well, that blonde may well prove to be his downfall.' He half smiled at the weakness of his own joke and then turned away, ashamed.

Tears licked Rudi's cheeks as his terrible secret bore

down on him in unbearable measure. A returning Heinkel passed obliquely overhead, casting a shadow on the figures beneath.

The Pathfinder

I

Group Captain Forbes-Harrison sat at his desk snatching small bites of his sandwich and washing them down with a glass of cool water. He was a tall man and looked uncomfortable on the small chair, his elbow now supporting his chin at a precarious angle. He had just had to inform the families of an entire crew that the Vickers Wellington bomber they had been flying had been lost over the ironically named Happy Valley district in Germany. His forehead, permanently creased, seemed to weigh down heavily on a face already deflated and craggy, the eyes deep-set, lips smacked into a jagged line of anguish.

There was a knock at the door and Squadron Leader Harringworth entered. In contrast to Forbes-Harrison, he was small and slight with fair hair and smooth, pale skin that was almost luminous. But the fifteen-year age gap between them seemed apparent only outwardly. War made men grow up fast.

'I've only just heard,' he said solemnly. 'I was only talking to Beech yesterday. He said how much he was looking forward to becoming a father. Rotten luck! All of them good men.'

'The best.' Forbes-Harrison looked at his watch and stood. This was no time for sentimentality. 'I take it you've seen my recommendations for the new aircrew?'

'You've put together a great team, but you don't mention a pilot?'

'No, it's taken me a while to find the right man. After all, this is not just a Pathfinder crew we're after. This is the Master Bomber. And that means we need a pilot with nerves of steel. Someone who is not just the first to arrive and mark out targets but someone who's prepared to stick around for the pillow talk, so to speak, communicating radio instructions, making damn sure the rest of the squadron hit their targets and find their way home.'

'Well, I'd be happy to put myself forward.' Harringworth seemed keen for the challenge. 'I know the men already and we work well together.'

'I appreciate that, Harringworth, but I've found someone. We're about to meet him.'

'Oh, do I know him?' Harringworth sounded

disappointed.

'No, no one here does. He's from Georgetown, British Guiana I believe.' He cast an eye at Harringworth. 'Very impressive qualifications. Great flying record. Completed two tours already. Went to Cambridge apparently. Name's Wing Commander Winston Cy Jellicoe.'

'I'm not sure the chaps will like that, sir. I mean, with a name like that.'

'What's wrong with his name? A chap can't help his name.'

Harringworth opened his mouth as if to speak and then closed it. After a moment, he said measuredly, 'Winston, sir. I mean the name Winston. Well, there can only be one Winston can't there?'

'Well apparently not! For all we know there are hundreds of Winstons in British Guiana. But that's not what you meant is it?'

'Well, sir...' Harringworth hesitated. 'No, sir, you're right, I think that some of the men might object to being ordered about by... by someone of colour, sir.'

'Well, if they don't like it, they can damn well lump it.' Forbes-Harrison recognised that part of Harringworth's objection was disappointment at not being offered the job himself, but he still didn't like the tone of his argument. 'There'll be zero tolerance for that kind of discrimination while I'm in command. We're not in America where Blacks and Whites are segregated.

The RAF embraces all colours and creeds. As far as I'm concerned, anyone who pays their own passage here to fight a common enemy has my backing. Thank God the colour bar was lifted. We need all the help we can get.'

'Yes, sir, I only meant…'

'The world is full of people who *only meant*, Squadron Leader.'

'Sir.'

'Go and tell the men. I'll bring him down as soon as he arrives. Ops are on tomorrow so if anyone has any problems with him, they can sort out their differences on the way to Germany.'

Harringworth was disappointed that he hadn't been chosen as the Master Bomber pilot in the Pathfinder squadron. It would have been quite an accolade for someone of twenty-four. But he knew that his record was rocky and that though the men generally liked him, they didn't completely trust his flying. He'd had a couple of near misses down to lack of judgement recently, but he felt he'd learned from those incidents and should've been given the benefit of the doubt. He had a lot of respect for Group Captain Forbes-Harrison. He was fair-minded and competent. But he questioned the wisdom of putting the crew together with an unknown pilot, let alone one from British Guiana.

The aircrew were at the Lancaster checking their equipment when he caught up with them. They were eager to find out who their new pilot was. Poker, the navigator, understood that trusting a pilot was imperative if a crew were to fly with the necessary confidence. He also believed that attitude was everything on a mission. You had to believe you were returning or else you were damned. When he saw Harringworth approaching, his heart sank.

'To put you out of your misery,' Harringworth said, 'I'd just like to assure you, you're going to be in very capable hands.'

'You're not our pilot then,' joked Doddington, the rear gunner, who always said what others thought but dare not say.

'Careful! Don't forget that little thing called insubordination,' warned Hammy, the wireless operator.

'I'll ignore that this time,' said Harringworth. 'Actually, your pilot is a chap called Winston, and no, I don't mean Churchill.'

'Winston! I didn't realise there were any other Winstons,' Doddington said.

'Oh, the name's quite common in some parts of the Caribbean,' said Poker, his face expressionless. 'You'd better start practising your Creole, Doddy.'

'My what?'

'You know,' said Foxy, the bomb aimer. 'Creole!' He shook his head in despair and said in his best Caribbean accent: 'So we can understan one anudda, chat about dis un dat ya know, before im tink im tek di plane away wid mi in it.'

The crew broke into laughter. 'Not bad,' Harringworth encouraged.

'Good morning, gentlemen.'

The crew turned to meet the furious face of Group Captain Forbes-Harrison and another man, equally as tall and imposing but with skin the colour of burnished coffee and a smile that extended gradually over white, even teeth.

'This is Wing Commander Winston Cy Jellicoe,' Forbes-Harrison continued. 'He's your new pilot.'

The crew were speechless with embarrassment.

Jellicoe pointed at Foxy. 'Wah yuh name, bwoy?' he demanded, raising an eyebrow.

Foxy was dumbstruck.

'He wants to know your name,' Doddy whispered.

'Foxy,' said Foxy. 'I mean, Sergeant Fox, sir.'

'Well, Sergeant Fox,' Jellicoe said in a clipped English accent. 'I can see that you're the joker of the pack. Flying into enemy territory is a serious business. We brush with death every time we fly. So it's good to know we can rely on you for some entertainment along the way.'

'Sorry, sir,' Foxy said. 'We didn't mean any offence.'

'None taken, I'm sure. A minor peccadillo. Now, let me see...' He studied the men in front of him and pointed to them in turn. 'Foxy, bomb aimer and comedian; Doddy, rear gunner; Hammy, obviously the wireless operator; Poker, navigator, so called because he never shows any emotion; Dixon, flight engineer. We're going to be sitting pretty close, Dixon, so don't forget to use your carbolic soap.' He winked. 'Then we have Mad short for Maddocks, mid-upper gunner. I hear you get pretty profane in that turret, Maddocks. Not my style, but if it helps then go ahead.' Maddocks had no idea what 'profane' meant but nodded his assent. 'Last but not least, Radish, radar operator and second navigator.' He paused. 'In case you were wondering about me, my crews usually refer to me as Bear.'

'Bear, sir?'

'A diminutive of Winston changed to a hypocorism.' The crew looked mystified. 'You know, from Winnie the Pooh. He was a bear, I believe! Anyway...' He cleared his throat. 'I hear you're all the very best the Royal Air Force has to offer, which is good as I only like to work with the best.'

'I'll leave you to get acquainted,' Forbes-Harrison said. 'Harringworth, a word in my office, please.' He turned to the men. 'You don't have long. Your first sortie together is tomorrow so get acquainted and then get some rest.'

'Sir.' Dixon, the flight engineer, looked uncomfortable. 'Presumably Wing Commander Jellicoe, I mean Bear, will be Second Dickie until he has some experience of the route and the German defences. I mean, that's the usual practice, to fly with a more experienced pilot for the first couple of missions. It

hardly seems fair to throw him in the deep end like this.'
Or us, he thought privately.

'It's true, that's the usual way of things.'

'Especially for us Pathfinders,' Maddocks said. 'And we're the Master Bomber.'

'I'd be happy to offer my services,' Harringworth suggested, 'until you get the hang of it.'

Jellicoe laughed, undermining Harringworth without intent.

'That won't be necessary,' Forbes-Harrison said firmly. 'The fact is, there is no one as experienced as Wing Commander Jellicoe and we are short staffed. Now...' He turned once more to leave. 'If you'll excuse me, I have work to do. Gentlemen, good luck.'

Jellicoe turned to the men. 'Okay,' he said, 'it's just us now and I want to get to know you all. I want to know how you think and react, what your thoughts are when you're in that turret, Maddocks, what motivates you all, your speech, your body language. I realise that it's a huge leap of faith, trusting a pilot that you don't know. But I will answer any questions you have now, about me, my experience, anything in fact that allows you to feel more comfortable with me and with my abilities. We are all brothers when we fly, whatever our race or politics. We rely on each other implicitly and we look out for each other like family.' He smiled his slow, white smile. 'I can't change serendipity but I can be the best and safest pilot I can be.'

The Pathfinder

After they had spoken at length, Jellicoe made them sit in their allocated places in the Lancaster and talk to each other in mock-up situations. Tomorrow they would fly this old lady to Germany, where she would face every assault imaginable while they sat in her cramped, metal fuselage with a 12,000lb bomb beneath them for company. He made it clear that he wanted all airmen at the primary briefing with the commanding officer. This was unprecedented but in Jellicoe's opinion, a unified crew meant a successful one.

The next day, everyone arrived promptly, uncertain but excited for what was to come. After the commanding officer had spoken and the Met and intelligence officers had made additions, they all knew exactly what was expected of them. Copious notes were taken concerning German anti-aircraft defences, search lights and where the German fighter planes were most likely to intercept. Jellicoe understood that as part of the Master Bomber crew, the navigators were under additional pressure to achieve accuracy, otherwise their target illuminators would be squandered and following aircraft would waste their expensive bombs on the wrong targets. And he was not a man for whom failure was an option. Both his parents had been academics and he had grown up in a large family, whose general maxim was that whatever you chose to do, you did it to the best of your ability, whether that involved sweeping the backyard or defending your country. It was a question of self-regard.

After the second briefing and when the Lancaster had been rigorously checked by the ground crew, Jellicoe led his men to the crew room. 'Time to suit up.' He grinned. 'And don't forget to collect your parachutes and your Mae Wests. I hear the English Channel's pretty cold right now.'

Juniper green trucks, their canvas roofs tapped by rainfall, drove them to their awaiting aircraft.

'Wait a minute,' Foxy said, as they were about to embark. He relieved himself against the tail wheel. 'Some aircrew have mascots,' he said cheerfully 'but that's my mascot, that wheel. And I don't have to worry about losing it. I know men who have been driven mad by losing their mascots.'

The quiet tension was palpable. 'Right,' Jellicoe said, 'let's get this little lady started. Good luck, everyone.'

Checks completed, he taxied around the perimeter track onto the runway and awaited the green affirmation. Coaxing the control column forward, he opened the throttle to the take-off position and the Lancaster eased down the runway, its tail raising slightly as Dixon assisted with the throttle. 'Smooth as butta,' Jellicoe said, directing his speech to Foxy. 'Nuh need ta fret yuh self, bwoy. Wi a comin' home.' He laughed his loud belly laugh as the nose of the Lancaster lifted effortlessly and they were airborne.

Later when the crew returned and spoke of their first mission with Jellicoe, all they could remember was the joy of flying with him. Never before had they experienced such a symbiosis between man and plane. Their target had been located swiftly using H2S, the ground scanning radar system, and illuminated with precision so that the following aircraft could mark it further and allow the Main Bomber Force to plant their incendiary bombs successfully. It had worked like clockwork, any aircraft located off course being quickly redirected by Jellicoe. The mission was deemed a complete success and despite heavy anti-aircraft defences, the Lancaster had returned without a scratch.

After half a dozen such missions, the crew agreed they never wanted to fly with any other pilot. Bear, they said, was a cool customer, his confidence contagious, his wit sharp and his judgement savvy. Quietly, he demanded a great deal of the men, but only when they entered the plane, and they adhered to this. From that point onward, any other concerns had to become secondary. One momentary lapse of concentration could spell disaster. Sometimes flights would last eight hours or more and for that, physical and mental vigour were needed. For his part, Jellicoe was extremely disciplined. He didn't drink and made sure that he had six hours sleep if possible. Everything about him exuded competence – his erect stance, his unwavering gaze, his calm, uniform eloquence – and this transferred to his crew, creating a happy, professional allegiance, consolidated frequently at the mess.

The officers' mess flowed organically from its antechamber, an amalgam of styles both in architecture and décor. Its tall, ornate ceiling edged by elaborate cornicing begged a grander hue than the plain pendant lights could provide. Similarly, the oak panelled walls demanded original canvases as opposed to the rather drab prints that embellished them. The furniture was also a composite of burnished Chesterfield sofas and occasional chairs, tables of woods both hard and soft, flooring a mix of parquet and carpet. It was a comfortable room, lacking ostentation yet hinting at formality and it was here, under wall sconces, in a faded wingback chair that Jellicoe liked to relax and read the morning papers after breakfast. Now and then Poker, Radish and Dixon would join him, Poker reading with him in contented silence while Radish and Dixon exchanged light-hearted riposte.

'Hey, Bear,' Radish said one morning, 'why don't you come out with us? There's a swing dance tomorrow evening as it happens. Some great music, pretty girls, lots of alcohol. What more could you want? It beats sitting in the mess with your head buried in those newspapers full of shameless propaganda. I sometimes wonder if we're fighting the same war when I read how we knocked Jerry out of the sky with no losses. We should take those journalists with us one day.'

'It's called boosting morale,' Poker said, without looking up. 'No one wants to hear about Allied losses.'

'Never mind about that,' Dixon persisted. 'Come on, Bear, it should be fun. Ole Poker face here is coming, aren't you?'

'Not unless I have to.' Poker's face was barely visible behind his newspaper.

'Oh, I don't know,' Jellicoe hesitated. 'You know I don't drink and there's nothing worse than being the only sober person in the room.'

'Drinking alcohol isn't compulsory. I'm sure the barmaid can fix you up with a cup of tea or an orange juice if you ask her nicely. Incidentally, I've never known anyone drink so much tea.'

'Yes, it's obscene,' Dixon laughed. 'Not the image we aircrew like to project. Elderly ladies drink tea, not bomber pilots.'

'He probably can't dance either,' Radish said. 'I expect that's the real reason that he doesn't want to join us.'

'Can't dance,' Jellicoe laughed. 'It's in my blood. I just don't want to make you chaps look bad.'

'No chance of that,' Radish smiled. 'I've been compared to a serpent on the dance floor. Old snake hips they call me.'

'That's not what I've heard. I overheard you danced more like a dog.'

'A dog?'

'Yes, with two left feet.'

'Very amusing, Dixon.'

'Oh, go on then.' Poker put down his newspaper. 'I'll go if Bear does. We're obviously not going to hear the last of it until we agree.'

'Okay,' Jellicoe said, with a grimace. 'But you boys had better be able to hold your liquor cos I'm not carrying any of you home.'

They arrived at the dance in a jaunty mood, Jellicoe having driven due to his sobriety. They had no flying the following day so could drink without regulation. The strain of the last weeks began to unfurl. The town hall was vast and the big-band sound was exactly the kind of musical ensemble that Jellicoe loved, and the perfect accompaniment for dancing. A platinum blonde soloist wearing a red polka-dot dress sang, her mellow, euphonic tones gradually seducing couples to the dance floor.

'I think we've made an impression,' Poker said as they entered. 'I can only think it's due to my debonair good looks.'

'It's Bear,' said Radish. 'Did you see that brunette? She couldn't take her eyes off him.'

'Yes, I suppose it's the novelty. There aren't too many men looking like me in this place.'

'Well if that's the case, I intend to use your novelty to our advantage with the ladies,' Dixon laughed. 'Look, there's Harringworth trying to chat up that cute blonde over there. She looks bored to tears. Let's go and rescue her.'

'I'm not sure we should interrupt,' Jellicoe said, but the others had already begun walking in Harringworth's direction, so he followed absently. The sound of the music was almost irresistible, and he felt himself swaying as he moved. He loved dancing but rarely found the opportunity. It felt good to hear the mixture of saxophone, trumpets and trombones in a congenial atmosphere with attractive ladies all dressed up, their finery and joyful demeanour making the war seem suddenly distant and inconsequential.

'I'm Dixon.' He heard Dixon introducing himself to the girl talking to Harringworth. 'And this is Poker and Radish. Oh, and this is our pilot extraordinaire, Wing Commander Winston Cy Jellicoe. Bear to his friends.'

Now that he was closer, Jellicoe could see that the girl was uncommonly pretty, with soft ash-blonde hair and eyes the colour of forget-me-nots. She was wearing a figure-hugging dress that accentuated her curves and her high heels showed off her slender ankles to perfection.

'I'm Rose,' she said, holding out her hand in his direction. He took it and noticed how soft and small it was.

'Of course you are,' he said carelessly, 'and a rose by any other name would smell as sweet.'

Dixon raised his eyes skyward.

She laughed. 'Do you always quote Shakespeare when you first meet a girl?'

'Only when the occasion calls for it.' Jellicoe felt awkward. 'I'm afraid I'm rather out of practice at meeting young ladies. I hope it wasn't offensive?'

'Offensive? Good grief, no! It was sweet.'

'They've managed to drag you out then,' Harringworth said. 'It's unusual to see you at a dance, Jellicoe. I didn't think this would be your kind of thing.'

'Why not?' Dixon asked.

'Well, I don't know,' Harringworth replied. 'I just can't imagine you dancing to the waltz or the foxtrot.'

'What can you envision me dancing to?' Jellicoe said, 'jungle drums, perhaps?' He turned to Rose. 'Actually, I love to dance but I rarely get the chance.'

'Oh, would you like to dance?' Rose smiled, sensing the tension. 'They're playing swing and I'd love to improve my jitterbug. Do you know it?'

'Know it? Practically invented it.'

'I'm sure Jellicoe would like to get himself a drink before he starts dancing,' Harringworth said, with obvious irritation.

'I don't drink.'

'Perfect then.'

Much to the amusement of his crew, Rose led Jellicoe to the dance floor.

'I hope you don't mind,' she smiled, 'but I try to give

Howard a wide berth. He can be such a dreadful bore. I've been dying to dance.'

Jellicoe laughed and took her hand, moving effortlessly in time with the music, guiding Rose around the floor with an innate dexterity. Rose was a worthy partner and soon her movements became looser and their jive more abandoned.

'Let's try this,' he would say, and her dress would billow in the wake of another turn until it was mastered. Soon they had a small crowd around them. 'Let's give them something worth watching. How about a back flip?' And before she had time to object, she found herself flipped over his shoulder.

'And again.'

The dance was fast and their movements frenetic, and when it ended, she collapsed in his arms so that his senses were filled with a fragrant mixture of perfume and the salty secretions of intimacy.

'That was wonderful,' she said, her face all animation. 'Let's do it again. Show me some more moves. I want to be really good at this.'

Everything she said seemed ambiguous in his momentary state of intoxication. 'You already are,' he said breathlessly. 'You can't improve upon perfection.'

The tempo of the orchestra changed. 'Can you waltz?' She moved closer. 'It'll give us a chance to catch our breath.'

Once again, the sudden closeness of her, this time in

slow, rhythmic embrace, startled him. He was seduced and could not tell whether his seductress was aware of her powers or had executed them without intent. He realised that he had never been so close to a White girl before. His usual types were dusky-toned with svelte necks and a reed-like elegance. So he was surprised that this pale-skinned girl with her bright lips and ashen hair had beguiled him so completely. Despite the fact that she was surrounded by girls of a similar colouring she seemed exotic and set apart, sequestered by a strange aura of indestructability. Her unrouged lips were naturally ruby, stark against her pale skin, and the row of bright, even teeth would have been perfect were it not for the slight gap at the front. He found he liked the gap more each time she smiled – a minor imperfection, oddly erotic. He noted too when he spun her around, the lines drawn down the back of her slender legs. This appeared to be a common phenomenon, no doubt due to the lack of stockings available in wartime. How resourceful women were and how clever they must be to know that the simple act of drawing two lines down the back of their legs could arouse such an interest in men. He wondered how she had managed to draw them so evenly and thought how glorious it would be to assist her in this undertaking.

He did not notice, in his distraction, two men dressed in civilian clothes, faces contorted with rage at the sight of him dancing with a girl they would like to have claimed for themselves. They stood in angry, beer-fuelled discourse, their noxious words biting the air, as Radish and Dixon walked past them.

'Steady on, chaps, you happen to be talking about a friend of ours,' Radish interjected. 'Now, do you mind refining your language as there are ladies around. Keep your narrow-minded prejudices to yourselves. There's no place for them here.'

The taller one with red hair and lines of discord etched on his face pushed Radish backwards by the shoulder. Radish tripped, knocking over several drinks and a chair before steadying himself. 'You're aircrew, I suppose,' he said. 'You all seem to think you're above the rest of us.'

'Only when we're flying, old man,' Dixon quipped, 'then it's a literal certainty.'

'Don't try to get clever with me. You all think you're so bloody superior, don't you?' He turned to his small, muscular friend. 'Hey, do you know what they say the difference is between God and a pilot?'

His friend looked absently into his beer as if the answer lay steeped in its froth. 'No, what?'

'God *knows* he isn't a pilot.' He laughed uproariously. 'You should all just push off and take Mr Midnight with you, the black…'

'Just a minute,' Dixon said. 'Now, I'm overlooking for a moment the fact that you've just assaulted a friend of mine here and insulted another. If you just apologise, old man, then we'll leave it at that.'

The red-haired man shrieked with laughter, threw back his head and brought it down full force on Dixon's forehead, sending him reeling back over a table. Poker, who had been observing the scene from a distance, promptly walked over, face devoid of enmity, and delivered one precise blow, deviating the septum of a nose already distended and causing the man to fall heavily onto the wooden flooring. His friend began to reach for an empty bottle but Radish, incited into an uncharacteristic rage, hit him hard in the stomach so that he was winded and bent double with pain. By this time, the doormen had been alerted. They seemed to get the measure of things, so that the two agitators were expulsed from the building.

Jellicoe, who had been sitting at a table immersed in conversation with Rose, heard the commotion and seeing his comrades in a skirmish, excused himself, mortified by his own preoccupation. 'What on earth was that all about?' He helped Dixon to a chair. 'Are you okay?'

'Couldn't be better.' Dixon nursed his aching head.

Radish sat down next to him. 'Just a couple of idiots. Jeez, Poker, you kept that right hook of yours a secret.'

'I used to box. I hoped it might come in handy one day.'

'But what was it about?' Jellicoe persisted.

'Two idiots with big mouths spouting off,' Dixon

said. 'Morons who'd had too much to drink and wanted any excuse to let off steam. Just forget it.'

'We'd better get you home,' Jellicoe said.

Rose, who had followed him over, looked at Radish then Dixon and said judiciously, 'Was it about us dancing, Bear and I?'

'No, nothing to do with that,' Radish said, but Jellicoe knew by his expression that he was lying. He wanted to pursue the matter further but not in front of Rose.

'We have to go,' he said rather coldly. 'Thank you for the dance. As you can see, I was enjoying myself so much that I neglected my friends at their moment of crisis.'

'Well…' Rose stepped back, a little surprised at his formality. 'I hope to see you again. There's a dance next week?' She felt a little foolish when he failed to reply, and turned on her heels, disappointed. He glanced over his shoulder. His last view of her was of her blonde hair, which had escaped from its snood and cascaded down to her tiny waist, and beneath that those legs that had caused him such discomposure.

It was with difficulty that Jellicoe managed to discover the truth about the evening. Poker would not deviate from his story and Radish and Dixon were equally reticent. When Dixon finally acquiesced and explained the cause of the brawl, Jellicoe was saddened but unsurprised. Some of these people had never encountered a Black man before and the stereotypes were all-pervasive. His race was considered lazy and intellectually inferior, its only attributes an ability to dance unfettered and an alleged carnal athleticism. Both of these accreditations were no doubt ascribed to the primitive nature of his ethnicity. Propaganda paintings portrayed Black people slumbering as if a metaphor for their arrested development, and the American Secretary of War, Harry Stimson, had not helped matters when he had said that leadership was not embedded in the Negro race.

Jellicoe encountered this kind of ignorance on a regular basis and was used to dealing with it, but he objected emphatically when it interfered with his crew's leisure time. He was touched that they'd defended him, but he now felt indebted, and he did not like the feeling of obligation. In terms of recreation, he would prove to be a thorn in their side. He decided that he would not accompany them to future dances. Part of him rebelled, craving to explore the possibilities of the evening. But each time he looked at Dixon's face, he was sorely reminded of the consequences of his presence. Despite their protests, he adamantly refused to accompany them to the dance the following week.

'This is crazy,' Radish said one day, his large, pleasant features unfolding into a smile. 'Are your movements really to be defined by the lowest common denominator, by bigots and xenophobes? Anyway…' He glanced at Dixon. 'That blow improved Dixon's face enormously. Another one or two punches and he might look half decent.'

'Yes, come on,' Poker said. 'All the boys are coming tonight and you'll be letting the side down if you don't join us.' For once, a wry smile flickered across his face. 'I expect that beautiful girl you stole from Harringworth will be there. And we all want to learn to dance that Jitterbug thing. By the way,' he added, 'did you notice that Harringworth stayed well clear of the action when the fight broke out? Even seemed to find it amusing.' His face returned to its usual arcane expression. 'She did ask about you, as it happens. Can't think why considering how dismissive you were.'

'You *were* a little abrupt when we left the dance,' Dixon said. 'Poor girl must be wondering what she'd done wrong.'

'That's all very well,' Jellicoe was conflicted, 'but I don't want any more trouble on my account.'

'Are you joking?' Radish sighed and shook his head in consternation. 'Can't you see how ridiculous that sounds? We risk our lives most days flying in that pile of scrap metal, when we are fired at from anti-aircraft artillery, fighter planes and even so-called friendly fire. Do you honestly think that we're worried about a few delinquents jealous of your dance technique and your prowess with the ladies?'

Dixon agreed. 'Your novelty value actually helped. It was a great talking point. The girls were intrigued.'

Jellicoe laughed. 'Great, I'm pleased I have *something* to recommend me. If it helps you finally get a girl, Dixon, then I suppose the least I can do is risk being lynched by Neanderthals. I owe you that much.'

The crew seemed in good spirits, yet Jellicoe knew that they were tired. Ops were becoming more frequent and targets more difficult. Over the next few days, they would be revisiting the heavily defended shipyards and oil refineries of Hamburg. The element of surprise was no longer a possibility, and the pressures of precision bombing were enormous, particularly for the navigator. The policy of bombing only military targets, requested initially by Roosevelt, put an additional pressure on Bomber Command in terms of accuracy, and as the Master Bomber, there was no margin for error. They were the first to be met by the onslaught of pyrotechnics, the colourful yet deadly flak that got the party started, and the last to leave the gala of bursts and firecrackers that meant a certain death to a faltering aircraft. The pressure on the crew was almost unimaginable as they neared the end of their tour. Radish was right. It certainly put the antics of a couple of halfwits into perspective. 'Okay,' he said, 'I'll come.'

The following week they arrived at the party a little late due to a long debriefing. He spotted her the moment he entered the dance hall, despite the crowds. It was not difficult. She wore a red satin dress with a V-shaped neckline that suited her shapeliness. Her hair was loose this time, other than at the temples, where she had swept it back into two voluminous curls. She was dancing and he felt envious of her partner. It was foolish. He had no claim on this girl and had only met her once, under trying circumstances. Yet he found himself thinking of her in a proprietary sense.

Harringworth was at the bar watching Rose dance as he drank his third beer. The young soldier she danced with was lanky and clumsy and not a threat, he felt. He saw Poker and Dixon arrive and shortly behind them, Doddington and Foxy. He was glad that they hadn't brought Jellicoe with them. Not only had he taken over the job he'd wanted, but he'd had the audacity to virtually steal the girl he intended to court before his very eyes.

He had privately been pleased when the fight had broken out. Those two hicks had been out of line, but they had expressed the viewpoint of many. He could see that Jellicoe was an impressive man. He was highly qualified and a superb pilot. His men loved him and so, apparently, did the ladies. Well, if he was intent on a White girlfriend then so be it, but there were plenty of others around. Rose was his. Although there was no agreement between them, he felt that eventually his persistence would prevail, so he was dismayed to see

Hammy, Maddocks and Radish now appear with his nemesis, laughing and joking as they headed toward the bar. He cursed inwardly and looked vaguely around the dance hall for any signs of agitation, but there were none. People moved around happily, glad for some respite from the horrors of war.

Jellicoe was the first to speak. 'Harringworth, good to see you.' He patted Harringworth on the shoulder.

'Likewise. I see your boys have dragged you out to drown your woes.' He took a swig of his beer. 'Oh sorry, I forgot you don't drink.' His voice was furred with derision. 'I hear you had a close shave on Tuesday.'

'Oh, nothing to write home about. A bit of ice on the wings and a near collision when someone appeared to mix up their port and starboard. You could say it made an otherwise dull flight a little more entertaining.'

'I'll say.' Harringworth lit up a cigarette and offered one to Jellicoe.

'No thanks, I don't smoke.'

'Don't smoke, don't drink. What *are* your deficiencies?'

'I'd say that's for others to discover, wouldn't you?'

Poker, who had been listening to their conversation, handed Jellicoe an orange juice. 'I know one,' he said mischievously. 'He has a penchant for beautiful women, beautiful blondes I believe.'

Harringworth looked irritated. 'Well, as long as your preference doesn't include Rose then we'll get along just fine. She and I have an understanding.'

'Understanding about what?' Poker smirked. 'Understanding that she has no interest in you whatsoever. I've seen you talking together, watched the body language and there's nothing between you as far as I can see, other than hot air.'

Jellicoe had no desire for any altercation, but he felt compelled to clarify his position. 'I dance with whom I like as long as the woman is amenable to the idea.'

'So…' The softness of her voice was unmistakable. 'The boys have persuaded you to come out of hiding.'

Jellicoe turned to see Rose's lovely face. 'I thought after that fracas a few weeks ago I'd seen the last of you, which would have been a shame,' she added meaningfully, 'since I haven't found such a good dance partner since.'

'There you are,' Harringworth blurted. 'I've been waiting for the opportunity to talk to you.'

'Can it wait, Howard?' She gently nudged Jellicoe's arm.

'Oh, yes,' Jellicoe started. 'I'm sorry, but I promised to teach Rose some more dance moves.' He winked at Harringworth. 'You know, shakin mi native ass on de dancefloh.'

He led Rose to the floor.

'What was all that about?' Before he could answer, she continued, 'I didn't think I'd see you again. And that thought made me sad.' The music was beating slowly and she moved closer to him. 'And although our acquaintance is a fairly new one, I don't think I'm being presumptuous when I say that I think the feeling is mutual.'

'I'd be a fool to deny it.' He admired her candour but was rather unnerved by it. 'But it would spell trouble and I think that you're aware of that. We hadn't even known each other for five minutes before the prejudices of others intervened.'

'I love talking to you,' she persisted, 'and dancing with you.' She smiled and he was once more captivated by the small gap between her bright teeth and the resolute, forget-me-not eyes.

'You could take your pick, someone…' He hesitated. 'Someone less complicated.'

'You mean someone White?'

'Well, yes, since you ask. It might be amusing to you now, fun even, a novelty. But trust me, people can be very harsh, very unforgiving.'

'Hush,' she said, and put her finger to his lips. 'Should I find myself a more courageous love then? One who is prepared to fight for me a little.'

He faltered. 'It's you I'm thinking of, not me.'

'Meet me. We can talk about this, have a meal perhaps. It's difficult to talk properly at a dance. I know a place. I'll write it down for you before I leave and we can meet there on Wednesday evening, if you're free?'

He felt his objections melting away and the need to

be alone with her too fierce. 'I'll be there,' he said. He looked toward the bar and saw Harringworth watching them. 'Harringworth won't be very happy. You know he has a thing for you?'

'He has no chance. Whether you were on the scene or not.' She moved in closer still and he marvelled at how well she fit, her head nestled against his chest. She slipped her fingers between his so that their difference was brought squarely to him, like the different keys of a pianoforte.

On the day he had planned to meet Rose, he was up early to fly. The crew were high on nervous energy. This would be their penultimate trip together as a crew before the end of their tour.

'Bet she won't turn up,' Doddy teased cheerfully. 'If she doesn't, I might ask her out myself. She's a real corker.'

'You?' Foxy made a face. 'She wouldn't be that desperate. Anyway, you can't dance. You'll have to learn to do *this*.' He gyrated his hips lamely while the others laughed.

The route they took that day was a new one and nothing could have prepared them for the heavy anti-aircraft fire, both from flak and fighters, that shook the very bones of the plane.

'Much too close for comfort. For a moment there, I thought we were toast.' Poker shifted in his seat.

'I'll try anything to break that deadpan expression of yours.'

Poker's navigation was superb so that the docks were quickly identified. From an aerial perspective, the short, squat oil tanks, dwarfed by the tall fingers of the distillation towers, looked bleak and ugly, their intricate web of industrial pipes, pumps and furnaces spread out against a backdrop of black water. Moments later, unremitting anti-aircraft fire began, bright and colourful as if designed to add cheer to the dreariness of the place, its deadly purpose hidden momentarily by its prismatic splendour. As Jellicoe weaved toward his target at six thousand feet, angry bursts whistling past the Lancaster, a brief image of Rose's smile manifested itself, an augury of good fortune, and, despite the pelting artillery fire, he felt the warmth of her presence.

'Bomb gone,' Foxy announced, and they felt the aircraft lift as if with relief at its discharged load. Beneath them, the exploded oil tanks, gasoline and other pollutants had turned the air into a thick, inky cloud. Other aircraft now began to attack and Jellicoe flew higher into cloud cover, circling as each took their turn.

'Jefferson just bought it.'

'And Bates. I saw him go up like a Roman candle.'

Jellicoe nodded. The flak was fast becoming impenetrable, losses growing with each op. He was relieved when the last Lancaster began to wend its way back to the coast and they too could set the course for home.

After leaving their target, they progressed to the North Sea. Their aircraft shuddered a little upon approach of the coastline, as if fearful of the inevitable unwelcome reception.

'There might be a small problem with the port outer,' Dixon said, 'but nothing we can't work with.'

Suddenly, Maddocks' panic-stricken voice screamed over the intercom. 'Bandit at three o'clock. Prepare...'

Jellicoe had forced the plane into a corkscrew before his sentence was finished, just as a Focke-Wulf 190 came at them from their starboard side. Doddy and Maddocks opened up the Brownings, the hammering sounds echoing through the fuselage.

They dived through dense clouds, their passage illuminated by tracer fire, in a descent that seemed endless and perilously close to the ocean. The Focke-Wulf followed them down and the Lancaster quivered and shook as shells pounded either side of them. There was an almighty thump and the deafening sound of exploding shells.

'We've been hit!'

Jellicoe pulled up the nose sharply and Maddocks, seeing his chance, fired a long blast into the blinding glare of enemy fire. The Focke-Wulf blew up and, now a giant incendiary, advanced toward them at terrifying speed. Jellicoe pulled the Lancaster skilfully out of its path, feeling the heat as it passed, and climbed hard and fast, thrashing the engines to their last beat until they reached twenty-five thousand feet. The noise was deafening now, and the airspeed indicator dropped suddenly. The entire plane began vibrating violently and the altimeter reading showed a sudden loss in height of one thousand feet. The oxygen supply had been cut and the reserve supplies were already being used by the rest of the crew. He struggled to regain control as the plane rattled and jolted through pockets of air.

'It's mighty cold all of a sudden,' Radish complained. He could see that Jellicoe was trying to avoid any other fighters by gaining height, but he felt his fingers bitten by frost. 'Has someone left a window open?' he joked. 'My nose is starting to resemble a stalactite.'

Maddocks laughed. 'You must be going soft. I'd let you have my heated flight suit but it's a bit colder in the turrets than where you're sitting.'

'Not right now it isn't.'

'Rear Gunner Doddington,' Jellicoe said, with a heavy heart. 'Are you okay?' The silence was deafening.

'I'll check on him. He's probably fallen asleep knowing him. Lazy bastard.'

'No, Maddocks, stay in your turret. Hammy will go. There may be other fighters around.'

Jellicoe knew that Maddocks and Doddy were best friends and had never flown without each other.

'I'm already half-way there, Skip.'

Jellicoe glanced briefly at Dixon next to him as the plane wavered. He knew they both shared the same fear. Everyone knew the vulnerability of the rear gunner, trapped in his Perspex dome for hours upon end, face fortified against the slipstream by thick grease and sheer willpower. Few were capable of conquering the inevitable sickness, the isolation and the exposure to the elements, while identifying enemy aircraft in a split second. A good rear gunner was a rare animal and Doddy was the best.

'Jesus, oh dear God.' They heard Maddocks' voice. 'It's not even... I can't help him... his head...'

'Return to your turret,' Jellicoe commanded. 'You can do nothing to help him.'

'But I can't... he's... he's everywhere... I can't... the bastards...'

'Maddocks, go back to your position. We need you there. There are still other fighters around.' Jellicoe was aware of the impact of death. The loss of a crew member was devastating. He had witnessed the death of comrades before and he could well imagine the sight that confronted Maddocks. He said calmly, 'Doddy would have wanted us to get the old lady home. He would have wanted us to carry on. And we need your eyes. Especially now.' He turned toward his flight engineer. 'What's the situation, Dixon?'

Dixon's face had turned a sickly grey colour. 'Two of

the engines are out, the pitot tube is gone, rear turret blown away, wings perforated. The fuel and coolant systems are damaged and looks like we're losing fuel fast. Also, the hydraulic systems are substandard, Skipper. It will be touch and go whether the undercarriage lowers and landing gear releases. That's if we can get to a landing strip in the first place. The final two engines appear to be faltering.'

Jellicoe nodded. 'And the good news?'

Dixon shrugged. 'Well, one way or another, we're going down!'

II

Rose waited at the bar. She was beginning to feel self-conscious. She had arrived fashionably late, hoping that Jellicoe would be seated waiting for her, but he was nowhere to be seen. Luckily, a couple of acquaintances were at the far table and they beckoned her over.

'I'm waiting for a friend,' she explained, 'but it looks like I might have been stood up.'

An hour later they left for the cinema and she decided she had waited long enough. She knew that Jellicoe had had reservations about meeting her, but she had not imagined that he would leave her waiting alone. She felt conspicuous now and a couple of men at the bar, emboldened and rendered opportunistic by alcohol, were openly leering at her. One winked. 'On your own, sweetheart? Fancy a drink?'

Ignoring them, she put on her coat and walked out onto the pavement. The evening was dry but chilly and she turned up the collar of her camel coat. It was very dark now and she deliberated over the best way home. It was not often that she misjudged a person. She had been sure that the connection between her and Jellicoe had been a very real one, yet he had left her standing alone in a bar, humiliated and consigned to the salacious glances of drunks.

She began walking down the street and turned a corner that seemed to be an obvious shortcut. It was only then that it occurred to her that something may have happened to him to prevent him from coming. After all, his job was a dangerous one. He was literally in the line of fire every single day. She suddenly panicked. She had no way of finding out. She had no address or telephone number. No, she was being silly. She was making excuses for him to appease her own wounded ego. It somehow alleviated her sense of abandonment to imagine him unavoidably detained.

It was a quiet street, so she instantly identified footsteps behind her. Turning, she saw that the two men from the bar were following her. Her instinct was to quicken her pace, but the shoes she was wearing were decorative and impractical. She had been foolish to take this route but she told herself that it was probably just a coincidence and the men were walking home. She

The Pathfinder

decided to cross over as a precautionary measure and then return to the bar. There she could call for a taxi, despite the expense. She crossed the road but to her horror, they crossed too, and as she turned to retrace her steps, they stood menacingly in her path. One muttered something to the other and they laughed, confirming in her own mind their ill-intent. She decided she had no option but to confront them. To walk yet further into an empty, ill-lit street might prove disastrous. Nervously, she walked toward them.

'Forgotten something?' He was quite tall with red hair and she recognised him now as one of the two men who had objected to her dancing with Jellicoe. He was chewing gum, which he spat out as she approached, as if adhering to some vulgar stereotype of masculinity.

Rose said nothing.

'Not very friendly, is she?' The other one was shorter and thickset, with a thatch of black hair. He caught her arm as she passed. 'Maybe it's got something to do with the colour of our skin. Not dark enough for you?'

She wondered how far her voice would carry in the still air, and as if anticipating her thoughts, the taller one mocked, 'You can scream all you like in this street. Look around you. Not exactly crowded, is it?'

When she'd appeared at the public house, he'd recognised her immediately. He'd been hoping that Jellicoe would arrive so that he could exact some kind of revenge for being thrown out of the dance. But a woman alone in a dark, empty street was even better. He'd been jailed for less than his intentions. Intoxicated, both by ale and the possibilities of the encounter, he cut a fugitive-like figure, his eyes agitated and bitter, his body arched and mutinous.

As he leaned forward, Rose caught the distinctive odours of beer and stale sweat. She silently processed her options. She could remain stiffly motionless and await the crimes they chose to commit, or act quickly before she was overpowered by these callous hands of thuggery that now wagged their stiff, stabbing fingers in her face and onto the lapels of her camel coat. Instinctively, she rammed her knee hard into his groin and ran. He groaned, cursing her loudly, nursing his injury with cupped hands as his stocky companion ran in pursuit.

She had taken off her shoes as she fled, ignoring the pain of her feet, bloody from the loose cobbles. Exhausted, she reached the street corner and screamed but the noise she made seemed small and encumbered. She could hear his panting behind her and felt the belt of her coat yanked as she was thrown against the wall. She screamed, louder this time, and bit his hand as he covered her mouth, so that he yelped in pain, granting her precious moments to swing the tapering heel of her stiletto into his face. It landed securely in the socket of his eye and, incensed from the pain, he raised his fist. She cowered, anticipating the blow, but instead, heard the distant echoing of her name and, suddenly, as though he were a genie conjured from a bottle, Jellicoe appeared, flooring her assailant with an ease fuelled by fury.

The man spat a mixture of teeth and blood from his mouth while his accomplice, now revived, carried with him a metal bar, which he attempted to use as a cudgel. Rose, rooted by fear and fatigue, could only watch as Jellicoe deflected, throwing him backward with a lateral blow then a left hook to his jaw. It was a measured response to an inmate's brawl – controlled, rhythmic and implacable.

'You'll regret that...' He struggled to his feet, invective spewing from his bloodied mouth.

Jellicoe took a cursory glance at Rose's small, anguished frame, barefoot, her clothes torn, her face smeared with blood and tears, and hit the man so hard that Rose feared he might have killed him. But still he stirred and Jellicoe approached again, his knuckles poised.

'No,' she said. 'That's enough. You'll end up killing him and he's not worth the aggravation that would cause.'

Incandescent now, Jellicoe knew that in that instant, he was capable of anything. The calm and reposeful man he had always fought to cultivate had so quickly been replaced by this pugilant, hateful aggressor. He could see Rose, her eyes filled with tears, and beside her, in his mind's eye, Doddy, being carried out of the damaged plane in pieces. He regressed momentarily to their journey home in the crippled plane.

Most of the crew had abandoned her as they had circled the green pastures of Northamptonshire.

'Hurry,' he'd urged. 'I can't keep this altitude much longer. She's wrecked. The engines have all gone.'

'What about you, Skip?'

'I'll follow,' he'd said. 'Now go, all of you. Come on, Maddocks. You too, Dixon.'

As the others had aborted the plane one by one, Dixon remained resolute. 'You're going to try to land dead-stick, aren't you?' he'd said. 'A heavy old girl like this. And there may be no suitable landing sites within reach.'

'We're not far from Grafton Underwood. Fingers crossed there will be no traffic on their runway. Now go!'

'I'll take my chances with you and the old lady rather than jump,' Dixon insisted. 'Never did trust these brollies. I'd probably end up impaled on some church spire. Let's see if we can take Doddy home. I've heard of occasions when Lancs have been landed with no propulsive power, just never witnessed any first-hand.'

Jellicoe was brought back to the present by Rose, stooping to retrieve her shoes as the two men on the ground groaned and choked and nursed their injuries. This was his fault. He had put Rose in danger by his tardiness. He had not intended to come at all but to send her a message explaining, in brief, his day and the circumstances that precluded an evening out.

However, the message had not been delivered and by the time he and Dixon had been returned to base and reunited with the rest of the crew, it was late and he had no choice but to go himself. To leave her waiting without an explanation would have been indefensible.

'Let's go,' she said, smiling weakly, and she began to walk but the stabbing pain in her feet prevented her.

'I'm so sorry.' He lifted her easily and carried her along the cobbles to the road where the staff vehicle was parked.

'I was waiting,' she said. 'What happened?'

'I'll take you home,' he replied. 'Your feet need attending and you probably need a brandy.' Thoughts of Doddy clouded his mind. 'Then I'll explain everything.'

Doddy had been the only fatality. Radish had sprained his ankle when landing, and Hammy had been caught in a great oak tree and had to be freed by the fire brigade. Each had their own story embellished into anecdotal readiness. Maddocks was met by men with pitch forks who thought he was German and Foxy, in contrast, had been greeted by a young woman, who, he proclaimed, he would marry instantly if she proved to be single. Poker, phlegmatic as ever, had walked to the nearest pub, downed a beer on the house and been driven back to Elsham Wolds. Jellicoe had successfully landed on the runway at Grafton Underwood, helped by Dixon, who was as steadfast as ever, never once doubting Jellicoe, his steely concentration adding to the air of calm resolve. They had started this mission together and if he had anything to do with it, Doddy would be returned for burial where he could be honoured and mourned by those who loved him.

The ground staff at Grafton Underwood were impressively prepared and medics and fire staff were immediately despatched, racing along the runway to greet the plane as it descended. Jellicoe and Dixon had done everything they could to maximise their chances of survival. Jellicoe gauged their height and air speed, the wind speed and the distance to the landing strip as best as he could, but they both knew that a certain amount of luck was needed.

'Look on the bright side,' Jellicoe said, 'the fuel has almost all gone so we have little potential to explode.'

'Very reassuring.'

'You might want to try once more to coax that landing gear out.'

'It's not budging.'

Jellicoe could feel the wind beneath the vast body of the plane and worked with it as much as he could until the runway was in sight.

The Pathfinder

'Here goes!'

Without engines or wheels, the belly of the plane touched the runway and dust and sparks showered them, impeding their vision. The fuselage vibrated wildly and as they shuddered their way to the end of the runway for what seemed an endless space of time, the plane tipped and spun port side, shredding the wings before it drew to a clumsy and abrupt halt.

The ground crew said it was the bravest and most ingenious landing they had ever witnessed. Jellicoe and Dixon were taken to the officers' mess, where they were offered eggs and bacon, which they would normally have devoured, but neither had an appetite, their thoughts very much weighted with the loss of Doddy. They were back at Lincolnshire within three hours, by which time they had discovered the fate of their crew. They were reunited with a sense of relief and joy, tinged with overarching sadness for the loss of their comrade. Squadron Leader Harringworth met them for the debriefing along with Group Captain Forbes-Harrison.

'Well, chaps,' Harringworth began. 'I see that quite a number of you are now members of the Caterpillar Club. Thank goodness for parachutes, eh?' He gave Jellicoe a sardonic glance. 'Though it appears there was no need for dramatics after all.'

Jellicoe and his crew said nothing.

Forbes-Harrison cleared his throat, embarrassed. 'I'd like to say how very sorry I am,' he said. 'Doddington was a first-rate gunner. I know you were all very fond of him.'

'Yes, we were.'

'I'm writing to his family directly if there's anything anyone would like to add?'

'Thank you, sir, but I'd like to visit his family personally to deliver the news,' Jellicoe said resolutely.

'There's no need to put yourself through that,' Harringworth said curtly. 'Surely a letter will suffice?'

His words, a little slurred, grated but Jellicoe remained calm. 'I think it may help his family to know the exact circumstances of his death and how much he was loved and respected.'

'Well of course,' Forbes-Harrison said. 'If that's what you wish. You are, of course, all on leave for a couple of days now. We will sort out a new rear gunner for you in the meantime.'

'He nearly made it,' Maddocks said.

'I beg your pardon?'

'One more trip and we'd have finished our tour. Just one more trip to go. If only…'

'Yes, well,' Harringworth muttered, 'best not to dwell on these things. One has to move on.'

'Perhaps not quite yet,' Dixon said. 'They've only just finished scraping parts of his body from the floor of the plane.'

The room fell silent.

After debriefing, Dixon reminded Jellicoe of his

date. 'You can't leave the poor girl standing there. Doddy wouldn't have liked that.'

'I've left a message with Flight Sergeant Hardy. He usually goes into the village. I'm sure he'll pass the message on.'

'He's been deployed. Short notice. You'll have to go yourself.'

Jellicoe looked at his watch. 'Damn.'

Foxy patted him on the back. 'If you don't go, then I will. She's a real doll and clever with it too. Did you know she's a WAAF? A radio telephone operator apparently, based here. Fairly new. That's how Harringworth met her. Love at first sight I believe, for him at least.'

Jellicoe was embarrassed to acknowledge that he hadn't known this. He and Rose had spoken about so many things, but she had been dressed in civvies and the topic of her occupation had never arisen. In the brief time that they had known each other, their connection had been through dance and neither of them had been inclined to discuss their work. It appeared they had both yearned for a little escapism.

'Here.' Radish threw a set of keys at Jellicoe. 'Take the staff car. We've no need for it now. We're off to drown our sorrows at the bar and raise a glass to Doddy.'

'Raise one for me. I'll be back to join you later.'

He drove quickly but realised that he was hopelessly late. She would surely have gone home or made alternative plans by now. He searched the pub but she was nowhere to be seen. After words with the doorman, who recognised her description, he wandered along the road for some moments, hoping to catch a glimpse of her. He suddenly had a desperate urge to see her, to hold her drowsy, velvety frame and remind himself that in this bitter, bloody war, tenderness and humanity still prospered. It was then that he had heard her screams, almost illusory in their quivering timbre, and, frantic, he had ran toward her, all the anger and frustrations of his day sheathed in the crook of his fist.

III

Squadron Leader Harringworth had had a bad day and it was getting worse. Group Captain Forbes-Harrison, having just congratulated Wing Commander Winston Cy Jellicoe for his presence of mind and loyalty toward his crew, had suggested to Harringworth that he take some time out from flying and spend more time at his desk. Try as he did, it was difficult for Harringworth to view Forbes-Harrison's remarks with any positivity. It was true that he had lost two planes and several crew members on his last few missions, but this was not unusual, given the nature of his work. What had put the nail in the proverbial coffin were a series of complaints by members of his crew concerning not just his capabilities as a pilot, but also his commitment toward them. One of them, his rear gunner, Charlie Rake, having heard about Sergeant Doddington's fate, had appealed to transfer to Jellicoe's crew with immediate effect.

Before the arrival of Jellicoe, things had been going well. He'd had high hopes of a promotion and the prestige of the Master Bomber position. Then, suddenly, Jellicoe had appeared from nowhere, cool as a cucumber, with two tours behind him, and his ambitions had been thwarted. He had wanted that position more than anything else in his career, as it was an affirmation of distinction. The Master Bomber crew had the most dangerous and challenging task of any airmen and everyone knew it. They were the trailblazers, circling their target, transmitting their instructions to others, in constant danger of interception. It was a job for consummate professionals and a job that he thought was meant for him, until the arrival of Jellicoe, whose reputation as a pilot was unrivalled. He had only been at the squadron briefly before he'd secured the trust of his crew to a devotional level, and not just the aircrew but the ground crew, who would wait up all night and cheer upon his return.

Conversely, his own crew were turning against him. His navigator had labelled him arrogant and self-interested, accusing him of blaming his own mistakes on navigational errors, and his mid-upper gunner had insinuated to Forbes-Harrison that his drinking put them all unnecessarily at risk. And now his rear gunner had joined them in their abandonment. Charlie Rake the snake. This humiliating set of circumstances had left him dejected and bitter. Forbes-Harrison had suggested he was exhausted and needed time to reflect. Now he was expected to sit in an office and push paper. It was a stupid waste of his talents and he intended to say so at their next meeting.

He suddenly felt the need for a drink and some sympathetic company. It was then that he was reminded of Rose. Until now, she had declined his offer of dinner, but he was wildly attracted to her and not easily discouraged. He knew where she was billeted and, eager for some respite from his despondency, he decided to call in on her on his way back from the bar.

At that moment, Flight Officer Rose Stevens was bathing her feet in a bowl of warm water. Jellicoe put a mug of steaming tea in her hands.

'I don't think you'll be doing the jitterbug for a few days.'

Rose smiled at him. 'I'm sorry about your rear gunner. He sounded a good sort.'

'He certainly is… I mean was,' Jellicoe corrected himself. 'Only had one more sortie to complete the tour. Then he could have seen out the rest of this damned war in relative safety.'

'Doesn't sound like he would have though from what

you say.' She looked at him somewhat defiantly. 'It takes a certain type of person to do a job like that, and it's not the kind of person that's seeking safety, in my opinion. He would have risked another tour and then, if he'd survived that one, another. And at some point, his luck would inevitably have run out.'

'You're a cheerful soul, aren't you!'

'What's the matter? Am I touching a nerve? This is your third tour, isn't it?'

'You seem to know a lot about me.'

'Yes, I made a point of finding out who you are.' She smiled at him warmly and he was once more captivated by the small gap between her pearly front teeth.

'And who am I exactly?'

'Someone who interests me. Someone I'd like to get to know better.'

'I'm flattered.'

'You should be.' She took another sip of hot tea. 'Third tour! You know you're living on borrowed time, don't you?'

Jellicoe laughed at her candour. 'Yes, but not for much longer. This is my last run. Then I will happily surrender myself to a dull future complete with pipe and slippers.'

'So you have one more mission, theoretically?'

'Yes, one more, theoretically or otherwise. That goes for the whole crew.'

'Tomorrow?'

'The day after. We have tomorrow off for Doddy. And of course, while another rear gunner is found.' He sighed. 'And I need to speak to Doddy's family.'

'The first mission without Doddy.' Rose watched him closely. 'That's bound to affect you all quite dramatically.'

'Of course, but it's an occupational hazard. There is no war without casualties.'

'You say that so resignedly.'

'How else is there to see it? It doesn't mean the grief is any less. But you must know that, being a WAAF yourself.'

'Well, yes, I've lost friends.' She beckoned to him to pass the hand towel, draped loosely over the sofa. 'And a fiancé.'

'Oh, I'm sorry.'

'Yes, it was on the last day of his second tour. He was a flight engineer.'

Jellicoe sighed. 'I didn't know.'

'Why should you!' She smiled ruefully. 'I told him not to go on a second tour. As if he hadn't done enough for King and country, but would he listen? I kept thinking afterwards, if only I had managed to persuade him.'

'It's not your fault. Every man has to make up his own mind.'

'I said to myself then that I'd never get involved with another flyer.'

Jellicoe lifted her feet from the water and wrapped the towel around them, tenderly patting them dry. 'And are you?' He looked at her intently. 'Getting involved with another flyer I mean?'

'I think you already know the answer to that,' she replied, leaning forward to kiss him.

Outside, Harringworth looked up at the window. He caught a brief glimpse of Jellicoe framed in the sepia room before the curtains were swiftly drawn and the lights dimmed.

Exasperated, he butted the steering wheel of the truck so that his pallid skin broke and bled. Was there no area of his life where he was not superseded by Jellicoe? It seemed to him that he had deliberately and wantonly stolen every aspect of his existence that offered meaning and purpose to it. Beer had made him morose and he slumped against the wheel, determined to confront Jellicoe. But tiredness prevailed and his head, weighted in equal measure by alcohol and despair, remained anchored to the wheel until he was awoken a few hours later by the sound of a revving engine. Stirred into a hazy consciousness, he tried to block Jellicoe's path, but his truck lurched forward into the side of the staff car and stalled.

'Idiot.' Jellicoe leapt from his vehicle. 'What on earth... Harringworth, what are you doing here?'

'I might ask you the same question.' Alcohol had

fuelled Harringworth's convictions. 'It appears it's not enough to undermine my position here. Now you want to take my girl as well.' He raised a fist and swung it lamely in Jellicoe's direction, wincing in pain as he missed, hitting instead the heavy window frame of the Humber Snipe.

'Don't be ridiculous, Harringworth.' Jellicoe pushed him roughly into the staff vehicle. 'You're drunk. I'd better take you back to base. You certainly can't drive in that condition.'

'Condition?' Harringworth laughed. 'I'm perfectly able to drive. What makes you think you know anything about my condition?'

'Look, I know you've had a bad run of things,' Jellicoe said, eager to defuse the situation, 'and that can drag a man down. God knows I know that. I've just lost my rear gunner and it's the worst feeling of loss. You think, why him and not me? But you need to rise above it if you want to keep flying. You have a crew to take care of. They depend on you. So I'd start by sobering up.'

'What for? I've been grounded.'

Jellicoe sighed. 'So that's what this is all about? If Forbes-Harrison has grounded you, then it's probably for your own safety. In times of war, you don't just ground your best pilots.'

Harringworth looked surprised. 'You're including me amongst the *best*?'

'Of course. You know,' he said solicitously, 'it was touch and go whether I got the Master Bomber position. I know you were a big contender.'

'I was?'

'Of course. I happen to know that you were very highly regarded from all ranks. Crews were queuing up to fly with you.' He paused. 'But you know what sometimes happens when men are good at their job?'

'What?'

'They get cocky. Too damn cocky. Positively gung-ho! They start to think that they are invincible and then they take chances and before you know it, they've lost a few men, a plane or two, and then they start to get nervous and defensive and that turns their men against them. And a pilot, however good he is, is nothing without the support of his crew. I should know, it happened to me once.'

'It did?'

'Oh yes.' Jellicoe thought fast. 'I had to do some soul searching and pretty quickly before I ended up rattling around on my own in that old heap of metal.' He laughed, a deep, resounding laugh. 'I said to myself…' He gesticulated animatedly. 'Tings noh good, Jellicoe. Yuh gotta pull yuhself togedda, an smartish.'

Harringworth watched him warily. 'That's hard to believe given your present crew's devotion.'

'Trust takes a long time to earn but is easily broken. You need to talk to your men and convince them of your commitment to them. You have some bridges to build. And you need to stop drinking now. If you do that, I'll talk to Forbes-Harrison.'

'Why would you do that for me?'

'Because I know that you're a good pilot and a good man who's just lost his way a little. There is an enormous responsibility as the pilot to get your men home and when that doesn't happen, we take it personally. Sometimes that pressure takes its toll.' He paused. 'You must be aware by now that my last mission is coming up. I'm being transferred to an operational training unit at Upper Heyford as a flight instructor. No doubt they'll be looking for a new Master Bomber crew and if you could get your act together, I'm sure you'd have a chance. You've got guts, I'll give you that.' He leaned against the steering wheel and looked resolutely at Harringworth. 'But, as for Rose, she and I have an understanding.'

Harringworth began to speak but checked himself.

'Go on. I can see you have some thoughts on the matter.'

'Do you think you're good for her?'

'You mean because of the colour of my skin?'

Harringworth was slightly taken aback by Jellicoe's directness. 'Well, yes, if you like. It's nothing personal but you saw what happened at the dance. Things would never be easy for her, for either of you.'

'Yes, don't you think I've thought of that?' Jellicoe

paused just long enough for Harringworth to feel uncomfortable. 'You know, I read in the newspaper today that the Duke of Buccleuch is annoyed that his Black workers are integrating with what he termed as "unsophisticated country women". "I do not like this mix of colour" were his exact words, I believe. It's funny when you think that we Blacks volunteered to come and fight for Britain. We can lose our lives for this country, but we're not entitled to court its White women. That seems fundamentally wrong, doesn't it?'

'I agree, it's unfair.' Harringworth felt some shame. He could sense that he was in the presence of a unique and gifted man, whose charisma was undeniable.

'We are fighting a common enemy yet at the same time, we are still fighting prejudices from our allies. At least some of them.'

'But you are highly accomplished, a rare commodity. A lot of those prejudices won't be applicable to you.'

Jellicoe laughed. 'Oh, you think so, do you? Well, let me tell you, a Black man has to be twice as good as a White man if he wants to succeed. But, however good he is, however clipped his accent or well-cut his suit, there will always be those who won't see beyond the colour of his skin. So yes, I agree life would be easier for Rose if I walked away, but I can't. We all have to find our path in life and mine is leading me to her.' He started the engine. 'Time to get back to the base. I need to see my crew and you need to sleep it off.'

Two days later, Jellicoe was preparing for his final flight as a member of 103 Squadron. The previous day, he had visited Doddy's parents, and their anguished faces, desperate for answers, searched his own, interpreting each expression, monitoring each phrase, in order to relive the last precious moments of their son's life. He knew the magnitude of words at such times, that his would be all they had to cling to in their darkest hour. It was important that he got it right, that he released just enough detail to soothe rather than aggravate their daily torment. When at last he left, they thanked him for his time, and he them for their hospitality, two parties linked by tragedy, in polite exchange, in the wake of their worst nightmares. The irony was not wasted on him.

Their new rear gunner was a man called Tommy Smart, a Canadian from Beaver Creek, who some of the crew already knew and liked.

'Smartie, what are you doing here? Are you the best they could find?' Hammy clapped him on the back. 'Good to see you.'

'Wish I could return the compliment.'

'We're pleased to have you join us.' Jellicoe shook his hand, his slow, warm smile permeating the cool air. Tommy Smart relaxed and the nerves he'd been carrying with him all day began to dissipate. This was a natural born leader who had earned his reputation of supremacy. He was top drawer, anyone could see that. And if he was going to be shot out of the skies, it might as well be with this crew, the best of the Pathfinders. Rumour had it that this was Jellicoe's last mission and if that was so, he wanted to be a part of it.

They flew over the North Sea with a resignation borne of duty. Whatever their thoughts about Doddy, they resolved to suspend them for the duration of the mission. One moment's lack of concentration by anyone could spell disaster for the entire crew. They settled into the droning momentum of the plane, watchful for any threat to its safety. So far, there had been no sighting of fighters, but that could change rapidly. They were leading a raid of three squadrons and this would not go unnoticed by the Luftwaffe. It was just a question of time. Their targets were industrial, but at night it would be difficult to locate them and would inevitably involve low flying, which would put them at greater risk.

'Enemy coast ahead. Brace yourselves for our welcome.'

Sure enough, Poker had barely finished his sentence before a deluge of cannon fire awakened the torpid skies. Green, yellow and red bursts of light flak strained to reach them.

'Night fighters.'

'Don't worry, we have our own.' Jellicoe privately calculated the range of their escorts and bemoaned the fact that they couldn't be with them for the duration of the raid due to their limited fuel capacity.

'You okay back there, Smartie?'

'Oh, don't worry, Skip. I have them in my sights. But no point in drawing attention to ourselves until it's vital.'

'Good man.'

After another hour, they neared their destination. Poker masterfully identified the industrial instillations that were their target and Radish confirmed their position.

'Just a little further south-east,' Jellicoe said to Foxy, before he released the flares. 'That creepback is getting greater with every trip. Those boys are sure as hell eager to hotfoot it out of here, so let's make their journey worthwhile.'

Foxy released the flares and Jellicoe then began circling, conveying instructions to the following Pathfinders so that further marker indicators lit up the sky to direct the Main Bomber Force to its target. The flares were met by a thundering of cannon fire below as the battle played out in the terrifying inky arena.

'Great illuminations tonight.' Jellicoe glanced at his flight engineer. 'You could light your pipe on that tracer, Dixon.'

Though the Pathfinders were elite squadrons, Jellicoe saw several planes go down. It was, he knew, sometimes a question of averages, and all you could do was hope you weren't one of the unlucky ones. He continued to circle, issuing directions, constantly reassessing and giving new fixes whilst weaving amidst a barrage of exploding cannon shells. He knew as the Master Bomber, they stood out, like an orbiting satellite through a telescope, easily detected by master searchlights, the high-powered carbon arc lamps that traversed the skies like prowling wolves. They could illuminate a hapless target eight miles high and gather their pack, creating a deadly triangle of blinding light. Once coned, you were a pitiful sight – beams latched onto you like flees, glued tight, baying for blood, as anti-aircraft fire hammered into the shaft of light beneath you.

Every few seconds, Jellicoe changed course and altitude. It was not enough just to weave, as the trackers below could predict a regular criss-cross or curved flight path. It was a question of defeating their predictions. Inside the fuselage, the explosions of nearby light flak were muffled, the familiar smoke from shells filtering through, pungent and bitter on the tongue. In his mid-upper turret, Maddocks could be heard cursing about the amount of time it was taking the Main Force.

'Come on, you bastards, get a move on.'

Finally, after what seemed like an eternity, the last of the Main Force turned for home, silhouetted briefly in a sky ravaged by warfare.

'Jesus, that flak's so thick you could climb out and walk over it!' Dixon exclaimed. 'Let's get out of here.'

Suddenly, an endlessly threshing beacon of light

caught them in its sights. Immediately, other diagonal beams joined forces so that they were truly triangulated. Maddocks screamed out expletives as they were blanched by light, blinding and disorientating.

Smartie joined in. 'We've been coned. We've had it now.' He prepared for the worst. He knew that the radar-controlled searchlights locked onto them were signalling their range to the German gunners below.

'Hold tight.' As Jellicoe spoke, an almighty blast shook the Lancaster as shells pumped into the beacon of light beneath the undercarriage. The smell of cordite filled the air.

'Fire, the wing's on fire!' Hammy's panic-stricken voice filled the intercom.

'Diving port.' Jellicoe threw the plane into a steep descent in an attempt to put out the fire and escape the coning. He knew that he was taking a chance as sometimes the intense speed of a dive served only to intensify the flames, like bellows on glowing embers. Pulling violently out of the dive, Jellicoe regained height and immediately threw the plane into a reverse turn starboard side and then again to port in a ceaseless, desperate attempt to escape the menacing fingers of light directing the artillery. This he performed a dozen times, pushing the Lancaster to its maximum capacity.

He heard its pitch change, along with the noise of retching and groans of misery, but he kept on until the sky around him turned to darkness again, the impotent black puffs of spent flak now working in their favour and shielding them from danger. This time it had worked, and his dive had served the dual purpose of putting out the fire and shaking off the searchlights, but it had left the crew badly shaken.

'Damage?'

'We have a hole in the floor from the flak,' Hammy reported. 'Not quite big enough to fall through but if anyone needs the karzy, it could be quite handy! There's also a hole above where it exited. The radio equipment is shot up. A fragment went straight through the aluminium casing.'

'There's damage to the wing port side, one of the engines has gone and we have a smashed rudder,' Dixon added.

'Everyone still with us?'

One by one their names were recounted.

'Enjoying your initiation, Smartie?' Jellicoe knew that the rear gunners had the worst position for evasive manoeuvres.

'Wouldn't have missed it for the world.' Smartie, having not expected to survive the coning, hardly noticed that he was lying in a pool of his own vomit.

'Poker caught the blast. He was out of it for a bit. Lost consciousness after he hit his head in the dive,' Hammy reported. 'Lacerations to his arm from some metal fragments but otherwise okay.'

'You okay, Poker?'

'I'll survive. A bit disorientated.'

'Great, that's all we need to hear from our navigator,' Foxy joked.

'Don't worry, I'm sure the anti-aircraft fire on the way home will soon clear my head.'

'Out of the storm now,' Jellicoe said reassuringly. 'New heading, Radish?'

'Tricky! H2S non-operational at present. Magnetic compass broken. Unless we're close enough for you to get a heading on the TR9, I'm struggling. Looks like it's down to dead reckoning and celestial navigation if the sky clears. Oh, and damn good luck!'

'No problem.' Jellicoe was desperate to get them home but the dive had changed their course and he was keen for navigational aid. Without it, they may fly deeper into Germany or simply hit the ground, which was hidden mostly by dense clouds. At the moment, there were sufficient gaps between them so that he could recognise certain landmarks, lit briefly by tracers, to make his way to the coast. He was relieved to see the North Sea beneath them, despite its bleak, choppy appearance and the inevitable assault by anti-aircraft defences. The plane was still wavering and it was difficult to assess the total damage in these conditions. Poker was vomiting from the effects of concussion and Maddocks, whose turret had been shattered, was quietly experiencing flashbacks from their previous flight. He was shaking ferociously, his eyes closed, trying to rid himself of the image of Doddy splattered from turret to rear spar and beyond.

Jellicoe could sense something was wrong. 'Not long now, Maddocks. Hang on in there. Can you see anything?' He knew it was necessary to keep him awake and active. There was no reply. 'Check on him, will you, Hammy?' He continued to weave through the night sky as the Lancaster swayed unhealthily to one side in the darkness. The clouds had thickened and he could no longer see the ocean and how close he was to it. He increased his height as a precaution. Luckily, he could see the North Star above and several constellations.

'Problem with Maddocks, Skip. Unhurt but not responding.'

'We need him fully functioning. The last thing we want is a Junkers or Messerschmitt creeping up on us.'

'Come on, Mad,' Foxy coaxed. 'Don't miss the trip of a lifetime – spectacular panoramas, charming company, sea views...'

'Yeah, and you've got the rooftop terrace,' Smartie added somewhat bitterly. His new skip certainly knew how to make evasive manoeuvres. He'd seldom heard of anyone escaping a coning before.

'Get him out of there, Hammy,' Jellicoe ordered. 'He's no use as he is.'

'We can swap places. At least I can be another pair of eyes.'

'No, you'd freeze without a heated suit this high up.

He might just snap out of it if you bring him down.'

Maddocks, shaking violently and clinging with a vice-like grip to his hammock seat, was gradually talked down and sat head in hands unable to speak for several minutes. Then, as suddenly as his flashback had begun, it passed. 'Sorry, Skip, I don't know what happened there.' Patting Hammy on the back, he rose to resume his position. 'Not that I can see much. The Perspex is shattered. I'll have to punch some of it out.'

'Prepare for dive,' Smartie said. 'Junkers, I think. Thought I saw a flickering of its wings in the moonlight but I could be wrong.'

Fearful of the Lancaster's ability to dive in its damaged state, Jellicoe waited for clarity. He weaved and banked starboard and then he saw it. By the way it was flying, he could tell it was badly damaged and making its way home, probably on low fuel, with injured crew.

'It's heading home. I don't think it wants any trouble.'

'It's a bit out of range,' Smartie said, 'or I could blast it up its arse and help it on its way. Would have been one for you I think, Mad.'

It was the Junkers lucky night, Jellicoe thought. Best shot in the RAF and he happened to be having a breakdown.

'Sorry, Skip,' Maddocks said. 'It won't happen again.'

The Pathfinder

Jellicoe smiled to himself. They had passed each other, that Junkers and he, like two cripples on a street who could barely raise their sticks in acknowledgement. 'No matter,' he said. 'Let's get this old lady home. Not too far off now.' He turned to Dixon, who was checking the hydraulics and the fuel system and in the process of switching over tanks.

'Have you seen the starboard wing? A part of it's shot off.'

'Well, you've landed with no engines and no wheels but even for you, no wings would present a challenge.'

Jellicoe grimaced. 'Best get home quickly then. No scenic route today.' He looked at the dense cloud beneath them. 'I'm going to try the direction finding stations to see if we can get a fix. Let's hope we're within their range.'

'Isn't that a bit risky?' Dixon looked concerned. 'Jerry might pick up the signals. Those night fighters seem to be everywhere tonight.'

'It's a risk we're going to have to take, I'm afraid.' He tried to allay Dixon's fears. 'In any case, it's Oktoberfest. The Jerries will all be home now, dressed in lederhosen, drinking beer.'

He called into the receiver, 'Mayday, Mayday, Mayday.' He grinned at Dixon. 'Let's hope they haven't fallen asleep in the control tower.'

'Responding. Please state the nature of emergency,' a tranquil female voice replied.

'We've lost navigational instruments and have zero visibility. Hole in fuselage causing drag and badly damaged wing. Guidance urgently needed.' He had recognised her voice instantly.

'Tracking signals now,' she said calmly.

Within a few moments, their position had been located and instructions were given for a new course. 'Thank God,' Foxy said. 'The rate the winds were blowing us off course, we'd have ended up in the Atlantic.'

'Lovely voice,' Dixon mused. Contrasted with Maddocks' angry expletives, the anxious shrieks of the gunners and the thundering of the Browning guns, the softness of a female voice seemed incongruous, yet patently welcome.

Jellicoe nodded absently. Hearing her voice out of context both thrilled and terrified him. Its velvety modulations were undeniably a comfort, but her audible presence meant that she would also bear witness to any disaster, should anything go wrong.

'Wind drift,' she said. 'New heading. Press on two degrees north-westerly.'

Jellicoe heard a groan behind him. 'Sickness better, Poker? You've come around I see.'

'We must be the luckiest crew alive. I really didn't think we were going to escape that coning. Well done, Skip.'

'Hear! Hear!'

'Maintain heading.'

'Anything you say,' Jellicoe replied, in an attempt to introduce a note of levity. 'I'm yours to command.'

Rose had recognised his voice from the first syllable. She had returned to work that day with the knowledge that it was Jellicoe's final flight. She wanted to be a part of the operation in some way. For the last few hours, she had guided planes back to the base, though she was aware that many would never return. As the Master Bomber, she knew that Jellicoe would be one of the last to return, having made sure that the other Pathfinders and Main Force had every conceivable chance of hitting their target. Every minute that had passed without news of him had been agony. She had no idea if he had safely landed or had been lost in the raid to enemy fire. Then his call had arrived, and her heart had leapt.

'Any casualties?' she asked.

'Just a concussion so far.'

Given that there had been so many fatalities, some planes exploding on the runway and others returning with crews so badly injured that they were barely recognisable, she felt overjoyed, but she knew that they were not out of danger yet. If enemy fighters were still around, every time she spoke to Jellicoe, she was potentially endangering him further. Enemy radar may be picking up their signals at that very moment and directing their fighters toward him. There was so much she wanted to say to him, yet she was restricted to a few vital, yet impassive words witnessed by an entire crew. She felt it was a terrible irony that helping him could cause him harm and that her words could hide, in their measured authority, a devotion that was beyond dimension.

Jellicoe too fought to concentrate his thoughts. He needed to get his men home. He owed them that. He had grown fonder of them than any other crew he had served with, and their safety was paramount. Flying had been his life and he had seldom thought beyond it. But recently, since knowing Rose, he had begun to imagine a different sort of life, a life after the war, if he survived it. Things happened quickly during wartime and the tendency was to live for the moment, never knowing if there would be others. Now, listening to her voice, he wondered if he dare imagine a life beyond this instant, beyond the roar of the Merlin piston engines, beyond the length of runway to which she guided him. Could the acrid smell of fuel and cordite be replaced by her sweet perfume? Could the gradual unfolding of day and night playing upon his wings be succeeded by her tender smile? Could he leave behind in the slipstream that fearful rush of adrenalin and save his beating heart for love alone?

They were nearing home now and he was preparing for landing. So far, all had gone well. The starboard wing was damaged but still intact and the remaining engines purred loudly. The undercarriage went down and locked into position as his hands guided instinctively the throttle and propellers into descent. He could see the flare path beneath like an earthbound constellation ushering him closer to Rose, and beyond it, the control tower in which she sat, awaiting his return.

Rose sat transfixed as Jellicoe's beaten plane, like some giant, clumsy bird, materialised through the darkness, barely clearing the distant thicket. It would be moments now before this battle-scarred silhouette, clucking its protest, damaged wings outstretched and underbelly thrust forward to meet the awaiting landing strip, was home to roost. Her preoccupation allowed her only momentary joy before, to her mortification, another aircraft, coming in fast with no obvious intention of landing, swooped down over the vast ebony hangars that housed, like dormitories, its sleeping planes, and opened fire. Ground crew dispersed to nearby air raid shelters and anti-aircraft gunners hurriedly took their positions, their Bofors guns bursting their retaliation into the night air. Maddocks, still in his turret as they approached the runway, was the first to see the Messerschmitt and took aim.

The fighter had been over the Channel when it had picked up the Lancaster's signals. The pilot had had a lucky night claiming two bombers and fancied a third before he retired and made for home. These giant birds were easy pickings when they returned from a mission, usually damaged, often with injured crew and unable to defend themselves fully. He had flown inland to intercept with no resistance, and this had given him confidence. There it was ahead of him now, preparing to land. He was taking a chance coming in so far but the whole of England appeared to be sleeping. He would wake her up. He smiled to himself, thinking how startled the crew would be. He would make his kill and be home in time for breakfast. He dived toward the aerodrome as the Lancaster touched down. Rat-a-tat-tat. Cannon shells rained down over the hangars and the semi-cylindrical Nissen huts where the riggers, mechanics and electricians had fled for safety.

Jellicoe, for once powerless, could only watch in horror. He had done all he could. He had brought his crew home. But it was not enough. He heard the cannon fire piercing the corrugated steel of the huts, the yells of agony of those dying and the angry bursts of counterattack. Incendiary munitions filled the air and the fighter was hit in the wing, but it was Maddocks who brought it down.

'This one's for you, Dod,' he said, and fired a round with acute precision into the belly of the plane.

The fuel tank beneath the cockpit floor was hit and burst into flames. The pilot was mercifully spared the pain of cremation by a series of preceding bullets but the plane, now a funeral pyre, hurtled downward, much to Jellicoe's horror, in the direction of the bulky, yet stately structure of the control tower. Jellicoe and his crew evacuated their aircraft onto a runway fraught with fire engines and ambulances racing toward the inferno, while others escaped the nearby operations block, which the dense, black smoke from the falling debris was already claiming.

Jellicoe watched, rooted to the ground in abject misery, as the once majestic control tower crumbled and the place where she would have been sitting collapsed mockingly beneath him, along with his dreams of their life together. He knew no phoenix would rise from the ashes of those flames, which licked the skyline in murderous delight. But in this, he was gloriously mistaken. She had run down the steps of the tower before his landing, unable to contain her eagerness, and there, suddenly, she appeared, moving toward him, a small, dark mythical figure, outlined by the pale beginnings of a new and beautiful dawn.

One Too Many

I

The graduation was an interesting assortment of people of every shape and size. You might call it a human ark, one or two of every species, with one common denominator – the military. If they weren't active military, they were married to military, honoured guests of military or had military connections of some obscure fashion.

Dress was formal, as was the occasion, the general mood one of paternal pomposity. The young graduates sat proudly at their tables preening like peacocks, awaiting their moment of glory, when, finally, after weeks of intensive training, they would officially receive their pilot wings. Their instructors, older and more cynical, regarded them with a fond condescension and privately speculated how long they would last. Some, in the hope of easing tension, entertained their wives with amusing anecdotes of their pupils' shortcomings. Wives responded dutifully, despite the tedium of these timeworn narratives.

The graduation was held in the long dining hall at the officers' mess. Portraits of past aces hung on the walls, along with souvenirs of their squadrons' distinguished past. The décor was entirely sumptuous, belying any signs of the ravages of war. By the left aisle toward the front of the ceremony was a slightly larger table bedecked with roses of the deepest red and the finest quality port, which was reserved for the air vice-marshal, the president of the mess, the guest speaker and a couple of the more distinguished officers, one of whom was Colonel Warwick, a Texan, who had spent much of World War II in England.

Warwick was a rare commodity in that he had distinguished himself in both world wars. During the first, he had received the Medal of Honor for the dogged courage he had shown while flying in France, despite being shot down once over Douai. He maintained that it was Manfred von Richthofen who had fired the interminable burst that brought him down. It was no secret that there had been a grudging respect for the Red Baron by the Allied powers, and Warwick admitted that he had felt it a dubious honour, even as he was crash landing and beating out flames with his gauntlets. If you had to be shot down, he felt, then let it be by the ace of aces in his crimson Fokker Triplane, the sight of which struck fear in the hearts of even the most sanguine of fighter pilots.

Warwick, oddly perhaps, considering his promotion was presently under review, seemed to have deliberately programmed himself to getting drunk. He had lately grown to despise these occasions – the pomp and ceremony, the overtly coiffured women, particularly his wife, and the speeches full of empty words that dispersed like vapour trails in an empty sky. He needed to drink to immobilise the hostile words that were bound to punctuate a more sober dialogue. He was a sedate drunk. He arranged his face in what he assumed to be a dignified pose and tried with worthy tenacity to keep in focus the faces of those around him as he raised his glass in tribute.

'To the King of England, to our allies, to the Chief of Staff, to our fallen comrades...'

There had been so many of the latter, as empty seats had demonstrated, young men whose faces he could still visualise and who had all paid the ultimate price for the glory of those wings. And here they sat, the new invincibles, smiling, laughing, telling jokes, keen to have their shot at bringing down the Hun. Some he had trained himself, and he knew with woeful certainty those who would soon be represented by a sprinkling of salt and a lit candle. Even the good ones, and these were few, had had too little time to be trained effectively. It was a question of lambs to the slaughter in the hope that, out of luck and the law of averages, some would manage to shoot down a few enemy planes before they were done for. When the women were finally seated, the men once more raised their glasses: *'To our ladies and our honoured guests.'*

Warwick sighed loudly. The toasts were part of the unchanging programme he could most easily tolerate as they provided him with an additional excuse to drink. He acknowledged their closure with regret. Looking to his side, he saw the wavering and distorted profile of his wife. She turned towards him, smiling icily at the empty wine glass he was waving precariously while awaiting a refill.

'Darling...' The smile was feigned. 'Don't you think you've had more than your share for one evening?'

His glass was filled by the passing waiter and he watched the blood-like rivulets drip from the goblet, tracing a red pattern on the starched, white tablecloth before they reached his eager lips. 'Sorry, what was that?' he replied disingenuously, emptying his glass.

Her face, plump and shiny, took on something of the expression of a large, oleaginous toad. The image delighted him, and due to his newly found Dutch courage and the knowledge that his wife had an abhorrence of public scenes, he felt relatively safe. He was reassured by experience that he would fall deeply asleep, fully clothed as soon as they got home and would snore blissfully through the inevitable lecture. Not that she was particularly worried about the long-term consequences of his increasingly excessive habit. But she knew that his drinking, which encouraged conduct unbecoming an officer, reflected on her as an officer's wife – soon, she hoped, a brigadier general's wife. She deserved this. He was, after all, a hero of two wars, some might say, one war too many.

Lt Colonel Webster, the guest speaker, sat opposite the Warwicks. He was the leader of the American Aerial Demonstration team and he had come to save Britain. He wore a hero's halo, due entirely to self-promotion. Modesty had never been one of his vices. It had taken him a long time to perfect the speech that he would direct at these young men, who already knew more about sorties than he and who were eager to encounter the enemy, an enemy that was still, to him, a rumour. He had rehearsed his speech endlessly in front of his approving wall mirror, yet he hoped it would look and sound spontaneous. The toasts were finally over.

This was probably a blessing, he felt, judging by the way fellow American, Colonel Warwick, seated opposite him, had been belting down the wine. Thinking again of his speech, he smiled to himself, inadvertently in the direction of Mrs Warwick, who reciprocated with a fixed, somewhat synthetic expression set in her moon-round face.

Warwick had heard of Webster's reputation as ambitious, egocentric and hectoring. These qualities he would not have minded so much, inherent as they appeared to be in many high-ranking and successful officers, had it not been rumoured that Webster's incompetence had once caused the death of two young flyers, who, following his instructions undeviatingly, had collided in formation. The whole incident had been dismissed as a tragic accident, but it added to Warwick's nagging sense of unease in Webster's company. Warwick had struggled latterly to remember why he had chosen a military career, though of course the propaganda for the Great War had been persuasive and had instilled some foolish notion of heroism – the romantic ideas one had about wars when young, having never lived or fought through one.

And he had been a success, had qualified as an ace before any others in his squadron, just as he had the second time around. And this was his reward, he thought glibly, to be seated at this table, listening to the fabricated exploits of the illustrious Lt Colonel Webster. He emptied another glass.

Dinner dragged on. Thunder rolled angrily outside. Sheet lightning flashed through the curtains, flooding the dimly lit hall so that the glare from the portraits seemed, he thought, almost accusatory. No doubt a further symptom of his intoxication. Warwick had always loved storms. They reminded him of his first solo flight in a Nieuport all those years ago in the war to end all wars – that hadn't – when a storm had raged all around him and he had felt the chill of death. *'I'm going now, old comrades,'* he had sung to himself to combat his fear, *'to heaven or to hell.'* Lightning had struck as, simultaneously, a German Fokker had come out from nowhere. Adrenaline had taken over then and a dogfight had ensued until he'd fired a deadly blast into the Fokker's tail and watched it burn in the storm, so closely that the debris had nearly taken them both. After that, his only fear had been of burning alive, so much so that he'd taken to carrying a loaded pistol in his plane. As the war had progressed, his participation had become mechanical. War became the enemy, not these poor wretches that he'd blown out of the sky, who, like him, had just been following orders. He'd killed them out of a necessity to survive and felt revulsion when he heard of pilots shooting down planes and returning to rake survivors. No doubt if they had been allowed parachutes during the Great War, some would have found sport in strafing men during descent.

Fewer and fewer of his comrades had returned and the skies, empty for countless unbearable hours, had haunted his waking days. He had stopped forming friendships and kept his own council, yet had become one of the most respected and popular flight commanders, due perhaps to his steadfastness at times of crisis and his benign manner with those who lost their nerve. He had never judged and was always there. When a young pilot had failed to return, he drank alone and everyone knew not to disturb him in the mess, but to keep their distance and allow his thoughts to convalesce. He had not expected to witness another war, let alone participate in one. But it had happened, though somehow from the offset, things had been different. He was older and more cynical. He loathed flying Mustangs and missed his Nieuport with its Lewis gun mounted on the upper wing, crouched like a praying mantis awaiting a kill. In the Nieuport with its open canopy, he could smell the enemy, like a shark could smell blood. But he'd adjusted and fought bravely in combat, his Mustang often riddled with bullets, clawing its way back to that hallowed piece of ground, the landing strip.

Warwick had known little of love when he'd married. Courtship had taken its course without too much reflection. He had liked the look of her – her loose hair and the suggestion of more behind the buoyant expression. His family had thought her the perfect military wife, a viewpoint he understood more fully as his years in the service had passed. Neither were blameless. She had chosen a lifestyle rather than a husband and he had assumed marriage meant companionship and a warm bed. A detachment had formed between them as the years passed, yet neither had considered separation. They had no children. His wife's friendships were superficial, her interests few. He felt he owed her at least the appearance of a successful marriage.

His only real experience of love came years later, between wars, when, on a six-month exchange in Italy, he'd met a girl and fallen for her instantly. Oddly perhaps, it had not been her looks that had first attracted him but the air of independence in her stride and the easy way she laughed without bluff or inhibition. Laughter had been something of a rarity for him, and to feel his tensions subside, if only briefly, had given him a sense of gratitude toward her that had remained steadfast. Her skin and hair had had the dull scent of wind and sand, her voice and conversation, an earthiness. But there had been no talk of permanence.

They had never spoken of his life back home. There had been a silent understanding that despite the flaws in his marriage, he had committed to it and must, therefore, see it through, like any other feat of endurance in the line of duty. But her influence on him had been profound. It was his brief, arcadian sojourn in southern Italy that had given him the strength and fortitude to remain in wedded enmity.

Warwick returned from his musings just in time to see Lt Colonel Webster striding to the podium with great enthusiasm, grasping rapaciously at the microphone. This was his moment. He began with exaggerated animation, recounting much embellished stories of his exploits as Aerial Demonstrations Officer. His language was descriptive as he recounted how he had coped with unfortunate elements, heavy crosswinds and zero visibility, outsmarting his opponents with quick-thinking and dexterity. The young graduates were enthralled. They forgot momentarily that he had not yet fought in any war, nor witnessed a threat to his homeland. He had years of experience and was here to win the war, and his enthusiasm was contagious and much more helpful than Colonel Warwick's silent, tormented form. Here was the man to help them, to assist in the defeat of the enemy. Finally, Webster reached a close.

'Two things, boys,' he said dramatically. 'Always expect the unexpected and never forget to check six.' With that, he turned around quickly to demonstrate the importance of observing the blind areas, lost his balance and almost fell from the podium. Regaining his composure, he straightened his jacket, looked toward the assembly, raised his fist and shouted, 'Fight proud, boys. Fight proud.'

Warwick began to laugh uncontrollably. The gathering grew quiet, embarrassment rising with every peel of Warwick's laughter. He found he could not stop. Terrified that his chances of promotion had been ruined, his wife tried to join in the laughter, as if his outburst had been a private joke between them. Warwick too felt an odd hysteria rising, partly because he had revealed himself, though, more than that, because he realised that he had left it too late for the life he should have chosen, too late for his dusky Italian girl and a life of peace. He was married, physically, traditionally and historically to this stranger beside him and to war, enmity and bloodshed. He was a man who had seen too much, who had lived too long. For a moment, he wished a candle could replace his absurd form. Then his grief began to fall in tears and his wife, mortified by his exhibition, stopped laughing and hung her head in shame.

Corkscrew Port Go

I

'Corkscrew Port Go!'

The words struck terror in the heart of Reg, the Lancaster bomber wireless operator, who instinctively prepared to counteract the effects of a precipitous dive by clinging to his seat and scanning the aircraft absently for loose, flying paraphernalia, not least, urine-filled beer bottles.

'Stuka below!' the panic-stricken rear gunner yelled, as the pilot banked the Lancaster bomber sharply to port, ready to drop.

But it was already too late. The Junkers Ju 88 had slunk into their shadow and now used its upward-firing guns to rake the belly of their aircraft with twenty-millimetre cannon shells, severing the rear turret entirely so that it parted company with the rest of the plane and plunged, along with its trapped rear gunner, nearly four torturous miles into the greedy gullet of the North Sea. The bomb aimer, who was, at that moment, using the Elsan chemical toilet a few feet from the severed rear turret, followed him down, sucked into the atmosphere, derrière frozen solid to the seat, still clutching the portable oxygen bottle in abject terror. Cannon shells ricocheted inside the fuselage, one of them slicing through the navigator's torso with such violence that his agony was barely conveyed before being muted by hot steel. The mid-upper gunner, also mortally wounded, cried out like a child for his mother. Reg could hear the pilot shouting for the crew to bail before he too was silenced by machine gun fire, his bloodied torso slumped over the control column like a rag doll.

The starboard outer engine was on fire, showcasing their presence in the inky darkness, and the flight engineer fought to close the master fuel cock. But the plane, now unpiloted, began its unmanaged descent, initially buffeting reasonably through truculent pockets of air, before gathering speed. Meanwhile, the shattered astrodome kindled the flames of a fire now furiously licking the inside of the fuselage and filling Reg's nostrils with the smell of burnt metal, cordite and charred flesh. He wasted no time trying to extinguish it. He knew from experience that the aircraft was done for and his only hope was to bail before the fuel tanks exploded or the plane plummeted, rendering any attempt to evacuate impossible. He reached for his parachute and clipped it securely before deftly using his T1154 transmitter to send distress and positional signals back to base. Then he made his way to the hatch in the floor of the nose and yanked it open.

'Quick, Don,' he shouted to the flight engineer. 'There's no one else. Let's get the hell out of here while we can.'

The flight engineer, his face blanched and terror-stricken, mouthed barely audible words, 'I don't have a parachute.'

For a moment, Reg stared at him in disbelief, before clambering back over the main spar to search for the navigator's brolly, but it was engulfed in a seething mass of bright flames and he quickly returned shaking his head. 'The skipper's?'

'All shot up.'

Until this moment, their aircraft had been descending staunchly but now the engines began to change pitch. A stall and downward rotation was moments away. He had no alternative. He nodded his head at the navigator, tormented by his glazed, petrified gaze, and rolled out of the hatch. He was caught momentarily in the playful maelstrom of the slipstream, which pinned him briefly to the underside of the burning wing, before, seemingly tiring of this game, it released him, parachute alight with yellow flame, into the abyss.

*

Ena, Reg's wife, worked busily in the kitchen. She was a petite, striking woman with limpid brown eyes and Cupid's bow lips, set in translucent skin and framed by wavy, dark tresses. She had first met Reg in a tavern in Lincoln, where she'd been enjoying a quiet drink with her friend Joan, a fellow Auxiliary Territorial Service volunteer, when he had walked in.

The collar of his greatcoat had been turned up against the biting winds, his forage cap perched impracticably above red-tipped ears. He'd sighted them immediately and nudged his companion Fred, the crew's rear gunner and his closest friend. Together, they'd smiled their acknowledgement and eligibility and Reg's face, boyish and hopeful, had followed her in snatched glances as they'd moved toward the bar.

It was strange, she thought, in retrospect, how carefree they'd both seemed that night. Fourteen missions later, Fred would be dead. He was killed not in the heat of battle, on one of their numerous and perilous sorties into enemy territory, but during a training exercise where the fighter planes had fired blanks and evasive manoeuvres had been pre-arranged.

Joan had been heartbroken, and Ena, well aware that this could soon be Reg's fate, shed quiet tears, both timely and premature, onto Reg's stiff lapel. Friends had warned her of the perils of falling for a member of aircrew, but it was too late for logic and sober choice. She was in too deep; her heart was resigned to the agony of loss but not departure. And she had been in on it from the start, was as much a part of the crew, in her way, as Michael, Fred, Les, Frank, Arthur and Don. She was there as they honed their proficiency in preparation for operational postings, overcoming air sickness, practising evasive and combat manoeuvres, learning the bail-out and dinghy drills, as well as polishing their individual skill sets. Reg was now having to acquaint himself with new technologies such as radio direction finding, used to locate emergency transmitters and intercept enemy radios, and the Identification Friend or Foe system, which determined whether an aircraft was friendly or hostile. And if he ever had any doubts about his own aptitude for his ever-increasing responsibilities, Ena was there to allay them.

She was with him in spirit as he flew his first combat sortie soon after learning that his brother Art, also a wireless operator, had been lost over the Ruhr valley in Germany. She'd wondered how he must have felt that first night, flying operationally over the area where, only shortly beforehand, his much beloved brother had disappeared. The torment of not knowing Art's fate must have played heavily upon his mind as he crossed the dappled waters of the North Sea. He must surely, as she had, have wondered whether he too would fail to return.

Such speculation was unhelpful yet unavoidable, but she managed, at least, to keep her thoughts concealed and, afterwards, in the joy of reunion, her curiosity curbed.

Art, they later discovered, had survived, had been miraculously catapulted through the cabin roof of his exploding plane, thankfully with his parachute intact. He had landed in a meadow and, immobilised, had been quickly captured and taken by his German captors to a hospital. There his critical head and facial injuries had been tended to, before, after a period of rehabilitation, he had become a prisoner of war.

Ena, a woman of great resourcefulness, had decided early on in their courtship that if she was to have any peace of mind, she would have to adopt an attitude of pragmatism towards Reg's occupation. Never overly imaginative or prone to hysteria, she told herself, quite sternly and without complaint, that until the worst scenario had been confirmed, she would think positively. If she ever wavered from this resolution, it was when Reg was uncommonly tardy with a promised call or he failed to turn up to a much anticipated rendezvous. But this was an infrequent occurrence and Reg, similarly disposed and quick to refashion a perilous offensive into a jaunty escapade, would soon have her laughing about some aspect of his trip or its aftermath in the sergeants' mess.

But there were also times when he kept things from

her, things he felt she needed protecting from, images that haunted his dreams and the shame he sometimes felt for surviving when so many of his friends had not. In time, he would reveal these thoughts to her, but only when their rawness had dissipated and they were no longer private maladies, just occupational hazards over which he had little control and even less accountability. And he found great catharsis in painting in oils the aviation scenes that he lived daily and which would never leave him.

Ena enjoyed her work in the ATS, where she and other employees occupied a large office block by the river in Lincoln. Her particular undertaking was to ensure that food was distributed to the surrounding airfields as efficiently as possible. She was a diligent worker and popular with others, due much to her unpretentious attitude. She treated everyone with the same initial circumspection, whatever their rank or sex, not easily fooled or flattered by the ambitious, particularly those with an aptitude for delegation. She looked after those in her charge, defending their liberties as she would her own, and, despite her love of practical jokes, understood when an occasion demanded austerity or discretion.

Her home life had not been an easy one, her father a sailor, with the proverbial girl in every port, her mother cowed by his casual cruelty and heavily reliant upon her sympathetic and capable daughter. After her husband had brought home one of his girlfriends, however, belly full-swollen with child and an ultimatum of her acceptance or departure on his drunken lips, she had taken up essential war work in Lincoln to be near to Ena, whose loyalty and protectiveness toward her had been unstinting.

Reg respected Ena's devotion to her mother and, missing the fulcrum of family life, he embraced the company of Mildred as if she were part of his own. In turn, she grew to love him like a son. He and Ena would visit her at her lodgings, where Reg would sink into the flabbiness of the lettuce-green armchair by the fire and listen to the affectionate chatter of the two women, trying hard to stay awake. Ena had assumed that his sudden tiredness signified boredom, but the truth was that he delighted in the ordinariness of their conversation, the ritual of tea and the softness of their female voices. After the masculine and robust tenor of his day, this female world, at once alien and familiar, was one that he relished.

His own small contributions to their conversation received far greater consideration than they would have amongst his male drinking companions and, he thought, far more attention than they genuinely deserved. But he was happy to be fooled, happy to bathe in the warmth of their ceaseless devotion. After a while, he and Ena would leave for the cinema or to treat themselves to a meal out, keen now to be alone, to talk in the unfettered manner of those young and in love.

Ena rolled the pastry onto the floured surface. She remembered how much Reg had always loved the pie and chipped potatoes at Boots restaurant in the early days of their courtship. She was not a natural cook by her own admission, but she had practised this recipe several times now and smiled inwardly, thinking how thrilled he would be when she gave him the news. She had also bought something a little stronger than the usual cup of tea to accompany the meal.

*

Reg was now falling at over 100 mph through the frostbitten air, attached to a burning parachute. His lungs craved oxygen, deficient in the sub-zero temperatures, and his gloveless hands and face throbbed from exposure. Tossed like a coin through a sky of thick molasses, lungs obstructed, face turned blue from hypoxia, he knew that soon he would lose consciousness and this horror would end. Perhaps it already had and he was in purgatory.

He searched frantically for the D-ring handle of his burning parachute. The faces of lost friends flashed vividly before him – young, fresh-faced men with their entire lives ahead of them, a hopeful readiness in their eyes, emblematic of their courage and willingness to serve their country. These faces, which he had barely observed in their everyday settings, whose features he would have struggled to describe, now appeared before him with a new and piercing clarity – jaunty, buoyant and deathless. And yet he outlived them, albeit fleetingly.

Thoughts turned to his beautiful wife. The life that he and Ena had eagerly planned together would never befall. How mortified she would be by his death. He grappled, in a last-ditch attempt, beating with one hand at the fire licking his harness and tugging at the metal D-ring handle with the other. He heard his frozen fingers snap like icicles in chorus with the roaring tongues of flames. With an agonising jerk on the rip-cord, an ignited canopy haloed his tumbling silhouette. Any moment now, he would be detached from the engulfed parachute and fall through the melded darkness of sky and sea to join his comrades-in-arms.

And sadly, it was not the comforting image of Ena that would take him to his grave but the torturous sight of Don, left behind in the Lancaster to face an inevitable and solitary end. Don had so often shunned the need for a parachute on a training exercise and had sealed his own fate. But still, his face haunted Reg, all the more piteous for its lack of accusation, and wistful resignation for what was to come. But the legacy he left Reg was a terrible and unceasing one. It would have been better, Reg thought, if he had stayed with him so that their final, agonising moments would have been alleviated by a shared communion. But it was too late.

At ten thousand feet, the suspension lines burned away from the last remnants of canopy and Reg rocketed toward the cobra-like waves of a hostile North Sea.

*

'Reg, wake up, wake up!' Ena, hearing the familiar sound of her husband's sleeping torment, was keen to reassure him. 'You've been having one of your dreams again, haven't you? What was it this time? The Battle of Berlin? Don and the others?'

Reg, slightly disorientated, looked around the sitting room, comforted by the familiar sight of the gramophone and mahogany sideboard. He held out his hand shakily. 'Come and sit with me a moment.'

'I can't.' Ena beckoned to the kitchen. 'The dinner. It's almost done. I don't want it to spoil. Not after all the effort I've made.'

Reg studied his wife admiringly. 'You're all dressed up. What's the occasion? I haven't missed a birthday, have I? Or an anniversary?' Still shaken by the vividness of his dream, he was grateful for her presence, luminous and manifest in her Sunday best.

'No,' she laughed. 'Though I wouldn't put it past you.' She smiled, stroking the slight curve of her abdomen. 'I have some special news, Reg.'

'You don't mean…'

Corkscrew Port Go

'Yes, I certainly do. We're going to have a baby, Reg. Don't look so surprised – you did have some part in it.' She studied him fondly. 'You look as if your mind's still somewhere else. Still in the bomber stream with your crew I expect. But that's all over now, Reg. You're safe, remember, and we have a future to look forward to, unlike so many others. So we have to make the best of it, for all of them.'

'You're right.' Reg, his happiness intensified by his recent conviction of impending death, shook his head in disbelief. 'That's wonderful news. Are you sure? I don't quite know what to say.' He reached for her small hands, his eyes straying in tenderness to her midriff.

'Well *I* do.' She reached for the fortified wine and the bottle opener beside it and passed them to Reg.

'Corkscrew, port, go!'

They laughed uproariously, glad to be young and alive. But as he uncorked the bottle, amidst the mellow, wood spice aroma, it was the acrid smell of cordite, exhaust fumes and burning oil from Merlin engines that pervaded.

Lion Hearts

I

Mrs Muggeridge put on her faded grey overcoat in the same perfunctory way that she did each morning. Her figure, slightly stooped, seemed older than her fifty-six years, her movements slow and passive. She walked toward the staircase with her strange gait, half fatigued and half resolute, shuffling slightly but with a momentum that suggested she dare not stop should she not start again.

'Gordon,' she called, in a voice that reflected her tiredness. 'Hurry, dear. You don't want to be late now do you?'

There was a loud thumping noise from the wooden flooring as Gordon appeared on the landing. In contrast to his mother, his expression was one of enthusiasm, his round face alert and smiling, his body, though bulky, full of vigour.

'Are we going to see the planes?' His speech was sluggish and childlike, and his small, oblique eyes shone with excitement.

'No, dear, I told you, you're going to help Mrs Partridge in the corner shop. Do you remember? We've been practising with different coins every day, haven't we? If it works out, you can have a full-time job there and earn your own money. Now wouldn't that be marvellous?' She made an effort to smile. 'Shall we practise some more? For example, if I bought something for half a crown and gave you...'

'I want to be a pilot like Michael.' Gordon descended the stairs and began racing around the house with his arms extended like plane wings, making a whirring noise. His right arm caught the blue vase on the sideboard, which tumbled onto the worn carpet. Miraculously, it stayed in one piece.

'Oh, Gordon, please be careful. We don't want any more breakages. Especially when you start working at Mrs Partridge's shop. She won't stand for any breakages. Promise me now, Gordon.'

'*Nnneeaoowwwwwww...*' Gordon continued to race around the front room making plane noises, occasionally exchanging them for the sound of machine guns.

'Come along then, Gordon, we don't want to be late.

If you're late on your first day, Mrs Partridge is unlikely to want you back. And it's not like job opportunities are exactly plentiful.'

Gordon stopped in his tracks. 'You look sad.' He smiled at her, the bottom lip of his small, round mouth protruding slightly. When she didn't respond, he took her hands and kissed them, his smile turning upside down to reflect her mood. 'Don't be sad. Let me give you a cuddle.' He put his arms around her and for a moment, she held on to him, tears of tiredness and worry prickling her eyes like needles. Then she pulled away and looked him square in the face.

'You can help me not be sad by putting on your coat and shoes and coming with me to the corner shop. Mrs Partridge will be waiting.'

Gordon put on his coat and shoes in his usual slow and fastidious manner. He hated to see his mother unhappy. He wished his brother Michael was home instead of flying aeroplanes. Everything seemed nicer when Michael was around.

Mrs Muggeridge locked the door behind them and they walked down the street together, Gordon sometimes skipping ahead, then waiting until she caught up. Knowing his mother was sad, he ran and hid behind a lamp post, his rotund body bulging from both sides, his head peeking out, smiling so broadly that his eyes almost disappeared into the folds of the lids.

'Peekaboo!' he said.

This was a game they had sometimes played and which he knew always cheered her up. But today her head hung low, giving her the look of a turtle, and her grey eyes looked dead, as though they anticipated disaster.

'Don't be silly, Gordon. You're fifteen now and a worker and you have to try to behave in a professional manner. Look! Look at those boys over there. They're laughing at you. You have to start behaving more grown up.'

Gordon was stung. 'You said it doesn't matter if people laugh, that I should just be myself.'

'Yes, well never mind what I said then. I'm telling you now that you're a grown-up and grown-ups have to earn money and they can't do that if they're busy hiding behind lamp posts and making silly faces.'

Gordon stopped walking, his face forlorn and confused. Two teenagers walked past and whispered, giggling to themselves. Gordon waved at them. 'Hello,' he said, but neither of them replied. As they turned the corner, one of them nudged the other and shouted out the word 'looney', before dissolving into loud and collaborative laughter.

'You see!' she said to Gordon. 'What have I told you about talking to strangers?'

'I was just being friendly.' Gordon, now submerged in his mother's gloom, stopped in his tracks and hung his head. 'I'd like to go home now.'

His mother stopped too and faced him defiantly. 'Oh, you would, would you? You'd like to go home and read your comics maybe, while I make a nice cup of tea?'

'Yes please.'

'Well you can't! You just can't.' Her body shook as tears ran down her face. 'How many times do you think I've wanted to just stop and please myself over the years? More than once, I can tell you. More than a dozen times. But I've kept on when people said you should be put in a home. I wouldn't have it. And when people said you wouldn't be able to learn, I told them what for. And so many times I wanted to just stop but I didn't. And here you are, a man now and able to earn a living. Your adding is better than most who go to school I'll bet, but you still have to prove it over and over again because of your…' she struggled for the right word, 'your ways.' The tears flowed now and Gordon put his arm around her.

'You don't like me anymore. You wish I was like everybody else.'

His mother stopped crying. 'No,' she said firmly. 'No, I don't. I love you just the way you are. You're kind and gentle and loving. It's not you. It's everyone else I want to change. I want them all to see you through *my* eyes.' She hugged him then and smoothed his brown coat, which she had bought for him the year before in a sale and which was a little tight across his chest. 'That's enough,' she said, as though a cloud had lifted. 'You're going to help Mrs Partridge and you're going to do it brilliantly. Just like we've been practising. Okay? You're the man of the house now that Michael's not here.'

'Okay.'

'And Gordon…'

'What.'

'Don't ever change.'

'No, I won't.' Gordon was happy again now and ran ahead a little. The shop was only a hundred yards away. Suddenly, as if from nowhere, a plane came into view. Gordon had learned to recognise the various war planes from his brother Michael, who was a Spitfire pilot.

'Look, look! It's Michael flying his Spitfire. Wave. Go on, wave.'

Mrs Muggeridge dropped her bag and waved at the plane flying overhead. 'Stay safe, son,' she shouted. 'Come home to us soon.'

'I want to fly too, just like Michael.'

'Well, maybe you will one day,' Mrs Muggeridge said, 'but one step at a time. You have to conquer the corner shop first. As it is, I think that Michael flew this way especially, just to wish you good luck on your first day at work. And you don't want to let Michael down now, do you?'

'No.'

She gripped her stomach. Nerves had caused her cramps. They walked on until they reached the shop.

They were fifteen minutes early so needn't have rushed. Mrs Partridge showed Michael where to put his coat and where the kettle was. He was given an old mug to use when he had his tea, and Mrs Muggeridge handed over his sandwiches to Mrs Partridge.

Mrs Partridge said that they could take it slowly and that there would be plenty of time that morning to familiarise Gordon with the till. Mrs Muggeridge was pleased to see that the till was exactly like the small model she'd drawn at home, which had been central to their practise with real coins.

Mrs Partridge ushered Mrs Muggeridge away. 'I'm sure Gordon and I will get on like a house on fire. And I'm sure you can do without your mammy watching over you, don't you think,' she said kindly, her large frame shaking with mirth. 'Off you go, Mrs Muggeridge. We'll see you at three o'clock and I'll tell you how it all went.'

Mrs Muggeridge went home. She was annoyed with herself for her earlier outburst. She had always told Gordon that he should be proud to be himself and there she was getting upset with him for no fault of his own. Why couldn't other people accept him for who he was, especially those who should know better? When he'd been born, the midwife had cried and rushed him off to the doctor. Mrs Muggeridge's heart had been filled with dread. The doctor had told her it would be better if she didn't hold him, in fact, if she had no contact at all. She could only lie in the hospital bed wondering in terror what kind of monster she'd given birth to. When she felt a little stronger, she had demanded some answers.

'Your baby has Mongoloid idiocy,' the doctor had said solemnly. 'You'll be lucky if he lives past infancy. It's better for your whole family if he's institutionalised straight away so that you don't have time to bond. He'll be much better off amongst his own.' Even if the baby survived, he'd continued, it wouldn't be able to lead an independent life. It would be unlikely it would be able to potty train, feed itself or understand the simplest things. 'Trust me, Mrs Muggeridge,' he'd said, 'the best thing for you and Mr Muggeridge would be to pretend that this pregnancy never happened.'

Mr Muggeridge had agreed and said it might be best to tell the relatives that the child had been stillborn. It would be such an embarrassment to the family. He couldn't understand how it had happened and it definitely hadn't been from his side, he'd insisted. His side were a family of professionals. They were a highly evolved lineage of solicitors, accountants and the occasional professor. The error must have come from her genes. His side couldn't possibly have given birth to an idiot child.

Mrs Muggeridge had cried herself to sleep for two nights and on the third day, had demanded to see her baby. She'd had no idea what to expect and had braced herself for the worst. Any child repellent enough to make the midwife cry must be very ugly indeed. The baby had been brought to her swaddled in a blanket so that its face was obscured. Nervously, she had taken it in her arms and pulled the cover aside. Then she'd smiled for the first time since she'd given birth. Her baby was beautiful with a round, sweet face and the bluest of eyes. She'd half wondered if the nurse had brought the wrong baby. His little, cherubic mouth was pink and moist, and he gurgled happily, oblivious to the drama that he'd created. She knew then that no one would part her from him, whatever the consequences. And there had been many.

Mr Muggeridge had left her after twelve months, saying only that he couldn't cope. He couldn't bear to be in the same room as their younger son. She had moved in with her widowed mother and got a job working night shifts, at first in a textile factory and then, later, as the war neared, a munitions factory, where the work was more lucrative. The latter involved handling toxic chemicals, often filling trays of shells with a high explosive called TNT. Collecting the cans of explosive from a large mixer was heavy work and the stench was awful. Sometimes, the TNT spilled onto Mrs Muggeridge's skin and scars from the burns were an inevitability, along with the slight yellow hew of her skin. But the job had enabled her to earn a reasonable living and night shifts meant that she could be with her children during the daytime.

She had slept for a few hours each morning after she had fed and clothed them both, during which time her arthritic mother had supervised them. In the afternoons, Mrs Muggeridge had played with her children and taught them to read.

She'd been worried that the amount of time she'd needed to devote to Gordon would cause Michael some resentment, but she shouldn't have worried. Michael had doted on his younger brother from the beginning. As he'd grown older, he'd taken on the role of the absent father. He'd helped to feed him and soothe him when he'd cried. He'd spent hours helping him to read and add up, so that Gordon had learned surprisingly quickly. Mrs Muggeridge had been determined that if the schools wouldn't take Gordon, she would do her best for him at home. She wasn't a well-educated woman, but she was clever and excelled at mathematics. Whatever the doctor had said, she felt that Gordon was very capable of learning as long as she took it slowly and showed him patience. After all, she had been advised at the hospital that he wouldn't be able to dress himself or learn to talk, and he had managed both.

She knew he would have to endure hardships. People were cruel, though she hadn't realised quite how cruel until Gordon had come along. The taunts from other children she had expected, but it was the prejudices of adults, most of whom shunned him as if he were a leper, that had most upset her.

Michael had begun to form friendships at school and he'd been keen to have his friends come home to play. Time and time again, he'd invited the children in his class and each time, despite their keenness, they'd been forbidden to go. Mrs Muggeridge and Gordon would wait for Michael outside the school gates as the other mothers chatted in groups and invited each other for cups of tea. They would look through her as if she didn't exist, not wanting to associate either with a disabled child, or a woman who had produced one. Children who showed any curiosity had quickly been told to look away. Mrs Muggeridge had stood with her turtle head bowed low, waiting for Michael to find her, before hurrying him away through the hostile crowds.

Then something curious had happened. Mrs Bright, who was the most popular, glamorous and wealthy woman in the neighbourhood, began speaking to her, hesitantly at first and then with less reserve. Soon, she had broken from her usual crowd and began standing next to Mrs Muggeridge instead, making casual remarks about the weather or the state of the country.

Mrs Muggeridge, so used to being ignored, couldn't at first imagine why this attractive, luminous creature had chosen to pass the time with her. She would listen politely, nod and gesture at what she felt were the right moments, but contributed little to the conversations.

Mrs Bright had seemed to understand her shyness and had persevered, and eventually a friendship was established, much to the amazement of the other mothers. Mrs Bright also had a young son called Andrew, the same age as Michael, and the two had become firm friends. Andrew's home was the largest Michael had ever seen and terribly grandiose. There would have been so much space to hide in, but Mr Bright, who did something terribly important for the local government, had declared certain rooms out of bounds, and, as he liked his peace, he was much happier when his son played at Mrs Muggeridge's modest terraced property instead, while Mrs Bright and Mrs Muggeridge cemented their friendship over tea and the occasional iced bun.

And, as is the way with the dullest of beasts, this had started a trend amongst the waiting mothers, who now viewed Mrs Muggeridge with an excited curiosity. Perhaps, they thought, they had overlooked something about her. She had, after all, managed to secure Mrs Bright as a friend. Suddenly, Michael became popular, everyone wanting an invite to his home in the hope of finding out more about Mrs Muggeridge and Gordon. But Michael, as if understanding, even at such tender years, had used his younger brother as a yardstick to measure friendships by. Those who accepted Gordon and were happy to include him in their games, returned, whereas those who proved themselves unkind or impatient had soon been discarded.

Mrs Muggeridge had been thankful for Michael's sake that they were no longer ostracised, but understood that most of the mothers were viewing her family as an oddity, useful fodder for gossip and for reclaiming the popular Mrs Bright. But Mrs Bright remained steadfast in her friendship, gradually earning Mrs Muggeridge's trust through her kindness and patience with Gordon. Gordon, in turn, had flourished in his learning and confidence.

Mrs Bright would lift him onto her knee and talk to him tenderly and with affection as Mrs Muggeridge made the tea. She would tell him what a handsome boy he was and how clever when he repeated words that other children of his age had long since used in full sentences.

Sometimes Mrs Muggeridge thought she saw a tear in her eyes, as though moved by the smiles and giggles, and was quick to reassure Mrs Bright that she shouldn't be sad on her account. Gordon had already brought her untold happiness. She was, she said, the luckiest of mothers to have not one but two beautiful sons with the kindest and most loving temperaments. Her only wish was that Gordon could one day fulfil his potential and learn to lead an independent life like his brother. She would do everything within her power to ensure that he did.

'But do you think that's possible?' Mrs Bright had

said. 'I mean, from what I've heard...' She had looked guiltily at the little boy on her knee. 'From what I've heard, there may be limitations imposed by his particular, er... ailment.' She'd blushed.

Mrs Muggeridge had replied confidently that the only limitations were those that we imposed upon ourselves. 'Oh, I'm not saying that he'll become a barrister or a brain surgeon, but there will be something that he can do to contribute to society, I'm sure.'

Mrs Bright had replied that she hoped she was right, her pillar-box-red lips smiling down at Gordon as he'd clutched his favourite toy, a wooden plane, in his small, plump hands.

The children in the neighbourhood had grown used to the sight of Gordon, though Mrs Muggeridge was protective of him and rarely let him out of her sight. She would sit by the window as he played outside on the cobbled street with Michael and his friends, playing British Bulldog or Hopscotch. His favourite had been What's the Time, Mr Wolf? when he would become so excited each time Mr Wolf answered that he would shriek and run whatever the reply, no matter how many times the rules had been explained.

'Everyone else is faster than me,' he would say. 'I don't want to be eaten by a wolf.'

'It's not a real wolf,' Michael had explained, and the group would collapse with laughter, including Gordon.

'Look,' Michael would say, '*you* be Mr Wolf.'

But every time Gordon was asked the time, he would shout, 'Dinner time,' and chase after them, a loud belly laugh slowing his already laboured run.

'Don't say dinner time *every* time,' Michael would advise. 'You have to keep us wondering. Say one o'clock, then three o'clock, *then* maybe dinner time. Okay?'

'Okay,' Michael had answered. 'One o'clock, three o'clock, dinner time.' And he'd turned and chased each one around the street, chortling loudly until he'd complained of a stitch.

As they'd grown older, they'd played in the streets until dusk and Michael and the others had run races around the square earnestly, as though it had been the quadrangle of some famous Oxford college. Gordon would always flag them off and wait patiently with a stopwatch to greet the winner, though he'd frequently become distracted and made them run again. 'I forgot to start the clock,' he would say merrily, or 'I got chatting,' as though the boys' energy was ceaseless.

'Oh, for goodness sake, Gordon!' they would chide.

Mrs Muggeridge had watched contentedly from the window, happy to see her boys enjoying themselves and making friends. Outside their street, the world had not been so kind. And as he'd grown older, youth had seemed less forgiving. At twelve years old on a trip to the post office, Gordon had been taunted and chased by two thugs who threw stones at him and called him words he had never heard before. One of the stones had hit him in the face and after that he'd refused to leave the house for several weeks, despite his mother and Michael's encouragement.

Eventually, he'd accompanied his brother, his ration book and pocket money in his hand, seduced at last by thoughts of barley sugars, pear drops and liquorice pipes. After a few days, he'd tried a solo visit, though Michael had followed at a discreet distance with Andrew Bright. They'd done this for several days, Michael almost willing the thugs to reappear, and when at last they did and had confronted a terrified Gordon, they'd been ambushed by Michael, who, incensed with rage, bulldozed into the pair, knocking them to the ground and pounding them with his fists.

'If you ever touch him again, you won't know what's hit you.'

'Too right,' Andrew had echoed, though he'd remained a spectator. 'Keep away from him, or else.'

As it turned out, the thugs had not been fighters and had taken to their heels, one holding a bloodied nose, shouting threats only from a safe distance.

'You saved me,' Gordon had said. 'You're the best brother.' He'd given Michael a bear hug. 'You can have one of my sweets.'

'Don't forget Andrew helped.'

'He only watched. But he can have a sweet too.' He

offered the bag of barley sugars.

'What about the pear drops?'

'They're my favourites.'

Michael and Andrew had laughed. 'So much for being your heroes! Okay, we'll take a barley sugar.'

'Only one each.'

Michael was a boy of immense character. He was never once resentful of the time his mother devoted to Gordon, or the fact that she had little time or money to spend on him. He was happy to contribute to Gordon and his mother's happiness and well-being in any way he could. His curiosity about his father had long since diminished and any attempts his father had made to contact him or offer him treats had been rejected. Michael understood, without being told, that a relationship with his father would exclude Gordon and for this, he felt nothing but contempt.

He saw how hard his mother worked, sometimes through illness and exhaustion, and how this had made her old beyond her years. When he visited Andrew's house, he noted that Mrs Bright always had time for relaxation. And one weekend every month, she took a trip to visit her sister-in-law in the countryside while Mr Bright looked after Andrew. Mr Bright bought her fresh flowers every week that filled a vase on the dining room table and he never failed to compliment Mrs Bright on how attractive she looked. Her hair was always perfectly styled and she wore lipstick that matched her various outfits. His mother's daily uniform was a worn apron full of stains.

It occurred to him that Mrs Bright lived the kind of life his mother would have led with his father had Gordon not been born. He couldn't remember a time when his mother had spent money on herself for a new dress or a hairstyle. And she never wore lipstick. At first, his grandmother had helped around the house but as her arthritis had worsened, he'd watched his mother look after her too until she'd died, with never a complaint. Yet her tiredness was getting the better of her. He could sense that in these last years, it had seeped into the very bones of her. Her cheeriness now had a feigned quality to it and her energy a lack of conviction. And the war wasn't helping. He knew she was terrified of the bombs, terrified of the confinement of the Morrison shelter and most of all, terrified that her sons would be harmed.

When the war began, she had considered sending them to the country, but she knew that Gordon would be reliant upon strangers who would never understand his ways. And Michael would not leave either of them. As the war progressed, most of the children in the street had been evacuated, waved tearfully goodbye from sooty stations clutching their few belongings in brown paper parcels. As Mrs Muggeridge put it, 'Left to the tender mercies of billeting officers and perfect strangers.'

Michael, much to his mother's pleasure, had attended a local grammar school, having won a scholarship. His mother had always vehemently extoled the virtues of a good education and, even as a young boy, he had acknowledged the advantages of a positive work ethic.

Andrew too had managed to secure a place and the two boys had remained firm friends until an incident – detestable for one and shameful for the other – had broken their boyhood ties irretrievably. Mrs Muggeridge had found it hard at the time to understand why their friendship had cooled but Michael had simply explained that they were both busy and had grown apart. He knew that she would find the truth decidedly less palatable.

One day at school, Michael had overheard the class ruffian asking Andrew why he spent so much time with someone from such a lowly background.

'His mother looks like an old sow,' he'd said, 'and his brother's a Mongol, a simpleton.'

He had pranced around the classroom giving an impression of Gordon, his distinctive speech and facial expression, his tongue protruding from his mouth in callous distortion. This in itself had been disquieting to Michael. But it was not the perpetrator who had upset Michael so much as his friend's response. Instead of defending Gordon, he had actually laughed, a nervous but consensual chortle.

'They are family friends,' he'd replied, as if trying to

excuse their association. 'My mother has a tender heart. She likes to befriend those less fortunate than herself.'

The words had stung. When Andrew turned and saw Michael standing forlornly behind him, he knew exactly what he'd done. Their friendship would never recover.

Michael had continued to show great academic promise. It was felt he would have made an excellent engineer, but he knew exactly what he wanted to do and that was to fly Spitfires.

The war was in full thrust and he saw many of his younger teachers leave to join the forces, and less qualified and committed teachers take their place. One, however, saw his obvious potential and knowing of Michael's ambitions, arranged for an officer at RAF Uxbridge to pay his class a visit. From then on, Michael was determined that this was his future. Like many young men, he was obsessed with the idea of flying and had read every aviation magazine and manual available. After writing several letters, he'd been invited to the air base and at eighteen years old he was accepted onto a flying programme. Mrs Muggeridge had wept when she'd heard his news, but Gordon, who didn't understand the gravity of the war and the short life expectancy of a fighter pilot, had jumped up and down with glee.

'I want to fly with you,' he'd said. 'We could get rid of all the baddies together.'

'No, someone has to be the man of the house,'

Michael had replied sternly. 'Who would look after things at home if you went to war? And what about your job at the corner shop?'

'But that's not a proper war job. And I won't get to fly in a plane and shoot down all the baddies.' He'd sat looking defeated then and added as an afterthought, 'Or get a badge for being brave.'

Michael had laughed. 'The bravest thing you can do is to stay here in London and look after our mother. She needs you now. So you need to be a good boy and help her in any way that you can. Do you understand?'

'I suppose so.'

'Good boy.'

'Will you take me to see your plane?'

'Not yet, but maybe one day I can take you to the base. We'll see.'

'Okay.'

Every day he had awoken since Michael's departure, Gordon had asked if they could go to see Michael and his aeroplane.

'No, dear, it's top secret,' Mrs Muggeridge would answer. 'No one is allowed in unless they are in the RAF. But maybe one day, Michael will get you a special pass.'

'Which day?'

'I don't know, dear, but someday soon.'

'Okay.'

Mrs Muggeridge tried hard to hide her fears from Gordon, but at times she found she burst into tears at the most unpredictable moments. Mrs Bright, whose son Andrew had been exempt from military service due to his poor vision and chosen career as a teacher, was her only real confidante. She had proven herself a good and loyal friend these last years, though Mrs Muggeridge still sometimes wondered why and what she could possibly offer to such a popular and enchanting woman.

'I don't know what I shall do without Michael,' she confessed, as though his death were a certainty. 'He's been my rock, you see, ever since Cyril left.'

'He'll be fine, you'll see,' Mrs Bright reassured her. 'He's such a talented boy and I'm sure he won't take any unnecessary risks.'

'I suppose I've always relied on him too much,' Mrs Muggeridge continued. 'It's not fair on him, I know, the way he's always had to protect Gordon and run errands for me. He had to grow up far too quickly. And now he sends me money every month. I've told him not to but do you know what he said?'

'What?'

'He said I was to buy a lipstick and a new dress. As if I can think of such luxuries when he's out there flying in combat, probably as we speak.' She shuddered visibly. 'And they're outnumbered, you know. I overheard a conversation the other day and apparently there are two German planes to every one of ours. What chance does he have? They say that about six weeks is the average life expectancy for a fighter pilot and Michael has been flying for six months now. How long can his luck last?' She began to weep quietly so that Mrs Bright put her arm around her.

'Please don't upset yourself,' she said. 'The worst time for our pilots was during the Battle of Britain, and, after all, the Americans are fighting with us now and they say the war won't last much longer. It's been going on for nearly six years. It will soon end and Michael will come home, you'll see. That dreadful tyrant will be killed and that will be the end of it.' She smiled. 'And in the meantime, you have Gordon. He must be a great comfort.'

'You're right,' replied Mrs Muggeridge. 'Michael has a day's leave next week and I don't want him to catch me like this.'

'I have an idea,' Mrs Bright said. 'You have such a pretty face beneath that worried expression. And with a little styling, your hair would look wonderful.'

'Oh no, I'm not sure...'

'But think how pleased Michael would be to come home to see his mother looking so well and happy. I'm sure he'd find it reassuring.'

'Do you think so?'

'Of course. He's said as much in his letter, hasn't he? He wants you to spend a little time and money on yourself.'

'What do you have in mind?'

'You'll see.' Mrs Bright took Mrs Muggeridge's hand. 'I've always admired you. It's about time you had a little time to devote to yourself.'

'You've admired *me*!' said Mrs Muggeridge in astonishment. 'I find it very hard to believe that someone with your beauty and talents could ever admire someone like me.'

'It's true,' Mrs Bright said. 'The way you handle Gordon and the way you've refused to allow doctors and a husband to force you to abandon him. I think that's truly admirable. I wish I were half as brave.'

'Well, that was an easy choice,' Mrs Muggeridge mused. 'When I saw his sweet face I knew I couldn't part with him. I mean, he's the kindest, most loving child a mother could ask for. There's not an ounce of malice or spite in him. He says exactly what he thinks and he has a sense of fun that's rare in these cynical times. Who wouldn't want to be around him? Yes, it can be exhausting but if I'd...' A tear appeared suddenly, which she absently wiped away with her handkerchief. 'If I'd put him in one of those institutions, well, who knows what would have happened to him.' She tucked the handkerchief back into her worn sleeve. 'That's why it's so important that he learns to become independent. Because if something happened to me, then what would become of him? I dread to think. I sometimes think it might almost be better if a bomb took the both of us.'

'Oh, my dear, please don't say that.' Mrs Bright dabbed her own perfectly made-up eyes. 'Nothing will happen to either of you. We'll all get through this damned war in one piece, you'll see.'

'Yes.' Mrs Muggeridge smiled determinedly. 'You're right. I'm sorry, I really mustn't be morbid.'

A few days later, Michael came home on leave. He was excited. 'They say Hitler's pretty desperate. This war can't go on much longer.'

'I do hope so.' Mrs Muggeridge looked at her elder son across the table, which she had bedecked with her best tablecloth to welcome him home. Gordon had picked some wildflowers from the roadside, which Mrs Muggeridge had put in a jam jar in the centre of the table. Michael smiled at her.

'I give it another few months, at most.'

Mrs Muggeridge smiled back. He had grown thinner in the face and there were dark circles under his eyes.

'When can I see the plane?' Gordon asked excitedly. 'You said I could see your plane, remember?'

'I've told you,' Mrs Muggeridge said softly, 'it's top secret. You can't go there. You need a special pass.'

'Why can't Michael get me one?'

'Because he's not allowed.'

'Well, maybe not yet.' Michael winked at Gordon. 'But before long we'll have ole Hitler licked, you'll see. Then I'll take you on a flight myself.'

'Be careful what you promise. You know how he holds tight to these ideas.'

'Well, we need something to hold tight to in these dark days.'

Mrs Muggeridge registered the tiredness in his eyes.

'By the way, you look smashing, Mum. I don't know what you've done to yourself, but you look wonderful. Easily the most glamorous lady on the street. I thought you were a film star when you first opened the door and that I must be at Ealing Studios.'

'Oh, you charmer.' Mrs Muggeridge couldn't help but feel pleased. Her dress, which was apple green with a white collar, had been given to her by Mrs Bright, who'd promised that she was going to throw it away if Mrs Muggeridge hadn't taken it. She had even made a few adjustments to it and sewn on a new button to replace the missing one, which almost exactly matched the others on the dress. The style emphasised what a small waist she had and the thrill of wearing it made Mrs Muggeridge stand taller and straighter than she was normally prone.

Mrs Bright had also taken the scissors to her hair and fashioned it in a style that she said was the latest rage. She had then set it in pipe cleaners so that it now bounced and waved around her face, disguising the thinness of it. The small, broken veins in her cheeks had been smoothed over with make-up and her lips gleamed with a peach-coloured lipstick. She couldn't remember the last time she had got dressed up and initially had felt a little self-conscious, but at the same time had enjoyed being pampered enormously. It reminded her how it felt to be a woman after so many years in her dreary apron. Wearing it now, along with the peachy lipstick and her new bouncy hair, she felt so happy. If only the world could stop turning right now, with her in her finery, feeling like a woman again, with her two sons at home, safe from the dangers of the world outside. If only she could suspend this moment in time, with Gordon laughing happily and Michael seated at her table instead of the cockpit of a Spitfire, all of them joking and having fun like in past times. She felt she would burst from the happiness of it all. She was so proud of them both. How could she have been so blessed with not one but two wonderful sons, as well as a kind friend like Mrs Bright.

'Mrs Bright gave me the dress,' she said proudly. 'I didn't have to spend a penny.' Thoughts of Mrs Bright reminded her of Andrew. 'You really ought to contact Andrew,' she said. 'I'm sure he'd love to catch up while you're on leave. You used to be so close.'

'Did we?' Michael's face clouded over. 'I think I would find it difficult now to find anything in common with someone so wholly disconnected to the war.'

'But Michael, that's not his fault. It's his sight. He wasn't able…'

'His sight and perhaps the fact that Mr Bright is so well-connected?'

'That's a little unfair. We don't know that. And the family has always been so kind to us. What with this dress and the time Mrs Bright took to make me look nice…'

'Yes, well I dare say it would suit Andrew to see you in one of his mother's old cast-offs. I don't like the way she lords it over you in that *noblesse oblige* fashion, while both the men in her household seem to have avoided any kind of combat.'

Mrs Muggeridge's face changed to an expression of sadness. 'I really don't know what you mean, Michael, and I don't want to. All I know is that she's been a kind and loyal friend to me. She wanted me to look nice for your return and it made me feel special and now…' She sniffed, trying to contain her tears. 'Now it's all spoilt.'

Michael was instantly contrite. 'I'm sorry. I really didn't mean to upset you.' He put a comforting arm around her shoulder. 'It's just the war, the damned war! You look wonderful, you really do, and you're right, Mrs Bright has been a loyal friend to you. But you shouldn't be *too* grateful because though you can't give her material things, you give her a great deal in other ways. Things she couldn't get from anyone else. I think in many ways she looks up to you for guidance because she knows that you're the better person. Everyone always looks up to her and wants to be her friend, but you're the one that deserves the most credit and she knows it. The way you have always looked after us and worked so hard and never complained. Well, that's admirable! As admirable as anything I've ever known. As admirable as being a war hero or an ace pilot. So you shouldn't feel so grateful for her friendship. I never say this but…' He hesitated. 'You are and always have been the best mother ever and I do so love you for it.'

'Me too,' echoed Gordon.

'Oh, do stop,' Mrs Muggeridge dabbed at her eyes with her handkerchief. 'You'll set me off. Come on, let's have some cake.'

'Tell me everything you've been doing, Gordon,' Michael said, happiness restored. 'Come on, what's my brother been up to?'

'He's been good,' said Gordon.

'I hear you're working very hard at the corner shop. I'm very impressed. Have you mastered the till yet?'

'It's easy,' Gordon said. 'Two boys said I got their change wrong but Mrs Partridge counted it up at the end of the day and I was right.'

'Yes,' Mrs Muggeridge said. 'Quite a few have tried that one. I think it's a surprise to all of them how good his adding up is.'

'I'll bet,' Michael laughed. 'Good for you. That's great news. It means you're earning your own money now.'

'And paying toward things.'

'He bought the ingredients for this cake.'

'And I made it. While Mum was getting beautiful.'

'It's true, he did,' Mrs Muggeridge laughed. 'I felt very spoilt, I must say, just sitting there getting my hair done while Gordon did all the work.'

'Well, well, and here's me who can't do a thing in the kitchen.'

'But you can fly.'

'Oh, but that's so much easier than baking a cake. Or at least it is for me.' Michael laughed and took a bite.

'Is it good?'

'Just a minute.' He swallowed a piece of the Victoria sponge and then clutched at his chest and rolled from his seat onto the floor groaning.

Mrs Muggeridge laughed. 'You're not fooling us, is he, Gordon?'

Gordon, startled for a moment, began laughing. 'You're having a joke,' he said. 'You're having a joke at my expense.'

'No, only at your cake's expense!'

Mrs Muggeridge laughed. 'Oh, it does my heart good to see you both enjoying yourselves. All of us back together.' She dabbed her eyes again. 'I can't tell you how happy I am. If only it could stay like this.'

'Don't worry,' Michael smiled. 'Like I said, this war will be over before you know it.'

The rest of Michael's leave was spent in happy reunion, Michael indulging Gordon's fantasies about flying and falling back into that seamless pattern of family life, before the bombs and the smell of death that now lingered, immovable in London's pungent air.

Michael said nothing about the friends he had recently seen burn before his eyes as their plane exploded on landing, their ineffable screams bursting his ear drums, their melting flesh transforming them like Dali clocks. He had belted at the flames with his bare hands until they were blistered and raw, but he had arrived too late and was pulled back, the agonies of their burning bodies now his own, engraved on his mind forever.

But being at home was helping. The sight of his mother dressed up, as if defying the greyness of her surroundings, had cheered him. But mostly, there was something cathartic about being around Gordon, who, as ever, seemed indifferent to the war and the devastation it brought. Other than the first time the air raid sirens had sounded, he greeted them nonchalantly, dusting himself off and returning to the house as if this were to be the general pattern. It was always difficult to stir him from his bed, despite the anxiety in his mother's voice.

'Do hurry, Gordon,' she would shout. 'Stir yourself, do!'

'They'll be gone soon,' he would answer. 'There's no hurry.'

'You'll be gone soon,' she would reply, 'if you don't get a move on.'

Only the sight of aircraft animated him. He was very clear in his preferences and didn't even seem to mind whether they were enemy or Allied planes, thinking the Messerschmitt a better plane than the Hawker. But his favourite was the Spitfire. Michael knew that this was more to do with the general glamour surrounding the plane than the fact that he flew them. Being around Gordon was better than rehabilitation. Gordon made no allowances for mood or incident, and the world he inhabited, though small, was pure and recuperative.

The day after Michael returned to the base, Mrs Muggeridge received a surprise visit from Mrs Bright. She seemed agitated and her usually immaculate appearance had gone, her face pale and drawn, devoid of make-up.

'My dear, do come in.' Mrs Muggeridge ushered her into the kitchen and put on the kettle. 'What on earth is the matter? Are you unwell?'

It took a while for Mrs Bright to compose herself but finally she sat down by the stove and smiled weakly at her friend. 'Did you ever wonder,' she asked sadly, 'why Michael and Andrew stopped being friends?'

'Well, yes,' Mrs Muggeridge began. 'But I supposed it was down to the fact that they have very different lives now. People drift apart, don't they? It's only natural.'

'Yes, but not when they were so close.' Mrs Bright then relayed the story of Michael and Andrew's estrangement. 'I'm so sorry,' she said, as though Andrew's disloyal remarks had been her own. 'Andrew has never been the most courageous of boys. He is very easily intimidated. He should clearly have defended you all but when one begins a new school, one is so desperate to fit in. He confessed to me after bumping into Michael in the street yesterday. Michael won't speak to him. It must have hurt him very deeply.'

'Yes, I see.' Mrs Muggeridge understood Michael's reluctance to visit Andrew now.

Knowing her son as she did, she knew Andrew's betrayal would have hurt him profoundly. If only he had confided in her, she could have told him that it really didn't matter. She had dealt with so much worse over the years. Poor Andrew must have been so keen to make an impression and he had never been a fighter.

'I wish I'd known earlier,' she said, 'and I could have perhaps helped with a reconciliation. It's such a silly thing to lose a friend over, after all. And considering the times, we should all try to keep at peace with each other.' She took Mrs Bright's hand. 'Please tell Andrew that it's okay. We all, at times, wish we had responded differently to a situation. We wouldn't be human if we didn't.'

'You're a wise and kind friend,' Mrs Bright said. 'I'm so lucky that we met.' A look of relief settled in her large eyes. 'But that's not all. I too have a confession to make.'

'A confession? That sounds very ominous.'

'I've been meaning to talk to you for the longest time but the right time never really materialised. But it's important that you know.' She paused. 'You know that I'm visiting my sister-in-law this weekend. Well, I'd like you to come with me. We could leave early tomorrow and be back the following day. Please do say that you'll come. It's important to me. And don't worry about the train tickets or the accommodation. Vanessa has plenty of room.'

'But what about Gordon? I couldn't possibly leave him. He wouldn't be able to manage. I should worry. He's never been left on his own before.'

'Of course, he must come too. Wouldn't he just love to see the countryside? Think about it. How long has it been since you both had a break? Anyway, that's sorted then,' she continued, as if Mrs Muggeridge had already agreed. 'I'll come for you both in the morning.' She finished the last of her tea.

'But I mean, I'm not sure… What would I pack? I have no idea.'

'Please, don't worry. Everything will be tickety-boo, you'll see. Just bring yourself and Gordon and everything else will sort itself out.'

When she'd gone, Mrs Muggeridge was filled with a sudden panic at the idea of leaving her home. She hadn't spent a night away from it since she had moved in with her mother, and even the falling bombs seemed a less frightening prospect than a night spent beyond its comforting walls. Yet she was intrigued as to why Mrs Bright wanted her company after all these years and what it was that she needed to tell her. And, if she could overcome her anxiety, how wonderful it would be for Gordon to travel to the countryside. He had never had a holiday or seen anywhere beyond their cobbled streets. How thrilled he would be to be a passenger on a train and to see fields rather than the familiar backstreet terraces.

The following morning, they were collected by Mrs Bright, who put their small overnight bag in the boot of her shiny, black Rover and drove them to the station. Gordon clung to his mother's arm on the platform as though they were about to board a spaceship, his eyes darting about him, this way and that, trying to absorb the sights and sounds of the station.

'Can we speak to the train driver?'

'No, dear, he's too busy right now.' Mrs Muggeridge clutched her stomach. The excitement of the journey had given her butterflies.

'Oh, I forgot,' Mrs Bright said, dipping into a bag. 'I thought you might like this, Gordon.' She passed him a hat. 'I know you want to be a pilot like your brother but until then, I thought perhaps you might like to be a train driver.'

Gordon, unused to receiving gifts, let alone riding on

trains or visiting the countryside, was suddenly overcome with joy and planted a big kiss on Mrs Bright's cheek. 'Thank you, Mrs B. That's the best hat I've ever seen.'

'You shouldn't have. You're spoiling him. Both of us, in fact.'

'It's nothing. Maybe the driver will let him have a look around the engine room when we stop if I ask him nicely.'

Mrs Muggeridge secretly felt that there were few men who would not indulge Mrs Bright if she asked them nicely. She was as entranced as Gordon by the journey. It was April and the colours through the windows were spectacular, meadows full of wildflowers contrasting with the grey dilapidation of the city behind them. She was so busy calming an excited Gordon that she lost all sense of time until suddenly, they pulled up at a small country station.

'Here we are,' said Mrs Bright. 'Time to disembark.'

'Dogs bark?' said Gordon quizzically.

'Quite right,' Mrs Bright laughed. 'And you will see one in a minute. Vanessa, my sister-in-law, has a border collie. Of course, she has the room. It wouldn't be fair in London. In any case…' She looked sheepishly at Mrs Muggeridge. 'There's something I must tell you before her help picks us up. I've been trying to tell you for the entire journey, but Gordon's been so excited.'

'Yes,' Mrs Muggeridge agreed happily. 'He doesn't

see the countryside very often, well at all really, well, that is, only in picture books. I'm sorry he's so lively.'

'Don't be sorry, it's lovely to see, but I must tell you…'

At that moment, a car pulled up and a man got out. 'Hello, madam. Good to see you. I'll put your luggage in the back.'

'Thank you, Thompson. We'll get in.'

Gordon wanted to know where they were and chatted incessantly all the way to the house, which was set at the edge of a village, about five miles from the station. It had a long driveway that weaved its way past a colourful array of azaleas and rhododendrons to the large, panelled door with corniced windows either side.

'What I wanted to say…' Mrs Bright began, but just as she was about to continue, a girl about the same age as Gordon came skipping out of the house and knocked on the window of the car.

'Aunty,' she demanded, 'I've been waiting for such a long time. What took you so long?'

Mrs Muggeridge started. Gordon stared hard at the girl. 'You look a bit like me,' he said. 'You've got the same round face.'

'I don't look like you,' the girl said defiantly. 'I'm a girl.'

'Yes, but if you weren't a girl, you'd look like me. What's your name?'

'Millie,' she said.

'That's a pretty name.'

'Thanks. Come on, I'll show you where I live.'

They hurried off, leaving Mrs Muggeridge staring after them in disbelief. 'Why didn't you tell me you had a niece like Gordon? In fact, why didn't you tell me you had a niece?'

'Because I don't. I have a daughter.'

'A daughter!'

'Yes.' Mrs Bright nodded her head. 'I've never told anyone about her before. I'm so ashamed, you see.' She noted the look in Mrs Muggeridge's eyes. 'Oh, not ashamed of her, of course. But of myself. For not being brave enough to keep her like you kept Gordon. I was told it would be best to have her institutionalised and that was what my husband wanted. Much like yours. He said our lives would be ruined if we had to care for a disabled child. Well, I couldn't bear to think of her in one of those places, so devoid of love. Then Harry's sister said she would have her and raise her as her own. She is unmarried and has no children, you see. It just seemed the obvious solution. Of course, we send money for her upkeep and I come and visit each month. She thinks I'm her aunty. We thought it best at the time but I've often longed to hear her call me mother.' Her eyes welled with tears, which she dabbed delicately with a white, lace handkerchief.

'And Andrew?'

'He knows nothing. At least he didn't. Until he told

me what happened at school, how he dismissed Gordon, all for the sake of appearances. It sickened me. I couldn't believe that he would be so disloyal, that he lacked the moral fibre to defend his friendship and ours. I was so angry with him. And then I thought about my conduct and what I'd done. I deprived myself of my own child, and for what? My reputation? Or to avoid being ridiculed by those stupid women who ignored you and Gordon in the playground? It was then that I realised my son had merely inherited my own cowardice and I couldn't very well chastise him for that, could I? Children learn by example, don't they?'

They had moved inside the house by now and Mrs Muggeridge sat down shakily. 'So is that why you befriended me? Out of a sense of guilt?'

'No, of course not. It was out of admiration. You were like a beacon of light and courage. You held your own and stood firm. To do what you've done, without the monetary or emotional support of a husband, is remarkable in my eyes. And so, I was ashamed to admit that I'd rejected my daughter. I've seen, through being with you and Gordon, how being different can be so joyful. But I lacked your bravery. Please, don't hate me for it. I couldn't bear it if you did.'

'Of course I don't hate you. You're my closest friend.' Mrs Muggeridge reached for Mrs Bright's hand. 'I only wish you'd been able to tell me earlier. To have kept such a secret for so long must have been a terrible strain.' She shook her head in disbelief. 'Did you really think I would judge you so harshly?'

The two women hugged each other, a tender and prolonged embrace like that of long-lost sisters.

Millie had already shown Gordon her prize possessions – her stamp collection, her model aeroplanes, which, impressively, Gordon had identified, and her cricket set. They took the latter outside to the field just beyond the garden, where Gordon began hammering in the stakes with the mallet.

'I don't really know how to play,' Millie said. 'I don't have any friends to play with.'

'I'll show you,' Gordon said. 'My brother showed me when I was younger. We used to play in my street with the other children.'

'Why didn't you play in a field?'

'We don't have any where I live in London.'

'Why not?'

'Don't know. I suppose there's only room for the factories and the houses and the corner shop where I work.'

'You must be clever to work in a shop.'

'Mum and Mrs Partridge say I am. But it's only for a while, till I learn to be a pilot like my brother, Michael.'

As if conjured up by his thoughts, the hum of a distant plane broke through the stillness of the countryside. Looking upward, shading their eyes from the bright sunlight, they watched, entranced, as the plane headed in their direction until its form could be clearly identified between puffs of milky clouds.

'A Spitfire. That's my brother, Michael,' Gordon said confidently. 'I expect he's come to watch me play cricket. He likes to check up on me, like when I had my first day at work. Wave,' he ordered. 'Make sure he sees us playing cricket.'

They began waving, Gordon frantically, jumping up and down with the cricket bat and yelling Michael's name at the top of his voice. The plane was almost directly overhead so that the colours of the roundels could be clearly determined.

'Why has the cloud around it turned black?'

'I don't know,' Gordon replied. 'Maybe it's because it's going to rain.'

It was then that he realised something was really wrong. The dense grey did not belong to the cloud but was pouring from the engine of the Spitfire, and the pilot seemed to be struggling to control the flailing plane, which snorted and lurched and began heading toward the ground. Gordon began to scream loudly so that Mrs Bright and Mrs Muggeridge rushed out to see what the commotion was about. They all watched in horror as the Spitfire swooped overhead toward a small spinney, flames now licking the tail of the plane. It hit the ground clumsily but surprisingly did not explode, the thick, ebony palls of smoke and bright orange flames instead working their way slowly and fiendishly toward the cockpit. The pilot had managed to slide open the canopy and partially lift himself out before losing consciousness, so that he fell limply onto the wing like a rag doll.

'Michael's been hit. He's going to burn. Help, help!'

Gordon raced toward the plane. Despite the sickly smell of burning glycol and the mounting heat from the burning engine, he fought his way through the spitting flames to the wing and began to drag the pilot away from the burning wreckage. He had dragged him about twenty yards when he stopped, his eager yet defective heart pounding from the exertion.

'Help me,' he cried weakly, his voice stymied from terror. Millie nervously gripped the other arm tightly as, together, they dragged the pilot's limp body yet further from the smoking plane just before it exploded. Gordon watched, both repelled and beguiled, as a raging mass of bright flames engulfed the Spitfire.

'Michael, Michael, wake up.'

The pilot's face and goggles were covered in oil and Gordon wiped them with his sleeve. He grappled with the helmet, which clung stubbornly to a head both clammy and scorched.

It was then that he realised the pilot was not Michael but a stranger, the same build as Michael but with different facial features entirely. Unused to running, Mrs Muggeridge arrived breathless and shaken.

'Oh, my dear, let me see.' She checked the pulse of the young man lying in front of her and then carefully removed his goggles. 'He's alive,' she said, 'but it looks like he's had a bad knock to his head.'

'It's not Michael,' Gordon said.

'No, dear.'

'I thought it was Michael.'

'You were very brave, dear,' Mrs Muggeridge said, her heart beating rapidly, her skin grey with anxiety. The same thought had occurred to her. It could have been Michael. He could be facing the same danger now, somewhere over land or sea. She mustn't dwell on it. This time it had been some other mother's son, older than Michael by at least a decade, but still young. The pilot began to rouse and opened his eyes to see Gordon staring at him fixedly.

'I thought you were my brother,' Gordon said. 'That's why I saved you.'

'Well, lucky me,' the pilot replied, glancing at the wreckage. 'Jolly decent of you.' He winced. 'I think I've broken a leg and possibly several ribs. Didn't see that one coming. Just smacked me on my way in. Awfully bad luck, what?'

'What, what?' Gordon asked.

'Don't worry,' Mrs Muggeridge said. 'Help is on its way.'

'They say Hitler's done away with himself,' the pilot said hazily. 'Blasted war can't go on much longer.

Bloody Hun may have done me a favour.'

Back in London, Mrs Muggeridge wondered if she had dreamed the events of the last couple of days. She was still reeling from Mrs Bright's shared confidence. She had made such a difficult decision, one that had altered the dynamic of her life forever, and she would never regain those lost years with Millie. She imagined how life would have been without Gordon. Despite all the challenges he had brought, she wouldn't have missed one moment.

Millie was such a sweet girl and Mrs Muggeridge sensed the same loving heart with which Gordon had been blessed. But her upbringing had been much more isolated than his and she appeared to have few friends. Hopefully this could soon be rectified. She hoped to take Gordon to see her again very soon. There was no denying that the two of them had enjoyed each other's company. She thought too of the young pilot who Gordon had bravely rescued.

There was no doubt that but for Gordon's quick and fearless actions, he would have been burned alive. The thought filled her with terror. Not a day passed by when she didn't worry about a similar fate for Michael. Could it really be true that Hitler was dead and that the war was nearly over, or had the pilot been delirious? The idea that she could be privy to such news before the general public seemed ridiculous. But that evening as she and

Gordon were enjoying a toast supper, a newsflash on the radio confirmed that the German führer was indeed dead. Mrs Muggeridge could have jumped for joy.

'Did you hear that, Gordon? Hitler is dead. This must surely mean the end of the war.' She clutched her stomach, which was a little bloated after the bread she had eaten. 'Such wonderful news.'

Gordon threw his arms in the air. 'The bad man is dead!' he shouted. 'Does that mean that Michael will be coming home?'

'I don't know, we shall have to wait and see. But wouldn't it be wonderful if he did?' She could hear celebratory voices in the street, whoops of joy and disbelief. Her neighbour, Mrs Braithwaite, banged on her window. 'Have you heard the news?' she shouted. 'Hitler is dead!'

Mrs Muggeridge opened her front door. 'It's wonderful,' she said, 'truly wonderful. Let's hope our boys can all come home now.'

A couple of days later, Mrs Bright came to visit. 'Can you believe it?' she said happily. 'Surely Germany must surrender now. They say that Goebbels, Hitler's right-hand man, has committed suicide, along with his wife, and that they forced cyanide down the throats of their poor children. Can you imagine such cruelty? I mean, your *own* children.'

Mrs Muggeridge said that she couldn't and that some

things were beyond imagining.

'I had a telephone call,' Mrs Bright stated, hardly able to contain her excitement. 'It appears that the young man that Gordon saved is a squadron leader at Uxbridge. He knows Michael. His father is someone terribly important in the RAF. He wants to thank Gordon personally. They've contacted Michael and they're going to organise something.' She smiled. 'Now, I have another dress that I never wear, two in fact, and some slacks I've brought along. They'd look far better on you and they're far too good to throw away.' She studied Mrs Muggeridge's face. 'Are you still in pain? You've had that blasted stomach-ache for far too long now. You need to see a doctor.'

'Good grief, no! I haven't seen a doctor in years.' Mrs Muggeridge smiled kindly at Mrs Bright. 'I know you mean well but I'd much rather not. With all the injured servicemen and women about, I'm sure they'd laugh at a touch of indigestion.'

'It's more than a touch. You've had it for weeks now. I insist. You must promise.' She gave Mrs Muggeridge one of her looks that meant she would not take no for an answer.

'Okay,' agreed Mrs Muggeridge reluctantly, 'but it will be a waste of the doctor's time.'

Mrs Muggeridge's fear of doctors was greater than her fear of illness. She hadn't seen one since Gordon's birth, when her trust in them had been irretrievably broken.

'Promise?'

'Yes, I promise.'

'Good, now let's discuss which dress you're going to wear for Gordon's special day.' She held up a pale yellow frock against Mrs Muggeridge's shoulders, then a blue one. 'I think the latter,' she said. 'It's quite regal, don't you think?'

'Far too regal for me,' Mrs Muggeridge laughed. 'You can't make a silk purse out of a sow's ear.'

'Really,' Mrs Bright scolded. 'You really are far too self-effacing.'

A few days later, Winston Churchill announced the end of the war. The atmosphere was euphoric and the streets were alive with people cheering and dancing, waving flags and banners and singing patriotic songs. *Land of Hope and Glory* blasted from every radio and the king and queen appeared on the balcony of Buckingham Palace to greet their people in victory, while the young princesses, nowhere to be seen, were mingling with the crowd in delightful anonymity.

Mrs Bright told Mrs Muggeridge about the sights around the capital, where young people, she said, were jumping into the fountain at Trafalgar Square and others dancing the conga around Piccadilly Circus. She had never seen so many people rejoicing, she said. It was the most marvellous sight. Mrs Muggeridge should really go herself to witness such a historic day.

'I'd rather stay here with Gordon,' she had replied. 'All the joys of the nation can be witnessed easily enough in this small, cobbled street.'

Neighbours shared rations to make cakes and children had their faces painted in red, white and blue. Gordon was in his element playing Hopscotch with the young ones and passing around his mother's cakes, the last of her rations, on a large plate. Mrs Muggeridge told Mrs Bright that she would not be completely happy until she saw Michael. 'Outside these streets,' she said, 'the war is still going on, despite the ceasefire.'

And she was right. Michael had narrowly escaped death that day returning a Spitfire to Biggin Hill. It would normally have been a job for the ATA, but many of their pilots had been demobilised, and he was happy to have a chance to fly this wonderful plane without the assertiveness needed in warfare. The Merlin engine roared impatiently. Like a racehorse champing at the bit, its eagerness was contagious, and he felt the adrenaline coursing through his veins as it lifted and soared into the ceaseless passage of sky. He enjoyed some aerobatics, skilfully coordinating the rudder, stick and throttle, easing the plane into a vertical reverse, then a snap roll, looping the feathery banks of spring mist effortlessly.

Beneath the vault of sky, the wispy clouds revealed a variegated spring landscape of spectacular beauty. He noted the filigree of roads and rivers, the fields of young corn and green meadows and the nearing town, its red rooftops gay and welcoming. Beyond it lay a silver-tipped cobalt of spuming waves. Descending in a shallow dive above the townscape, he threw the Spitfire into a victory roll. He could see crowds beneath now and imagined the euphoria as peace was celebrated.

He would sing along with them. *'We're gonna hang out the washing on the Siegfried Line,'* he began. Then, suddenly, there was a flash of light and a burst of ammunition. He throttled back violently and the airspeed indicator quivered to near stalling point as the wind smacked his face through the shattered canopy. The bullets, which had ripped through the Perspex, had miraculously missed him by inches and, as luck would have it, the instrument panel was undamaged. He dived just in time to see a Messerschmitt disappear through gossamer clouds into the distance. Shocked into fury, his first instinct was to pursue this lone raider, but he reminded himself that he had no ammunition. He had not expected to be attacked on the day of unconditional surrender, and 109s had not been seen so close to England for some time. No doubt it had been a last-ditch attempt from a conquered enemy to avenge his comrades.

He delivered the plane, shaken from the encounter but, moreover, annoyed with himself for being so careless. His last flight had been spoiled by the enemy, whilst defeated. He listened to Churchill's speech on the radio. '*The evildoers lay prostrate before us,*' the Prime Minister stated boldly. There had been nothing very prostrate about that Jerry. He thought about his mother and Gordon, who had recently risked his life to pull a pilot from his plane, mistakenly thinking it had been him. How futile and manifestly more painful his death would have been to them had it been preceded by a proclamation of peace. He suddenly felt the need to return, to reassure his mother that she need worry about him no more. Yet, despite the elation of his fellow countrymen, victory felt to him bittersweet. He had lost so many friends, yet he was alive. He suddenly felt laden with guilt. It wasn't fair. All those young men who had had a lifetime ahead of them. Bloody war. Bloody, bloody war.

Mrs Muggeridge had kept her promise and been to see a doctor. He was a middle-aged man with grey, thinning hair and he looked at her over his spectacles as she spoke, nodding now and then and writing notes with his silver fountain pen. After examining her, he concluded, 'I think we need to have a few tests taken, Mrs Muggeridge, just to eliminate anything sinister, you understand. I'll send you today and you can pick up the results this time next week.'

Mrs Muggeridge wanted to say that it wouldn't be possible to pick up the results then, as it was the same day that Gordon was to be officially commended for his bravery at Uxbridge. She didn't want anything to spoil things. But there was nothing for it. She would have to collect the results in the morning before they left.

The week passed quickly and the euphoria of her fellow countrymen began to subdue as the grim reality of the war's aftermath became clear. So many towns and cities had been reduced to rubble and so many families devastated by the loss of loved ones. But nothing could suppress Mrs Muggeridge's optimism as she awoke that morning. She dressed excitedly in the soft, royal blue dress that Mrs Bright had given her and took out a matching brooch from her mother's old jewellery box, which, until now, she had never found the occasion to wear. Mrs Bright once again made up her face with blusher and peachy lipstick and set her hair in a wonderfully bouncy style.

'Regal enough?'

'I feel like a queen,' Mrs Muggeridge replied. She hesitated. 'I have to visit the surgery for the results of some silly tests the doctor took,' she began. 'Of course, it's all very unnecessary but it was just a precaution he said. Such a shame to disrupt Gordon's special day.'

'I see.' Mrs Bright sat down in the wicker chair in Mrs Muggeridge's kitchen. 'Why didn't you tell me before? You didn't say a word.'

'I didn't want to worry anyone over such a trifle. I only mentioned it as I have to collect the results this morning, though I don't know how I'm going to walk in these shoes. The heels must be at least two inches.'

'You're not going to walk. I'll take you in the car and then I can accompany you into the surgery.'

'That's really not necessary.'

'I insist. Supporting each other is what friends do. And you're the dearest friend anyone could have.'

Two hours later, an RAF staff car arrived to take Mrs Muggeridge, Gordon and Mrs Bright to RAF Uxbridge.

'It looks like you'll finally get your wish to see Michael's plane,' Mrs Muggeridge said to an elated Gordon. 'I'm so proud of you.'

'I can't wait. I've wanted to see Michael's plane for ages.' Gordon nudged Mrs Bright's arm. 'You're very quiet, Mrs B.'

'Sorry, Gordon.' Mrs Bright made an effort to smile. 'I was deep in thought.' She cast a look at Mrs Muggeridge that showed her solidarity. 'Are you comfortable, dear? Are you sure you're up to this?'

'I'm perfectly fine,' Mrs Muggeridge said stoically. 'Really, I am. You mustn't fuss. This is Gordon's day.'

Michael was there to greet them as they arrived at the base, along with Air Commodore Whiteley-Stone.

'At last,' the air commodore said. 'I get to meet my hero. To risk your own life to drag my son from a burning plane showed great courage and tenacity.'

'I thought it was Michael,' Gordon replied. 'Can we

see the plane now?'

Michael laughed. 'Soon, but we're going to have lunch at the officers' club first, in your honour.'

'Okay,' Gordon said, disappointed.

The room was opulent and Mrs Muggeridge had never seen such a beautiful table as the one at which they sat. The cloth was the purest white and the silver cutlery adorning it glistened. The napkins were made of cloth and were tucked into silver rings, and an arrangement of beautiful flowers sat in the middle, where rose petals had been sprinkled loosely around the condiments. Air Commodore Whiteley-Stone stepped behind Mrs Muggeridge and helped her into her chair.

'Red or white?' he asked when the waiter approached.

'My mother doesn't drink,' Michael said protectively, 'but I bet you'd love a glass of dandelion and burdock, wouldn't you, Mum?'

'Yes please,' Gordon said.

'Actually, I think I *would* like a glass of red wine,' Mrs Muggeridge said, 'if you could recommend something. I'm afraid I'm no connoisseur.'

'Me too,' Mrs Bright said.

'Good choice, we'll have a bottle of Cabernet Sauvignon. Ah...' the Air Commodore sighed. 'Here comes my reprobate son. Late as ever. Always did have dreadful table manners. Still, better late than never, what?'

'What, what?' Gordon asked.

'It's just an expression, Gordon,' Mrs Muggeridge whispered.

Squadron Leader Whiteley-Stone approached the table on crutches. 'So sorry I'm late. It's this leg, you see, and the cracked ribs. They make getting dressed a nightmare. Still…' He faced Gordon. 'Could have been a damn sight worse if you hadn't acted so quickly. Can't thank you enough, old man.'

'I thought you were Michael,' Gordon said.

'Yes, so I remember.' The squadron leader clapped Gordon on the back. 'But I don't think your brother would have allowed himself to be ambushed like that.'

'I wouldn't be too sure,' Michael said, thinking of his recent flight. 'We all have our bad days.'

'Two lion hearts in one family,' Squadron Leader Whiteley-Stone continued. 'Michael's saved my skin several times. He's one of our best, an ace several times over, in fact.'

'What's an ace?'

'It means he's shot down a lot of enemies, Gordon.'

'Did you get Hitler?'

Everyone laughed.

'No, but I wish. Now that would have been a kill worth bragging about.'

'Let's not forget, gentlemen,' the air commodore said, 'that we have ladies present.' He glanced at Mrs

Muggeridge. 'I think that's enough about killing, don't you?'

'Quite, sir.'

'Good chap. Now...' He studied the menu. 'I can recommend the Dover sole meunière. Hugo swears by the coq au vin, don't you, Hugo? And I hear the beef Wellington is excellent.'

'Wellingtons are to put on your feet,' said Gordon. 'I'd like cheese on toast, please.'

'It's his favourite,' explained Mrs Muggeridge. 'I'm afraid he's never been very experimental with food and my cooking has always been, well, fairly plain, even before rationing.'

'If that's what he wants then that's what he shall have,' the air commodore said.

'You look lovely, Mum,' said Michael. 'That colour suits you.'

'Yes, I'm very fortunate,' the air commodore said, 'to have not one but two beautiful ladies as dining companions.' He raised his glass. 'To our two beautiful ladies!'

'To our ladies,' the men echoed. Gordon seemed to understand and raised his glass of dandelion and burdock.

The waiter returned. 'Can I take your order now, sir?'

'Yes,' the Air Commodore said assertively. 'Three times the coq au vin, two beef Wellingtons and, as a special request, our young hero here would like the biggest plate of Welsh rarebit you can muster.'

'Thanks,' Gordon said, 'but I don't want to eat any rabbits. I'd rather have cheese on toast, please.'

After dinner, Michael changed into his flight suit and they were driven to an awaiting Spitfire. 'Well, here it is,' he said. 'Would you like to sit in it, Gordon?'

Overcome with happiness, Gordon climbed into the cockpit.

'Where's the steering wheel?' he asked.

'Look,' Michael said, 'here it is. It's called a joystick and when you want the nose of the plane to turn upward, you move it this way and when you want to go left or right, you move it like this.'

'Here's the local press,' Air Commodore Whiteley-Stone said. 'They've come to take your photograph, Gordon. Don't forget to say cheese!'

'Or rather cheese on toast,' quipped Michael.

The photographer took a picture of Gordon in the Spitfire, then one of him shaking hands with Squadron Leader Whiteley-Stone, another with his brother and one of the entire group. He promised Mrs Muggeridge that he would send her copies of all the photographs. Gordon seemed to be enjoying his momentary celebrity, preening and posturing happily while answering a series of questions. When the journalist and entourage had gone, Michael took Gordon for a flight in a Tiger Moth. It was a perfect day for flying. The sun shone so that the sky, a vast blanket of unblemished blue, lit the faces of their spectators as they ferried past them on the runway. As the wheels left the tarmac, Michael could hear Gordon squeal with delight. He climbed higher and levelled the Moth at about one thousand feet. 'Okay,' he said, 'your turn now. Gently does it.'

Gordon, his introduction to aerial perspective an unequivocally empirical one, was hypnotised by the varying shapes and colours of the meadows below. His hand clutched the joystick, timidly at first, and then, after some minutes, like a man slowly liberated from a lengthy captivity taking his first joyous steps into the unknown, with increasing aplomb.

After a while, Michael regained control and headed back, turning sharply so that the wind, bracing against Gordon's face, lifted the small plane and dropped her as quickly into ever greater depths of cerulean.

The landing was smooth, the Moth licking the tarmac gently until it reached a standstill and was marshalled to its allotted space. Michael unstrapped his brother and helped him out of the cockpit. Mrs Muggeridge was waiting nearby wearing a huge smile. 'How was it Gordon?' she asked. 'Was it everything that you'd hoped for?'

'More,' Gordon replied. 'Today has been the best day of my life.'

The staff car was parked by the hangar ready to take them back home.

'I've had the most wonderful day,' Mrs Muggeridge said to Michael, as he opened the door of the Hillman. 'I can't tell you how proud I am of you, of both of you.'

'I'll be home later,' Michael said. 'I have some leave due and I want to be with you both tomorrow when the newspaper arrives. I'll have to get used to having a famous brother.' He ruffled Gordon's hair affectionately.

Air Commodore Whitely-Stone kissed Mrs Muggeridge's hand. 'It's been a great honour,' he said. 'Two very fine boys. As Hugo said, both lion hearts. And I suspect they have inherited that from you.'

'Me!' Mrs Muggeridge chuckled. 'Oh no, I jump at the mere sight of a mouse.'

They drove away from the base in the shiny Hillman. Gordon sat in the front chatting excitedly to the driver, while Mrs Muggeridge and Mrs Bright sat in the back seat.

'His feet have hardly touched the ground,' said Mrs Muggeridge, 'literally.'

Mrs Bright, her usually ready smile absent from her ruby lips, hung her head in sheer misery. 'When are you going to tell them, my dear?' she inquired, reaching out to hold Mrs Muggeridge's hand, which was shaking slightly from the impact of the day's revelations.

'Oh, I shan't be in any hurry,' replied Mrs Muggeridge. She looked out of the window at the blue sky, broken only by the small, wispy condensation trails high above. 'It's been such a perfect day.'

Into the Fray Goes Walter Pidgeon

I

At six weeks old, Walter Pidgeon was plucked from his warm bed of straw in the pigeon loft and given his first lesson in homing. At first, the distance back to his nest and the delicious tray of seeds and corn was short, but as he grew, both in confidence and stature, he was released further and further from his destination. From the very outset, Walter Pidgeon showed a great aptitude for navigation, arriving at his loft in record time, cooing proudly in anticipation of the fuss that awaited him, along with the prized treat of mealworms.

'It's Walter, Dad,' Peggy said gleefully one afternoon, her nose pressed to the window so that an observer might be forgiven for assuming she was referring to a favourite uncle paying them a visit. 'He's beaten all the others again. He must be tired after his flight. I'll go and make him a fresh bed.'

'He's a special one alright,' her father said. 'Your star of the silver screen.' He laughed. 'You've done a sterling job training him, Peggy. It's down to your hard work and dedication that he's learned as quickly as he has. The Confidential Pigeon Service will be proud of you.' He chortled. 'Walter Pidgeon, eh! Here...' He tossed her some coins from his pocket. 'That should be enough to treat yourself to the pictures tomorrow, along with an ice-cream I shouldn't wonder.'

Peggy took the coins happily. She loved the cinema almost as much as she loved her pigeons. During this bleak period with her brother Jim away at war, it provided her with much needed escapism and glamour. Her favourite film of all time was *Mrs Miniver* starring Greer Garson and Walter Pidgeon. Greer Garson was so glamorous and Walter Pidgeon, her screen husband, so handsome and debonair. How bravely he had volunteered to collect those men fleeing from Dunkirk, while, in his absence, his wife, disarming in every sense, had relieved a Nazi pilot of his gun. How unflappable they were in the face of adversity. Despite being touched by tragedy, they had survived and flourished. She wondered if it could really be like that. She couldn't imagine behaving with such reserve and dignity if anything should happen to Jim. But then their lives were not part of a Hollywood film. Mrs Miniver would never have cursed as her own mother was prone and Mr Miniver would never have managed a pigeon coop. The mere idea was absurd. But then, if films were about the ordinary and prosaic, no one would pay to watch them.

Her own life and that of her family's was unremarkable and unsung, like millions of others, lacking the glamour and allure of the great screen idols. Her mother knitted and cooked, her father bred pigeons and marched with the Home Guard, and she attended the local school and had trained Walter Pidgeon. She smiled to herself. Theirs was hardly a story of heroism or valour, hardly one to be snapped up by Metro-Goldwyn-Mayer.

Peggy's school friends teased her mercilessly for her interest in pigeons, calling them flying rats and disease-carrying vermin. But Peggy knew the debt that was owed to them. They had saved many lives during wartime. She had heard stories from her father about how they had carried messages back from the front line asking for reinforcements, and had been used as spies, penetrating occupied countries and returning with vital information. Some had even been double agents, "stool pigeons" her father had said, amused. And by training Walter Pidgeon for war work, she felt that she was doing her part in protecting Jim, though she was not quite sure how.

But she had worked with pigeons long enough now to recognise star quality when she saw it, and Walter was exceptional. She could simply tell by looking at his beak and crop and the proud way he held his head. He had stamina and intelligence and he was fast, perhaps the fastest pigeon they had ever bred. How he, or any other pigeons, managed to find their way home was something of a mystery. Some people thought they had an inbuilt magnetic compass that steered them home, while others believed that they just had a good memory for geographical landmarks. But, whatever it was, their unique ability to find their way home meant that their utility lay in being deposited in war zones and returning back to base with classified information.

As she went to sleep that night, she tried to visualise Walter Pidgeon being parachuted in a container behind enemy lines, awaiting release from a benevolent farmer who would send a message back to England in the Bakelite cylinder that would be attached to Walter's leg.

Perhaps it would be a message instrumental in ending the war. Then Jim would come home, her mother would stop crying herself to sleep and she would have a brother again. How she missed Jim. She awoke later in a cold sweat. In her dream, the hungry farmer had decided to eat Walter and no message had ever been delivered. She had waited by their coop for days in her dream, looking up at the bleak sky, where only the occasional hawk flew past searching for its own version of pigeon pie. This surely couldn't be the destiny of such an exceptional bird?

She dressed and ran hurriedly down the garden path to the loft. Walter cooed in welcome and she stroked his head and filled his food bowl with his favourite seeds. 'I'll fetch some fresh water. No doubt you'd like a bath today to freshen up after your marathon flight.' She put down a large tray of water and watched as Walter paddled toward it, his small, soft head with its keen, auburn eyes bobbing with each movement. She stroked the scarf of purple and green that seemed almost painted onto his plump chest as he frolicked, dipping his fleshy bill into the water and fluffing out his feathers. 'I wonder what the armed services have in mind for you, Walter? A pigeon spy maybe, a double agent? Intelligence gatherer?' She laughed. 'If you come across Jim, give him my love, won't you?' She heard her mother call. It was time to go to the cinema. 'Bye Walter, see you later.' She planted a kiss on the top of his head and he cooed his response. But when she returned a few hours later, Walter had gone.

'He's been conscripted for the war effort,' her father said rather grandly. 'It was all very sudden. I was asked for the very best pigeons I have, so I had to let him go. But he'll be back, you'll see.'

Peggy felt sick. 'He isn't ready yet,' she insisted.

'He's still so young.'

'Like half the young men in the army,' her mother replied. 'Like our Jim. He's just a pigeon, Peggy.'

Peggy fought back the tears. She knew her mother was right, but she had grown so attached to Walter. Training and caring for him had proven cathartic. He was no longer just a pigeon to her but a confidante, a kind and gentle friend to whom she could impart her most private thoughts and fears. And now he was gone.

*

Jim had known for some time that an invasion of France was imminent. He had been training for it daily on increasingly rigorous assault courses until every sinew in his body screamed from the exertion. Recent parachute drops had been from a variety of planes travelling at differing speeds and altitudes, often into bitterly cold terrain. He knew that soon, everything he had learned about battle would be put to the test. He was a lean, wiry boy of medium height. His thatch of brown hair had been shaven to within a quarter of an inch and his jaunty expression somewhat dulled by fatigue, so that overall, he appeared less personable than before. It was true that his training had hardened him, had channelled his natural athleticism and roguish nature into becoming an alert, disciplined soldier. He had passed selection into Airborne Operations with ease and carved a niche for himself amongst the Parachute Regiment.

Most of his boyhood had been spent exploring the countryside. He had loved nothing more than fishing, climbing trees and camping, initially with his father, who rigged up a small tent in the back garden, and later, alone, disappearing for days at a time with only the basic equipment to fish, cook and orienteer. He had slept beneath the stars and relished waking to a dawn chorus of robins, blackbirds and wrens, and cooking himself a breakfast of roach, accompanied by scrumped apples. This love of the countryside, added to his sense of adventure, physical prowess and disinterest in scholarship, meant that enlisting as soon as he could was almost an inevitability.

His father had accepted his decision reluctantly, but his mother had been so affected by it that she'd become ill, taken to her bed and cried for a week. She'd felt with a certainty that he would be killed and that no king or country was worth the death of her beloved son. Also, despite his obvious strengths, she'd felt he lacked the natural aggression needed to kill without thought or hesitation. She had seen the effects of war on her husband, whose stoical grip on his emotions had meant he had seldom spoken of the gory, brutalised world where boys were catapulted prematurely into manhood. But shell shock had dominated those early years of marriage. Her husband's fatigue and night terrors, as he had relived the sights and sounds of battle, had broken into their sleeping and waking hours like the unrelenting cannon fire that had provoked them. If it hadn't been for the pigeons, she didn't know how she would have coped. It had been the pigeons that had nursed him back to health and enabled him to function again. The pigeons had given him a sense of purpose after the Great War, had kept him outside, tending, training and fully absorbed in their care during those dark days of recovery.

Jim had enjoyed his father's pigeons as a child, especially fascinated by the tiny, peeping squabs with their cyclopean eyes and ungainly bodies. He had cried when he'd first watched them feeding from their parent's crop, their miniature beaks embedded deep in their mother's or father's throats, as though they themselves were being eaten. And later, he had used them when camping alone to communicate his whereabouts. But, as he moved toward his mid-teens, he had grown tired of them and left their care under the auspices of his father and little sister. He had even felt at times somewhat scornful of his father's devotion toward them, not understanding their significance to his rehabilitation. The pigeons, he felt, were like the members of the British Home Guard, to which his father belonged – clumsy, outmoded and rather ineffectual. It was really only as his training progressed into the realities of war that he began to appreciate what his father must have endured in the trenches under heavy mortar bombardment. Jim had now witnessed a similar carnage to the sights of no man's land, where bodies were burned black, limbs severed and guts spilled in an abattoir of human slaughter. He had heard men's screams fracture the air in piteous chorus to no avail. And now they were about to invade Normandy.

While part of 6th Airborne had the task of disabling a German battery on Sword Beach to aid the Allied seaborne invasion, Jim and his comrades had orders to seize the River Orne and Caen de Canal bridgeheads to block German reinforcements and facilitate their own passage over the waterways. The general consensus was that very few of them would return and they were encouraged to settle their affairs and write their last words to loved ones. Jim thought of his family and the pain his death would bring to them, especially to his mother. He would no longer be able to protect his little sister or explain to his father that he now understood.

He even remembered with affection the pigeons at the bottom of their garden, some of which, ironically, may be joining him into the fray. He smiled to himself. Along with cumbersome weapons, ammunition, rations, reserve and main parachutes, many of the paratroopers would have to carry a pigeon. Since radios would not be allowed, due to signals being picked up by the enemy, pigeons would be their only form of communication to mainland England, until their presence in France was established. Some of the men were uncomfortable at the thought of this and felt that the mere practice of carrying these birds rendered them comical and compromised their sense of invincibility, but for Jim they provided succour, reminding him of childhood and home comforts.

Just after midnight, 6th Airborne Division was despatched. Jim clambered into the Stirling, heavily laden with equipment and a pigeon strapped securely to his chest, adding a new dimension, he thought drolly, to the term pigeon-chested. As he looked behind him in the darkness of the congested aircraft, the men, with their blackened faces and avian companions, looked like strange marsupials carrying their young. The pigeons, encased in their pouch-like receptacles, showed little sign of the nervous tension palpable amongst the soldiers.

Jim was glad when the plane took off and the rumbling of the engines rendered laborious any articulation of fear. Let that remain unspoken beneath the bravado of war paint – there was no call for it now and nothing to be profited by it. He stroked the bird's crown. It was almost time. Beneath him, the seascape had changed to a barely discernible landscape, into which he was about to throw himself, along with his feathered friend. They were in it together, this guileless bird and he.

The despatcher announced that it was time to go and Jim stood and secured his static line. There was no room for error when jumping from an aircraft. He had witnessed the results of a parachute that had failed to open and it wasn't a pretty sight. He felt a rush of adrenalin and thought of Eisenhower's recent words: *'The eyes of the world are upon you. The hopes and prayers of liberty loving people everywhere march with you.'* Hopefully, their prayers would not only march with them but sail through the unsheltered arena of night sky, now illuminated with colourful tracers from anti-aircraft flak.

He followed half a dozen others to the exit at the rear of the fuselage. 'Good hunting.' The despatcher smiled, then the green light signalled and without a moment's hesitation, Jim dropped. The seconds it took him to land seemed interminably long. Paratroopers, he knew, were at their most vulnerable in descent. Without the element of surprise, they could be taken out like clay pigeons. He grimaced at the analogy. He was grateful for the number of Ruperts, the paradummies, that rained down amongst the men. Hopefully, the enemy would waste some time and ammunition on them.

Under a hail of shells and tracers, he landed smoothly by a small copse and moved toward it, the sound of rifles and submachine guns hastening his gait. Once sheltered, he reassessed his position, loaded his Sten gun and rearranged the pigeon onto his back. The bird was motionless beyond the confines of its jacket, petrified by the anti-aircraft fire, but comforting a bird in a theatre of war was a comical concept that he absently dismissed. Paratroopers were still being dropped and he checked their line of descent. He should reach the planned rendezvous point in no time if he could avoid German patrols and snipers. Being isolated in enemy territory was a soldier's worst nightmare, so he was comforted by the distinct sounds of the rallying call from a distant bugler. He followed the sound northerly over a landscape abundant with trees and hedgerows. Lurking in every shadow were other paratroopers, all drawn to the bugler, as though he were the Pied Piper playing his magic flute.

After some minutes, they all met, congregating by a dilapidated farm building. Greetings were warm but brief. Already there were casualties, some lying dead in the surrounding fields, others managing their wounds as best they could. There were no medics amongst them and no commanding officer. Jim spoke up. 'We need to keep moving. We should reach the bridge within twenty minutes, but we need to circumvent Bénouville, where there are bound to be snipers. Help the wounded at the back. If we can get to the bridge and the glider raid was successful, the bridge will be taken and there should be the beginnings of a Regimental Aid Post.'

By the time they reached Caen de Canal bridge, they

had lost six men to snipers and several more amongst them were injured, but there was elation nonetheless when they saw that the bridge had been successfully captured. Someone had even made a rudimentary sign calling it Pegasus Bridge, named after the emblems on the shoulders of the British Parachute Regiment. The bridge, it was established, had been secured within the first ten minutes of landing after Major John Howard and his men had so accurately navigated their glider that they had touched down only yards from their target. Dead bodies now festooned the bascule bridge and beneath, the carnage continued into the dark canal waters. They advanced cautiously then ran the length of the girders without hostilities.

'Well done, chaps. Good to see you.' Major John Howard led them over to the marshy ground by the canal to Café Gondrée, where Monsieur Gondrée offered them the last of the champagne he had dug up from his garden in celebration of his family's liberation. It seemed bizarre to Jim to be sipping champagne in the middle of a war operation, but he was grateful for the sparkly liquid that released the dryness in his throat.

'We've done the easy bit,' Major Howard said modestly. 'We've taken the bridges. The difficulty will be in retaining them. And that's where you chaps come in.'

'What about the demolition charges, sir?' Jim asked.

'Removed successfully. But counter-attacks are an

inevitability. We are in desperate need of more ground support.' Nearby, Jim noted soldiers were digging pits, simple fortifications from which to defend their positions. 'The problem is,' the Major continued, 'we've no way of communicating with the rest of our battalion. Some individuals will be stuck behind enemy lines, some trapped in small pockets of resistance, but we don't know where. I've sent out a small platoon to scout for them but they haven't returned. It won't take long for the enemy to regroup and form a pincer attack, and with our numbers so drastically reduced, I'm not sure we can hold out until the seaborne invasion is won.' He paused. 'We desperately need to contact the War Office to let them know that we've succeeded in taking the bridges intact and that we need reinforcements fast. But we have no radio yet.'

'We have pigeons, sir. About fifteen of them.' Jim had almost forgotten about the pigeon on his back and hoped that it was still breathing.

'Well,' the major said somewhat dismissively, 'I don't set much store by this Pigeon Service lark myself, but at this point anything's worth a go.' He hesitated for a moment, casting a worn hand over his eyelids, then spoke. 'Those of you with pigeons, write the following code for the capture of the two bridges.' Hands were trembling as the men followed the major's instructions. 'Jam and Ham,' the Major stated earnestly. 'Reinforcements needed NOW. Oh,' he added as an afterthought, 'and don't forget to sign your name and regiment if you can fit it in, so that the War Office knows it's not more German treachery.'

Jim stroked the head of his poor bird. It seemed stunned by its experiences and the noise of distant munitions. There was no alertness in its eyes like the pigeons in his father's loft that cooed and tilted their grey heads in response. 'Okay, everyone,' he said. 'Are the first flight of pigeons ready?'

'Pigeons ready.'

There was something comical, Jim thought, in that reply, which would normally have referred to firearms. Suddenly, in this theatre of war with all their weaponry, they were reduced to primitive measures, reliant on these gentle, gallant birds to carry their hopeful words across the miles. The skies were full of tracer fireworks. Only rarely silence prevailed, to be shattered rudely by distant bombing or machine gun fire as the enemy tried to reclaim the bridges. Eisenhower was right, he thought, in his assertion that the enemy would fight savagely.

The pigeons were released in a flurry of wings as they took to the skies. The men watched them go, cheering, willing their birds on as though there was a bet to be won.

'Come on, Nancy, you can do it.'

'Get your skates on, Chalky. Give our best to Old Blighty!'

Suddenly, the sound of gunfire drowned their cheers and one by one the birds were picked off by gunshot, dropping like stones to be engulfed in the swollen waters beneath.

'Bastards, they've shot the lot. Except for that one.' Jim's bird had flown to the nearest branch of a tree and remained there without movement. 'And that bird's not going anywhere.' The soldier sighed. 'What a bloody time to get shell shock. Never heard of a bird with shell shock before. I've a good mind to shoot it myself.' There was laughter but morale was low. 'Let's try the next lot.'

'We need a smoke grenade as a distraction,' Jim said. 'Ready?'

'Ready.'

The second flight of pigeons was released but several flew in the wrong direction. The others were shot just as the smoke cleared. 'Well, that's it then.' Spirits were low. 'The good 'uns are dead and the bad 'uns are searching for the nearest German pigeon loft to find some grub. Mind you, I don't blame the double-crossing rats. I'd do the same given half a chance.'

'One last chance.' A bird was handed to Jim. 'You seem good at handling them. Found him over there.' He pointed to a dead soldier lying in the dirt. 'Luckily, he fell forwards or this little blighter would have had the stuffing knocked out of him. A bit grubby, though. He's been lying in that soldier's blood for a while now.'

Jim studied the bird. 'He's not injured.' He poured some water from his canteen onto a piece of cloth and wiped the red stain from his feathers. 'It's a beauty. Look at its rounded chest and wingspan. A young bird. Look how keen he is, full of vitality.' Jim wrote a final note and clipped it to the pigeon's leg. He stroked it gently and it cooed. He kissed its head for luck. 'Off you go, my beauty.'

He thrust the bird upward as the sound of a German Tiger tank fired in their direction. The bird disappeared into the smoke screen as the men all cheered. They knew their last chance of assistance lay with this avian messenger. It had become more than a pigeon to them – an emblem of hope and liberation. It flew high, enjoying its new-found freedom, undeterred by the gunfire and explosions from the tank and artillery fire. There was something elegant in its flight as it took their hopes with it into the distant battle of night sky. Then, suddenly, just as it neared a safe height, a keen German marksman aimed his gun and fired. The men watched in horror as the bird fell through the air to what appeared a certain death. But then, miraculously, its wings began to flap and it gradually regained height. The men cheered their encouragement. More shots were heard but the bird was fast and undeterred and disappeared from sight, into the stormy sky.

'My God, that's a brave bird.'

'Yes, very plucky you might say.' The men laughed.

'It won't make it across the canal let alone the English Channel with that shot wound, will it?' The men looked at Jim for an answer.

'You'd be amazed what a good pigeon is capable of,' Jim said. 'That bird will get home, you'll see.'

The men, heartened by Jim's words and the pigeon's gallantry, resumed their positions.

'Well, men,' Major Howard said. 'If a damned pigeon can get through with a shot wound, then keeping possession of these bridges should be a doddle.'

*

Walter Pidgeon had been enjoying his bath when the gentleman from the Air Ministry had arrived. Walter didn't understand about the Air Ministry and its work and he didn't care to.

He was only interested in the simple pleasures – feeding his stout belly with corn, plumping his feathers with splashes of water and soaring into the vast expanse of sky, into which he was frequently released. He was also gregarious and loyal, and loved not just the family of pigeons whose coop he shared, but his trainer, the gentleness of her hand and the whispers of her private thoughts. So he was disappointed at the arrival of this stranger, whose palms were rough and without offerings and whose voice was stern and uncompromising.

Walter was put into a container and driven in a van to

a place he did not recognise. He could hear the sounds of other pigeons, housed in similar containers nearby, but none were from his coop and he missed the familiar cooing of his regular companions. Later in the day, someone entered the room where the containers were stacked and supplied Walter with water and grain, and, despite the upheaval of the day, Walter ate hungrily.

The following morning, Walter was put into another van along with the other pigeons and they were driven to a place where Walter observed lots of giant, metal birds flocked together along a grey branch-like structure. His eyes absorbed the great span of their wings and his ears heard their thunderous roar, but he was unafraid. Their beaks were absent and their claws the wrong shape for clutching prey, and groups of people walked about them without falling victim to attacks.

Walter sat patiently in his container, hoping that Peggy would arrive soon to release him. He was tired of the confines of his box and the oily fumes of the giant birds. He wanted to fly home to the familiarity of his own straw bed and frolic for a while in a small pool of tepid water before the close of day.

Walter had waited and waited for what seemed like an age until suddenly, the room in which he was held captive, long since shrouded in darkness, was shattered by a sudden burst of light.

Into the Fray Goes Walter Pidgeon

'Okay, gentleman, here we have His Majesty's pigeon post. Not to be scoffed at. These will be your companions for the foreseeable future so choose your bird wisely.'

There was some laughter. 'Flee-ridden rats.'

'One of those flee-ridden rats may save your neck, so get picking.'

One by one the pigeons were plucked from their containers by unsympathetic hands. Walter was grabbed by the neck and just as he spread a wing, it was stuffed unceremoniously into a vest on a soldier's chest.

'Come on then, mate,' the soldier said good-naturedly. 'It's you and me against the world.'

Walter looked about him. He was driven toward one of the great metal birds and before he knew it, was inside its giant belly. The metal bird roared loudly and began to move. Walter tried to spread his wings but they were contained by the pocket of material into which he had been placed. He was grateful at least that his head could move freely and that he was no longer in a box. His captive stroked his head occasionally as the giant bird rose high into the stormy sky. Walter was grateful for this as the belly of the great bird rumbled and shook its way through the night.

Eventually, someone shouted something and Walter's carrier stood and shuffled behind a long line of men toward the back of the giant bird. One by one, they disappeared out of a hole in its side and into the bleakness beyond. It was soon Walter's turn and he tried desperately to spread his wings once more as they fell into a shower of rain where the dark air was full of strange, luminous bursts of colour. They dropped like a stone and Walter, restrained from flight, felt terror run through his small, static body. Soon, though, he felt a tug and they slowed, sailing toward the ground beneath a circular, white wing until they touched down into a cornfield and moved hurriedly toward a dilapidated farm building in the distance.

Walter was slung onto the soldier's back, blocking his view ahead. He heard loud noises around him that startled and frightened him, but he felt sure that soon he would be released and could begin the journey home to the safety of his coop. He didn't like to fly at night and he disliked the harshness of the elements even more, but his instinct to fly back home to his flock and to the kindness of his handler superseded both of these concerns. He could see from his peripheral vision that they were approaching the ruin, a building similar to many he had flown over before and yet, the terrain and topography was entirely inconsistent.

The cacophony of sounds was also different and disturbing. The soldiers were growing in numbers as more and more appeared from the shadows, yet Walter could sense death all around him, in the stillness of bodies in the field, the stifled fear of the soldiers and the harshness of the reverberations. The soldiers walked and jogged for many miles, sometimes diverted by the turbulence of others actively fighting, firing and reloading their rifles, so that Walter's gentle heart quickened with each deafening shot.

'There it is,' someone said, 'the bridge. We've made it. Quickly, everyone! Over to the other side.'

Moments later, the crack of gunfire sounded from behind them and the soldier carrying Walter fell forward with some force, blood from the bullet wound only an inch from Walter's head. Blood began seeping out, covering the vest that sheathed Walter, the warm, red liquid bathing his contained body. Walter could do nothing but lie in the darkness, listening to the groans of the dying soldier as he uttered his final breath. Over an hour had passed before he was rescued. By this time, Walter was cold and saturated and had to consciously raise his head to stop from drowning in blood.

'Last pigeon standing, sir.'

Walter was passed to Sergeant Jim Harris, who wiped him down with cool water and wrote a message quickly on the thin rice paper provided, before returning it to the message capsule attached to Walter's leg. The soldier kissed him on the head and then raised his cupped hands skyward as the soldiers all cheered him on. After only a few moments, he could hear their elation turn to misery as they watched him fall heavily toward the canal below. They obviously thought his death was an inevitability, but Walter rose again, spurred on by the cheering crowd below, and began to gain height. This time, despite more gun shots, he continued undeterred until he was out of range of the snipers.

Initially, Walter had felt disorientated and his body and wings, bound for so long, had felt strangely ineffectual. But he was strong and young and determined to escape this horror to return to the safety of his loft. When the shot penetrated his chest, it hit with such force he had been propelled backward before dropping heavily toward the water beneath. He was in shock, yet he acted instinctively to save himself. He knew he had only moments before hitting the icy water where he would be dragged under the current. Despite the searing pain, he recovered his flight just in time, pounding his wings furiously against the gusting winds and rain, gaining momentum with each beat of his wings. Soon, he was near the coast where he once again met the giant, clawless birds, this time excreting their loads onto the beaches below, while men scurried about in avoidance.

Out at sea, rocket launchers fired onto gun batteries and trenches, catapulting men into the air, ablaze, their death screams shattering the approaching dawn. Walter knew nothing of artillery, except that it meant pain and death. The earth beneath him rumbled and quaked as he danced between the colourful tracers of anti-aircraft fire. His mental map was drawing lines of magnetic fields in front of him, giving him the coordinates he needed to direct his way across the vast expanse of the English Channel. In the early morning light on 6 June 1944, he relinquished the beaches of Normandy and powered over the stormy seas to Portsmouth.

Walter's joyful first sighting of England was diminished somewhat by a distant bluish speck circling above the coastline. This was the worst welcome he could have anticipated – a much faster, well-rested bird of prey looking for its breakfast. The peregrine falcon spotted Walter on his lone flight with its telescopic sight and immediately gave chase. There was nowhere to hide above the choppy waters and Walter was weary and injured. But he had also learned a few things on the battlefields of Normandy, such as resilience and fearlessness, and he also had a few manoeuvres of his own. It seemed to him now that the only thing that separated him from the safe haven of his pigeon loft was this falcon, and he was not about to surrender his life easily.

As the falcon began to gain altitude, so did Walter, instinctively knowing that his chances of survival were lessened if his attacker was able to dive at him from a great height. The falcon, desperate to secure his prey before the mainland provided a multitude of hiding places, managed to gain enough height to swoop just before Walter reached the shoreline. But Walter had predicted the dive and allowed his battle-scarred body to freefall, so that the outstretched talons of his predator fell into a vacuum as Walter raced toward the shelter of a nearby copse. By the time he reappeared from the far end, the falcon had found other prey. Walter arrived at his pigeon loft fifteen minutes later, exhausted, dehydrated and bloody, and Peggy, who had played hooky ever since Walter had been taken, saw him from the window and ran elatedly to greet him.

*

When Peggy's parents returned home later that day, a despatch rider had already called by to collect the tiny Bakelite cylinder that Walter had carried back from France. It was delivered post-haste to the War Office, where it was taken from its tube and unravelled, its contents treated with the highest priority.

'I know it's forbidden,' Peggy's father said to his wife that evening. 'But I would love to have known what that message said.' Peggy's face flushed crimson. 'Oh, Peggy,' her father groaned. 'You didn't? I've told you before, it's strictly forbidden.'

'I know,' Peggy had replied sheepishly. 'But I'm so glad I did. I've been dying to tell you both all day.'

Her mother wept when Peggy told her about the signature, feeling that this was a portent of her son's safe passage home, which it may well have been as Jim survived the war and was reunited with his family and the pigeon he had thrust, in desperate measure, into the war-torn arena of Normandy's night sky. After the message had been relayed in London, the War Office had managed to radio through to another company, who, along with lost sectors from the Airborne regiment, had regrouped at the bridge and fought indefatigably to prevent its recapture until the seaborne infantry had arrived. This swift action, made possible by Walter's monumental efforts, had undoubtedly saved the lives of many and, in all probability, Jim's.

Walter had been tended to by a vet, who said that the shot wound would heal with respite, and Walter was duly bandaged and cosseted. A week after he had returned home, a representative from the War Office called to say that in accordance with Walter's extraordinary valour in the face of adversity, Walter Pidgeon was being awarded the Dicken Medal, the animal equivalent of the Victoria Cross. His gallantry had helped save the lives of numerous soldiers. Peggy's heart had swollen with pride.

Walter's rehabilitation was assisted by Gladys Cooper, also known as Glad or Coo, who had been raised in the nesting box beside Walter's. They became lifelong mates, producing many squabs, the first of which was a splendid-looking cock bird.

'What are you going to name him, Peg?' her father had asked her.

'I've been thinking about that.' Peggy looked up from the *Picture Show Annual* she'd been thumbing. 'There's a new war film coming out soon called *Days of Glory*. And it says here that the leading man is set to become one of Hollywood's most celebrated stars.'

'Ah, I see what's coming,' her father grinned.

'Well, what's his name then?' her mother asked. 'Come on, Pegs, don't keep us in suspense.' Peggy held up the slick, glossy pages of her film star annual for her mother's delectation.

'Oh, very nice, I must say,' her mother said, absorbing the handsome features languorously, as she was prone with items of great beauty and value that were well beyond her expenditure.

'Never mind all that drooling,' her father said good-humouredly. 'What's his name?'

Peggy passed him the annual and he studied it before bursting into laughter. 'That's a good one,' he said. 'Gregory Peck! Well I never! Now that's what you call preordained.'

About the Author

Jacqueline Puchtler lives in Northamptonshire and works as a school librarian. Her interest in flying began when she lived in California in her early twenties. There she was introduced to the Mojave Desert from an aerial perspective in a friend's battered Cessna, 'that shook and shimmied its way over the desert.' She later married a military pilot based at George Air Force Base and eventually moved to Nordrhein-Westfalen. Her interest in flying was rekindled in recent years after enjoying some aerobatics in a Tiger Moth.

Reg Payne, (1923 -), inspiration for the story Corkscrew Port Go and artist of the front cover, revisits his position as wireless operator in a Lancaster bomber in 2013 aged 90 years.